THREESOMES - VOLUME 2

THE LESBIAN COLLECTION

VICTORIA RUSH

COPYRIGHT

Threesomes - Volume 2 © 2020 Victoria Rush

Cover Design © 2020 PhotoMaras

For the uninhibited...

VOLUME ONE

NUDE CRUISE

1

EXOTIC VOYAGE

My exhilarating encounters at the dinner party, the dark room, and naked yoga had whet my appetite for new adventures. But each of these experiences, as stimulating and fulfilling as they were in their own right, were one-time affairs. In each case, it hadn't taken long for me to yearn for something new, something more. I wanted an *all-in-one* adventure, where I could move from one new experience to another without having to search for the next one. I wanted my own erotic *Disneyland*.

I knew if I could find such diverse activities online, there must be a whole underworld of swingers looking for something similar. Surely some enterprising operator would see the potential in putting together some kind of package deal. I sat down in front of my computer, opened up my browser, and typed in the words 'all-inclusive erotic adventure.'

A surprising number of 'clothing-optional' resort listings came up. I clicked on the first one, but it just showed the usual pictures of pretty pools, beaches, and guests suites, with a vague description of an 'upscale retreat for an adventurous lifestyle experience'. A little further down the page, I saw a blog article titled *Inside a nudist sex resort*. The article described an adventure traveler's experience at a resort where couples romped on nude beaches, swam in nude pools, and 'hooked up' in private cabins.

Definitely a little too tame-sounding for me.

I clicked on the next page of search results, where I saw a link titled *Nude Cruise — Explore Your Erotic Fantasies.*

This looks interesting.

I clicked on the link and a webpage opened showing pictures of naked people climbing walls, dancing in water fountains, and wrestling in a muddy pit.

That looks a little different, I thought.

At the top of the webpage, there was a tab titled *Fantasy Menu.* I clicked on the link, and a list of sexy-sounding shipboard activities appeared:

> Peak Sensation
> House of Holes
> Fantasy Fountain
> Sensuous Steam Room
> Masquerade Ball
> Sexy Games Room
> Get Down Disco
> Cybersex Rules
> Private View Rooms
> Intimate Massage
> FourPlay

I clicked on the first one and a photo appeared showing naked men and women scaling a climbing wall with unusual foot and hand holds. Instead of the usual jug and pocket holds, the 'grips' were in the shape of dildos and artificial vaginas, where climbers could pause to 'rest' and 'recharge their batteries' as they scaled the wall. A description under the photo read:

Challenge yourself to a climbing wall like no other. The higher you go, the more stimulating the experience becomes. Reward yourself at each new level, where you'll find a new wall feature to stimulate and excite every part of your body, as you seek the peak experience at the top of the mountain. All while safely strapped into a comfortable harness that permits a maximum range of movement and accessibility.

That sounds like an incredible turn on, I thought.

The idea of fucking a dildo strapped to a wall while people watched me from below sounded insanely sexy. My pussy began to twitch as I imagined the idea.

What's this next one—*House of Holes*?

I clicked on the next listed activity, and a picture appeared showing various nude men and women pressing their hips and buttocks against a wall with scattered holes. The look of ecstasy on their faces left little doubt as to what was happening on the other side. The description read:

Hook up with a stranger on the other side of a wall through your own personal intimate portal. You can choose to 'give', 'receive', or 'merge' with a partner of either sex in an erotic and completely anonymous connection. Or you can choose to simply watch, as other couples get their groove on in this sensuous and erotic House of Holes.

Damn, that sounds dirty. And fun.

I'd heard of glory holes before, but I'd always thought of them as skanky places where gay men went to get an anonymous blow job. The idea of engaging in heterosexual sex or touching pussies with another woman through my own private portal was different. And highly stimulating. My left hand dropped down between my legs and I began to rub my clit as I continued exploring the website.

What happens in the Sexy Games Room?

I clicked on the next activity, which displayed a photo of naked men and women in contorted positions atop a polka-dot-covered mat. Their hips and asses were pressed together while they stretched their arms and legs around each other. The caption read:

Play interactive nude games with your fellow guests where the rules and rewards are wide open. With Naked Twister, stretch into increasingly difficult and erotic positions as you try to reach around, over, and under your naked partners. Or try Naked Poker where the 'loser' must engage in increasingly erotic situations in full view of their playing partners. Or jump into the Naked Mud Wrestling pit and try to wrestle your partner into submission, all while surrounded in sensuous mud.

Fuck, yes! I thought. *These guys know how to organize an erotic party.*

I didn't need to click any more of the fantasy activities to know this was the sort of erotic travel destination that I had in mind. It promised to be an immersive, stimulating experience with multiple partners and exciting activities. As always though, I needed to be sure it would be clean and safe. I searched the page and found a tab marked *Conditions*, which read:

Every Nude Cruise guest must provide a certified report from a verified medical testing lab, indicating negative for sexually communicated diseases. The report must be dated within one week of your ship's departure date. Clothing is optional for all activities. Security staff are available at all venues to ensure the safety of guests and to ensure that all interaction occurs only with express consent.

Fair enough, I thought. *The medical test requirement shows this is a class act. You can't be too careful about these things.*

I clicked the Booking tab and viewed the calendar for available dates. The next cruise departed from Miami in two weeks' time. I'd have to move a few things around and schedule a two-hour flight, but one of the joys of my job as a freelance graphic designer meant I could choose my own vacation days. I booked a private cabin with a Queen-size bed, then I tore my panties off and plunged my fingers into my pussy as I fantasized about all the shipboard activities I'd soon be participating in.

2

SETTING SAIL

On the scheduled day of my departure, my whole body was buzzing with excitement. This was my first cruise, and I didn't know what to expect. Besides my fear of seasickness, I was a little nervous about the idea of parading around nude in public. I'd picked up some anti-nausea pills at the pharmacy, but I had butterflies in my stomach for an entirely different reason.

So far, my excursions into the realm of public sex and nudity had been fairly anonymous. At the dinner party, I could hide behind my masquerade mask. In the dark room, the special light effects concealed my identity. Even at my naked yoga class, everybody was so busy concentrating on their poses that it was really only my partner who had a close-up view of me.

But on this 'clothing-optional' cruise, I'd be going about my everyday routines in plain view of hundreds of strangers. Granted, some of the activities sounded highly erotic and fun. But the idea of sitting down for dinner or even just sunbathing in the nude gave me the willies. I'd packed some skimpy bikinis in case I got cold feet, but I didn't want to be the only one wearing clothes if everyone else was naked.

When I arrived at the cruise terminal, it was a hive of activity.

There were hundreds of people waiting to go through security, and the building was buzzing with chatter and public announcements. I pulled out my boarding pass and looked for the sign directing me to my designated gate. Just like at airport security, there were multiple lines of people placing their bags on conveyor belts going through an X-ray machine. When it was my turn, I took off my shoes and opened my roller-bag to remove my liquids.

"That won't be necessary, ma'am," a handsome security attendant said.

"Oh?" I murmured, confused.

"No need to remove your shoes or any items from your bag," he said. "Security procedures for cruise ships aren't as stringent as they are for air travel."

I smiled and nodded sheepishly as I pulled my sandals back on.

"Unless you're carrying something metal, of course. That'll set our machine off."

"No, of course not," I said, blushing from all the attention I was getting holding up the line. But now I was worried about the vibrator I'd packed in my luggage.

Who needs to bring a vibrator on a naked sex cruise, anyway? I chided myself.

"I'll just need to see your boarding pass," the security agent said.

I showed him my pass, and he directed me to stand in line behind the pass-through body scanner. As I waited for my turn, I looked around at my fellow boarding passengers. Most of them were fairly young, in their 20s and 30s, but there were also some older couples who were apparently looking for a little adventure to spice up their marriages. I noticed a few people checking each other out. Most of them didn't make eye contact for very long, but I wasn't the only one undressing some of the hot passengers with my eyes.

I caught a tanned gentleman in the adjacent line running his eyes up and down my body. I'd intentionally worn skinny jeans and a tight blouse for the first day to show off my best assets. I stood up tall and lifted my chest to display my cleavage. He had a nice ass, strong arms, and beautiful skin. When our eyes met, he smiled at me, and I could feel the blood rushing to my face again.

Come on, Jade, I admonished myself. *Get a hold of yourself. If you're going to be this self-conscious fully clothed, how are you ever going to be comfortable walking around in the nude?*

I returned my attention to the X-ray machine as my bag disappeared under the cover. I watched the face of the security agent as he scanned the monitor for any suspicious contents, then breathed a sigh of relief when I saw my bag pop out the other end.

"Ma'am?" the agent at the opposite side of the body scanner said, motioning for me to step through.

I'd been so worried my vibrator would set off the X-ray machine, that I hadn't realized I was holding up the line again. I nodded self-consciously, then walked through the pass-through stand, making eye contact with the security agent to ensure I wouldn't set off any other alarms. After he nodded that I was clear, I picked my bag off the X-ray belt and looked for the sign to the check-in area. By now, I was sure that half the passengers in the security area were cursing in bewilderment at my awkward travel etiquette, and I was glad to find a respite at the end of a new line.

"That's a pretty big bag for a short cruise," a woman's voice said, as I heard someone step up behind me.

I turned around and looked into the eyes of a stunning brunette about my same height.

"Um, well, you know," I stammered. "It's mostly makeup and toiletries and that sort of thing. We women can't be shorthanded about these things."

I could feel the flush in my cheeks again, caught off guard by her disarming beauty.

"No, I suppose not," she said, smiling at my innocence. "Although something tells me *makeup* will be the least of our concerns on this trip."

Her confidence and bold manner was rapidly sending blood flowing to another part of my body.

"Is this your first time with this cruise operator?" I asked, not wanting to state the obvious.

"This is my third Fantasy Cruise. Once you dip your toes in, it's kind of addicting." Her eyes darted across my face, appraising my demeanor. "How about you?"

"It's my first time. I'm a bit nervous, to be honest. You know, about all the..."

"Yeah, there's a lot of that," she said. "But there's nothing to worry about. We're all in the same boat, so to speak. You get used to it pretty fast. It's actually quite liberating. Not having to dress up and put on airs. Nudity is a great equalizer."

I took a quick glance at her tight and tanned body. She was wearing loose fitting linen shorts and a tight T-shirt displaying a cruise ship sailing into the sunset. Her legs were long and shapely, and her firm breasts sat up high on her chest.

"Some of us are a little more equal than others, I'm afraid."

She scanned my figure and smiled.

"I don't think you have anything to worry about. You're gorgeous. As long as you don't mind being the center of attention with a body like that."

I puffed out my cheeks and exhaled heavily.

"That's exactly what I'm worried about. I'm not used to being the center of attention. At least not in a public setting with all my clothes off."

"What deck is your cabin on?" she asked.

I fumbled for my travel papers and pulled out my boarding pass.

"E deck," I said. "They told me that if I chose a cabin nearer the water line, I have a better chance of avoiding seasickness."

"That's my deck too. Stick with me girl, and I'll show you around. There are plenty of ways to take your mind off the motion of the boat. The key is to not stay in one place too long. With so many interesting shipboard activities, your stomach will be the *last* thing you'll be thinking about."

She held out her hand and smiled at me.

"My name's Heather."

"Jade," I said, shaking her hand softly. "Thanks, Heather. I could use a wing woman, or shipmate, or whatever you're supposed to call your cruise partner these days."

"It's a deal," Heather said, winking at me. "We'll be *partners in crime*."

I reached the front of the line and saw one of the check-in agents motioning for me to come to her station.

"I'll wait for you past check-in," I said, suddenly mindful of the increasing dampness building between my legs.

3
______

RECEPTION

After clearing through Check-in, Heather guided me through the final boarding process then we walked together toward our rooms on E deck. We agreed to meet thirty minutes later when we'd go to the guest reception in the main lounge on the top deck. Our rooms were in the same hall, so after saying temporary goodbyes, I continued down the hall toward my stateroom.

When I opened my door, I was surprised by how small my room was. The Queen-size bed seemed to take up almost all of the space, with a tiny adjoining closet and small desk beside the wall-mounted TV. I went into the bathroom and was disappointed to see a stand-up shower with no tub. I knew that space aboard a cruise ship was at a premium, but I wasn't expecting it to feel so claustrophobic.

I unpacked my toiletries and placed them on the tiny sink, then carried my small carry-on case and placed it on the bed. There was a small sliding window beside my bed, and I immediately walked over and slid it open to breathe in some fresh air. I could see a flotilla of small boats moving about the bay opposite our ship, and I immediately regretted not upgrading to a larger room with balcony.

I bet Heather has a bigger room, I thought. *I'm such a lightweight at this cruise thing.*

I was looking forward to picking her brain for other tips about optimizing my shipboard experience. Not to mention picking over the *rest* of her body. I couldn't wait to see her naked and run my hands over her tight ass and breasts.

The porter had taken my larger roller case, and I didn't have much of a change of clothes in my carry-on bag. Heather had said not to worry too much about what to wear for the reception since most first-time guests chose not to go fully nude at the first activity. Nevertheless, I wanted to get with the program and ease myself into the idea of being naked on board, so I removed my bra and unbuttoned my silk blouse three buttons to reveal my cleavage.

I went into the washroom and looked at myself in the small mirror. The soft silk rubbing against my nipples had already stimulated them to an aroused state, and they protruded against the thin fabric, creating two conspicuous nodes. I smiled at how full and firm my breasts looked in my revealing blouse and hoped they'd attract Heather's attention too. I put on a new coat of light red lipstick and touched up my mascara, then grabbed my purse and headed down the hall toward Heather's room.

When she opened her door and I saw what she was wearing, it took my breath away. She wore a see-through gauzy top that barely concealed her large breasts through the sheer material. I stared shamelessly at her figure, wanting to flip her loose top up over her waist and devour her firm, round tits. To top it off, she'd let her long brown hair down and it shone with iridescent hues of amber and gold. She looked absolutely ravishing, and I was already regretting my wardrobe choice.

"Damn, girl," I said. "You're a feast for sore eyes. Who needs hors d'oeuvres when the main course is standing right here in front of me."

"That can be arranged," she said. "Come on in. Let's freshen up before heading over to the reception."

Heather motioned me into her room and I stepped inside. As I suspected, her room was larger than mine, with a small sitting room next to her bed and French doors leading out to a balcony.

"I knew I should have upgraded to a suite," I frowned. "I'm already beginning to feel claustrophobic in my tiny little cabin."

I looked out her French doors toward the open bay.

"Do you mind if I check out your view?"

"Of course. Make yourself comfortable. You're welcome to hang at my place anytime you're feeling closed in. I'll just be a couple more minutes."

Heather disappeared into the washroom, and I slid the side doors open and stepped out onto her balcony. I could smell the fresh salty air from the sea and I closed my eyes as I breathed it in.

This is definitely the way to travel, I thought. *Next time,* I reminded myself, *remember to get a full-size suite with balcony.*

After a few minutes, Heather emerged from the washroom looking even more beautiful than before, and I couldn't help shaking my head.

"I'm feeling terribly overdressed. You look like you're getting in the swing of this nude cruise thing already. Should I find something skimpier to wear?"

"Nonsense," Heather said. "You look perfect." Her eyes traced a line down to my aroused nipples protruding against my blouse. "You're revealing just the right amount for the meet and greet. I guarantee you'll be getting a lot of attention in that tight outfit."

I glanced down at her tanned legs and sandals.

"But you're showing a lot more...skin. Am I going to be the only one covering up my whole body?"

"Not at all. Most first-timers come to the initial reception dressed pretty conservative. It takes a couple of days for people to get comfortable being in the buff around their fellow passengers. By the second or third day, everybody will be strolling around buck naked. After the reception there's a dance, where the lights get turned down. You'll have plenty of opportunity to shed some of your clothes then."

As Heather walked toward me, I watched her breasts jiggle under her sheer blouse. When she stood in front of me, I stared at her tits and soft brown nipples. I couldn't stop myself.

"May I?" I said, looking gently into her eyes.

"I thought you'd never ask," she smiled.

I lifted her top and cupped her breasts in my hands and squeezed them softly. They were full and firm, and perfectly shaped, straight out of a centerfold. I noticed her areolas contract and her nipples begin to extend. I rolled them gently between my thumbs and forefingers, and she leaned in to kiss me. When our lips met, I pushed my body toward hers and pressed my hips against hers. She grabbed the back of my head and pulled me closer as our tongues danced around each other's mouths. I could have fucked her right then and there, but after a long lingering kiss, she pulled away.

"There'll be plenty of time for this later," she said. "Let's go meet some new people at the reception. This is a *nude cruise*, remember? We don't want to be holed up in our cabin the whole time, do we?"

"I suppose not," I said, slightly disappointed. My head knew she was right, but the ache in my pussy disagreed. I wanted her right now, and I didn't feel like sharing her with anybody else.

"Come on," she said, grabbing my hand, pulling me toward the door. "Let's go trip the night fantastic."

When we got to the top deck, Heather led me to a large open lounge with floor-to-ceiling windows offering a commanding view of the bay. I hadn't realized the ship had already left the pier, and I saw that we were steaming past South Pointe Park toward the open sea.

There were hundreds of people milling around the room, and Heather clasped my hand as she led me toward the bar. I was glad almost everybody was fully clothed, ranging from shorts and T-shirts to camisoles and bikini bottoms. A few veteran Fantasy Cruise travelers had been bold enough to go topless, but for the most part, it was a fairly low-key affair.

"What'll you have, ladies?" a handsome bartender wearing a white dress shirt and bowtie asked.

"I'll have a watermelon vodka," I said.

"I'd like some sex on the beach please," Heather said.

"Coming right up," the bartender smiled.

"You're so naughty," I teased Heather.

"Hey, when in Rome..." she said.

I turned and looked around the room. Heather had given me good advice about what to wear, and I began to feel more relaxed.

"You were right about the dress code tonight," I said. "Though the bartender seems a little formal. Are the staff always dressed so prim and proper?"

"They're always *dressed*, if that's what you mean. It's company policy that staff always must wear clothes, even on a nude cruise. Something about maintaining their professionalism, I suppose. It kind of helps to separate the staff from the guests, especially when you need something. The officers dress in navy whites, and the servers typically wear black pants, vests, and bow ties."

I watched the bartender approach us as he returned from the other end of the bar.

"Are they allowed to...you know...*hook up* with guests?" I asked.

"Officially it's a no-no, but whatever enterprising staff chooses to do when they're off duty, is nobody's business. If they get caught cavorting with passengers they can technically be fired, but it's pretty hard not to dip your toe in the water every now and then with so many flirty naked passengers floating around."

"I see your point," I said, as a pretty topless girl walked past us.

"Here you go, ladies," the bartender said, placing our drinks in front of us.

"Come on," Heather said, picking up her glass. "Let's go mingle."

For the next hour or so, Heather and I stuck together as we wandered from one cluster of passengers to another, making small talk. Nobody seemed to want to address the elephant in the room, mostly sticking with safe subjects like where we were from, what we did for a living, and if we'd been on a Fantasy Cruise before.

But everybody was definitely checking each other out. Although most of us were technically fully 'dressed', there was plenty enough skin showing to get a good idea of what we'd look like naked. Most of the men wore tight T-shirts or open shirts, revealing plenty of chiseled pecs and abs. The women wore skimpy bikinis, or flimsy camisoles and miniskirts. It was a feast for the eyes, and I soaked it all in. After a little while, I spotted the tall gentleman who I'd made eye contact with in the security line, and I gently steered Heather in his direction.

"I see you managed to survive the security gauntlet," he said to me, as I shimmied up next to him.

"Barely," I laughed. "I wasn't sure who was going to arrest me first —the security guards for my smuggled contraband or the passengers who were steaming about me holding up the line."

"It wasn't so bad," he smiled. "Traveling on a ship is easier than a plane. Is this your first time?"

"Yes," I said. "How about you?"

"This is my second trip. I guess I had some unfinished business from my first time around. There's so much to do on this big ship— one week hardly seems to be enough time to take it all in."

I paused for a moment as I appraised his body. He was wearing creme-colored linen pants and sandals, with a loose-fitting short-sleeved Bermuda shirt. But it was unbuttoned enough to show the cleft rippling between his chiseled pecs as he motioned with his powerful arms. His dark eyes beckoned to me, as I began to fantasize about falling into his arms.

"I'm Marc," he said, extending his hand.

"Jade," I said, feeling his large fingers envelop me. I turned toward Heather. "And this is my partner in crime, Heather."

Marc smiled as he looked at Heather, trying to keep his gaze concentrated above her barely concealed breasts.

"Are you two sisters?" he said. "Because I have seen such a lovely pair since Giselle and Patricia Bundchen."

"If you're talking about Jade and me," Heather teased, "no." Then she grabbed her breasts and shook them provocatively. "But if you're talking about my girls here, I'll take that as a compliment."

"Either way," Marc said, "I mean it as a compliment."

A woman's voice suddenly came over the room's public address system to break the sexual tension. The three of us turned toward the stage, where a woman wearing white shorts and a pressed shirt was standing holding a mic.

"Good evening, Fantasy Cruise travelers!" she said, raising her voice in welcome.

A loud cheer filled the room from the attending guests.

"My name's Ashley, and I'll be your cruise director. For those of you who are traveling on your maiden voyage with Fantasy Cruise, welcome. And for those of you returning for more fun and games, I promise you won't be disappointed. We've added even more fantasy activities to uplift and stimulate you.

"All of you should have found the brochure with our full Fantasy Menu on your nightstand when you checked into your staterooms, but we have lots more here on the desk beside the stage. Whenever you have any questions, just come see me any time. I'll be here the rest of the evening, and you can find my office mid-ship next to the Poseidon Restaurant on Deck B. Or just ring me at triple-two on your in-room phone.

"But now, let's get this party started with our first Fantasy Dance!" she hollered.

The suddenly lights dimmed and flashing lights began circulating the room. The sound of Marvin Gaye's *Let's Get it On* began booming over the speakers, and Heather, Marc and I began swaying our hips together in unison. Heather turned toward me and began shaking her ass suggestively in Marc's direction.

He's dreamy! she mouthed to me.

Damn straight, I returned, widening my eyes in agreement.

Marc simply smiled at me as he pretended to grind his hips against Heather's ass.

My first fantasy cruise was off to a promising start.

4

———

GETTING DOWN

For the next hour or so, Heather, Marc and I got our groove on as the swirling lights from the disco ball flashed over the writhing crowd. With the sun beginning to set over the horizon, the room became increasingly dark, and some brave passengers began shedding their clothes. Heather was the first to take off her skimpy top, and after another ten minutes of bumping and grinding with her and Marc, I soon followed suit. Not long after, Marc ripped off his shirt and threw it on a growing pile beside the stage.

It felt fabulous to be semi-nude, and we shamelessly rubbed our bodies together as the sexy music played in the background. It didn't take long for us to remove our clothes completely as we got more and more worked up by the suggestive lyrics. When Donna Summer's *Love to Love You Baby* came over the speakers, we moved in close and rolled our hips and chests together, our passion rising in tandem with the singer's orgiastic moans. I could feel Marc's cock hardening against our bodies as my wetness commingled with Heather's on our skin. As usual, Heather made the first move.

"Let's get out of here," she panted in our ears, and we didn't even bother to pick up our clothes as the three of us pranced out of the lounge. Bypassing the elevator, Heather led the way down the closest stairwell while we raced down the three flights to E deck. We giggled our way down the hall past a few other half-dressed passengers as we headed toward Heather's room. When we got to her door, I looked at her blankly, wondering how we were going to get in. We were all stark naked, and none of us were carrying a room key.

"Shit!" I said to Heather. "What now? Maybe we can find a secluded spot on the deck—"

"Not to worry," she said. "I've been in this predicament before, and I've taken precautions."

She kneeled down on the floor and peered through the small crack under the base of her door. Then she reached into the space with her fingers and pulled a credit-card-sized room key out across the carpet.

"Shazam!" she said, standing up and displaying her room key triumphantly. "A lady is prepared for every contingency."

She fumbled with the key in the lock then pushed open the door, and the three of us scrambled into her room. As soon as the door closed, Heather jumped up onto Marc and threw her legs around his hips. He turned and pinned her against the door, and they started kissing passionately. I rubbed my breasts against his sweaty back and moved my hand between his legs. I could feel his hard cock pointing down between Heather's legs, and I rubbed it against her soaking pussy. It didn't take long for the three of us to be coated in her slippery juices.

I squeezed Marc's balls gently as he contracted his glutes and pressed harder against Heather. All three of us were panting, wanting a piece of his meat. Suddenly, he swung around and carried Heather toward the bed with her still clinging to his hips. He placed one knee on the bed and lowered her onto its surface, then pressed his body against hers. Not wanting to interrupt their rhythm, I stood and watched as my sticky hand moved between my legs.

At this point, I was so turned on I could have come just watching Heather and Marc make love. But Heather had other plans, and she twisted her body and flipped Marc over, straddling his hips. She motioned for me to join them on the bed and I kneeled down beside her and kissed her on her lips. I could feel her body writhing over Marc's midsection, and I ran my hands down her stomach to feel their connection. Marc's hard cock was flat against his stomach as Heather rolled back and forth over it with her wet pussy. I played with her clit and she began to moan in my mouth.

Then she began lowering herself until our mouths were inches away from Marc's throbbing phallus. She swung her leg over to Marc's opposite side and his penis popped up into an acute sixty-degree angle, pointing toward his head. In the soft moonlight streaming through Heather's balcony doors, I could see that it was large, straight, and magnificent. The head glistened with a mixture of pre-cum and Heather's juices, and we both wrapped our fingers around it.

While we gave him a slow, two-handed massage, Marc sighed and thrust his manhood into our pliant hands. After a couple of minutes, Heather lowered her head and took him into her mouth, as I cupped his balls and played with the space between his testicles and anus. Marc moaned and began to roll his hips more aggressively, obviously enjoying Heather's attention on his cock. I could hear his passion rising and I began to feel his balls tighten and rise up. I knew it wouldn't take long for him to come with the combined effect of two beautiful women attending to his erogenous area.

Heather must have sensed it too because she lifted her head off his dick and leaned over and kissed me. Marc began to raise himself up wanting to get in on the action, but Heather extended her right hand and pushed him back onto the bed. He quickly got the message and watched the two of us while we explored each other's bodies. I cupped Heather's tits again and rolled her nipples between my fingers, then we pressed our chests together and tribbed our nipples while we fucked each other's mouths with our tongues.

By this time, all three of us were ready for some direct stimulation, and I hesitated, unsure where to go next. It was my first time in a threesome—at least one where I had this degree of control—and I didn't want to leave anyone hanging. Heather suddenly lifted her right leg and swung it over Marc's stomach, then did the same with her other leg until she was straddling his hips from the side. She motioned for me to do the same, then we pulled each other forward until our vulvas touched Marc's throbbing member on opposite sides. It was an incredible sensation feeling the heat of his hard cock sandwiched between our two pussies. Heather and I wasted no time moving our hips up and down, giving Marc an entirely new type of erotic massage.

The three of us were now getting direct stimulation, and Heather and I moaned in each other's mouths as we rubbed our soaking pussies together against Marc's pointed cock. I could feel our combined wetness running between my legs, as I pushed harder against Marc's warm and wonderful joystick. I wrapped my arms around Heather's waist and pulled her closer toward me. By now, we were all moaning in abandon and nearing the tipping point. I tilted my hips downward a bit and pressed my clit against the side of Marc's cock. Heather and I were humping him hard now, and our tits rubbed together as sweat streamed down our stomachs. This was an entirely new kind of tribbing that I'd never experienced before, and the image of the three of us joined together soon put me over the edge.

I threw my head back and let out a primal scream as Heather and I thrashed our hips together and gushed all over Marc's throbbing hard-on. We kissed for another minute as we came down from our high, then we separated and peered at Marc. He had a silly smile on his face, but his cock was still pointing up, bobbing gently over his stomach from the pulse flowing through its veins. I ran my hand over my stomach to see if I could detect any sign of semen on me, then I looked at Heather and shook my head to signal that he hadn't come yet.

"Good boy," she said, leaning over to give him a long, lingering kiss.

Then she shifted her body until her hips were behind his head, and she looked at me, silently nodding. I knew her intent immediately, and I swung my legs over Marc's midsection, straddling his hips in her direction. She lifted herself up, placing her pussy over his face, then lowered herself onto his eager mouth. I could see her eyes roll back in her head as he took her swollen clit between his lips and began to suck her, and she began to grind her hips into his face.

I didn't need any more encouragement. I grabbed Marc's thick schlong and directed the tip toward my quivering opening. I teased him for just a second, rubbing his sticky head against my clit and vulva, then I lowered myself onto him until his mound pressed firmly against my clit. As Heather and I locked eyes, I convulsed in a mini-orgasm.

It was an unbelievably hot sight watching each other fuck this adonis from opposite ends as we watched our passion rising. I began to rock my hips in unison with Heather, and I could feel Marc's hips answering the call. I loved the feeling of his big cock filling me up, and he knew how to move his hips to give my clit direct stimulation. The combined feeling of my clit grinding into his mound and the head of his cock rubbing against my G-spot was driving me crazy. I began moaning more loudly as I stepped up the pace of my humping action, while Heather and I clasped hands.

I wanted to make this last as long as I could, but the sights and sounds of three beautiful people joining together in an erotic union was too much. I could feel my orgasm welling deep inside me and I made one final push down hard onto Marc's cock as I squeezed Heather's hands like a vice. When I finally came, I grunted like a wild animal as my body spasmed over Marc's hips while I looked Heather straight in her eyes.

I guess that was too much for Marc too, because he grabbed my hips with two hands and thrust his hips into the air, lifting me off the mattress as I felt his cock throbbing in rhythmic contractions inside my pussy. With him moaning into her pussy and her seeing me have a powerful orgasm, it soon put Heather over the edge. Just as I was beginning to feel the last of my contractions subside, her hands squeezed mine hard and her eyelids narrowed as she clamped her thighs around Marc's head. She growled like a dog in heat as I watched the pleasure roll over her pretty face. The whole time we never took our eyes off one another.

When she finally collected her breath and came down from her orgasm, she smiled at me. We were both thinking the same thing. My new partner in crime and I had found our first accomplice.

5

———

WATER SPORTS

Later that evening, Marc returned to his room and Heather and I continued to make love into the wee hours. By 3:00 a.m., we were both spent, and we fell asleep sprawled naked atop the bed sheets, as a cool breeze from the ocean wafted over our sweaty bodies. When the morning sun streamed through her balcony door, Heather rolled over and caressed my breast.

"Morning, Sunshine," she said, as my eyes slowly flitted open.

"Morning, Beautiful," I said, moving in closer to give her a kiss.

"That was quite a first night we had together."

"Mmmm, yes," I said, tasting her sweet tongue in my mouth. "Hopefully the first of many."

"I hope so too. But I don't want to steal all your time and attention on this cruise. The main idea is to mix it up and take advantage of as many activities as you can in the limited time you have available."

"Can't we do that together?" I asked.

"Some of them, for sure. But I think some of the other activities you might enjoy more on your own."

"What about our new friend Marc?"

"I'm pretty sure he'll want to get out there on his own and sow some more of his oats. But he left his room number on my nightstand, so we might have a chance to hook up with him again before the cruise is over."

I looked out the open balcony doors at the sun shimmering over the open sea.

"You've done this before. What activity do you recommend we try next?"

"Most people like to ease into this whole nudity thing. Let's head up to the pool and do some people watching while we work on our tans. There's also a cool fountain on the top deck that's quite fun and refreshing. But first, I think we should get something to eat. I don't know about you, but I'm famished!"

"Me too. I think we burned enough calories last night for *three* meals. But first I'd like to return to my cabin to freshen up. What do you recommend I wear to breakfast?"

"It'll be pretty hot up top. A bikini and sandals should be enough. You'll just be taking it all off pretty soon anyway. You don't want to have to carry a bunch of clothes around with you."

"That reminds me," I suddenly remembered. "I've still got to retrieve my stuff from last night in the lounge."

"Something tells me you're not going to need jeans and a blouse for a while. We can pick that up on our return to our cabins later in the day. Did you want to borrow my shawl to get back to your room?"

I smiled at Heather's thoughtfulness.

"I'm just a few doors down. Judging by last night, half the people on the ship are already nude, so a little more streaking down the hall shouldn't hurt me."

"You're going to need a key to get in though. I'm guessing you didn't think of my trick."

Heather leaned over and picked up her room phone then tapped some numbers on the dial.

"Yes," she spoke into the phone, "my friend's lost her key for room E48. Can you send someone down with a replacement? She's in my room, E32. Thank you."

Ten minutes later, there was a soft tap on Heather's door.

"Maybe I'll take you up on that shawl offer after all," I said.

Heather smiled and went to her closet and held the garment open for me as I slid my arms into it.

"Meet you in the Poseidon Restaurant in an hour?" she said.

"Deal," I said, giving her a quick kiss.

I opened the door, gave Heather a playful shake of my ass, then followed the porter back to my room.

***

After breakfast, Heather led me to the main pool on the top deck, where scores of people were lounging naked on deck chairs and playing in the water. A series of interconnected pools simulated the look of a tropical lagoon, complete with life-size palm trees and small cabanas. We found a couple of open lounge chairs not far from the bar, and Heather asked me to mind them for us while she went to get a couple of drinks.

While she was gone, I made a quick scan of the scene. Virtually everybody was already naked, and it was a busy hive of activity. On one end of the lagoon, a large waterslide deposited screaming guests into the splashing water. In an adjacent basin, a small group of people were playing water polo. On the other side of the patio, a few passengers were skipping through a water fountain like a bunch of playful toddlers. It was all pretty surreal, and I paused to take it all in.

"Checking out all the action?" Heather said, returning from the bar and handing me a drink.

"Mmm, yes," I said, taking a sip of my pina colada. "There's certainly a lot of...*diversions*."

"Are you referring to all the naked people or the activities?"

"Both," I said, scanning the bodies of some of the men walking around the pool. "It's strange, though. Everybody seems so...*asexual*. I would have thought more people would be, you know, *aroused*, seeing each other naked."

"That's the thing about us all being in the same boat, so to speak. Like I said earlier, nudity is the great equalizer. Everybody gets used to it pretty quickly, and before you know it they're walking around like it's a normal walk in the park." Heather paused as she appraised my demeanor. "Are you disappointed?"

"Not really. I just expected the men in particular would be showing more sign of, you know, *interest*. The cruise operator billed this as more of a sex cruise than a nude cruise."

Heather smiled, as she lay back on her lounge chair.

"Believe me, there'll be plenty of opportunity for you to get down and dirty on this cruise. There's more going on than might first appear. For instance, take a look at that woman standing in the fountain on the other side of the patio."

I peered across the pool and saw a naked woman in her twenties standing over some jets of water spraying up from the surface. She had a strange look on her face as she spread her legs and squatted over the stream.

"It looks like she's having an enema," I laughed.

"I think she's directing the spray to a *different* part of her body," Heather said.

The look on the woman's face changed to one of pleasure as she began to shimmy her hips over the water stream. Suddenly the spray started pulsing like a shower head, and she let out a low moan.

I crossed my legs, beginning to feel a tingle in my pussy.

"I see what you mean," I said. "Now I see why they call it the Fantasy Fountain."

Heather noticed me squirming on my chair.

"Do you feel like giving it a try?"

"In a sec. Let me enjoy her experience first."

The woman suddenly grabbed her tits with her hands and pushed them up, as the spray from the patio surface gushed up over her abdomen and washed over her face. She was grunting and groaning now and moving her hips more rhythmically over the jet.

"Fuck, that's hot," I said.

"Kind of a nice way to cool off on a hot day like this."

"It looks like it might take the edge off in more ways than one."

Suddenly, the woman began screaming, as her body convulsed and her hips shook in rhythmic spasms. There was no doubt to us or any of the many other spectators that she had just enjoyed a powerful orgasm. When she staggered out of the fountain back toward her lounge chair, a small round of applause rose from around the pool.

"What do you think?" Heather said. "Are you up for it?"

"Now that I know I'm going to have an audience, I wouldn't mind some company. Will you come with me?"

"I think I will," Heather said, winking at me. "Let's toss these bikinis first. We don't want anything getting in the way of all the fun."

Heather nonchalantly unclasped her bikini top behind her back then stepped out of her bottoms. I'd almost forgotten how beautiful she was, and her tanned body looked magnificent in the bright sunshine. Her shaved pussy left nothing to the imagination, and I could see her nub poking out of her labia at the top of her pussy.

"Damn girl," I said, opening my eyes wide. "You're never afraid to let it all hang out."

"It's called a *fantasy cruise*, right? Let's live out our fantasies. Get those clothes off and let's go have some fun!"

I pulled off my top and bottom and threw them on my lounge chair, then Heather and I scampered around the pool past a throng of curious onlookers. When we got in the fountain, it was actually quite refreshing. The water was warm, but it felt cool against my hot skin in the blazing sun. The water jets were spread a few feet apart, facing different directions with alternating pulsing patterns. Some were a constant stream and some stopped and started periodically, while others pulsed at different speeds like an overhead shower faucet.

Heather and I stepped into the sprays and danced around for a minute, laughing and holding hands. Then we came together and kissed, rubbing our bodies together as the spray shot up between us, soaking our faces. Suddenly, I no longer cared about being naked in full view of the other pool guests. I was lost in the deluge of sensations I felt from the water jets spraying against my ass and Heather rubbing her body against mine.

We shifted position until we found a spot in the fountain where a steady stream directed toward our pussies. Then we pushed our mounds together so the stream sprayed directly against our touching clits. I opened my mouth and gasped as Heather smiled at me. This was a once-in-a-lifetime experience, and I wanted to enjoy every moment of it with her.

Suddenly, two more sprays began jetting at a forty-five-degree angle from behind each of us, and we bent our knees to give the spray direct access to our rosebuds.

"Oh my God!" I said to Heather, as my eyes flew open.

"Is this *arousing* enough for you?" she said, grinding her clit against mine.

"Fuck, yes!"

Just when I thought it couldn't get any more intense, the steady spray directed toward our clits began pulsing in strong, flickering streams.

"Uhnn," I moaned, closing my eyes at the intense feeling of pleasure I was experiencing from every part of my body.

"Enjoy, Baby," Heather said, as she thrust her tongue into my mouth, swaying her hips in tandem with mine.

I could feel the passion rising quickly inside me, and there was no way I could hold it back any longer.

"Fuck, I'm coming!" I said, as my pussy clenched inside me and I became weak in the knees. "Ohh, Ohh, Ohh," I panted into Heather's mouth, feeling the waves roll over me. Heather grunted into my mouth and I felt her hips shudder against mine as she reached her own peak. We moaned out loud together as the warm water from the jets sprayed all over our ecstatic faces.

When we finally came down from our orgasms, we held each other over the gentle spray, leaning against one another in exhaustion. When we separated, a loud cheer rose from around the pool from the appreciative crowd.

I guess this won't to be so hard getting used to after all, I thought.

6

―――――

PEAK SENSATIONS

eather and I spent the rest of the day lounging around the pool, people watching. We made a few new friends and got some more cabin numbers, but mostly we just wanted to relax and scope out our next move. Heather said if we didn't pace ourselves, we'd either be too sore or exhausted to partake in some of the more adventurous shipboard activities. After perusing the ship's Fantasy Menu, we both agreed our next rendezvous would be at the climbing wall.

I went back to my cabin alone that night planning to get a good night's sleep, with visions of naked climbers exposing themselves as they scaled the cliff. I woke up refreshed the next morning, eager to try out the next erotic challenge. When I met Heather at the breakfast buffet, the room was filled with naked passengers filling their plates with hardly a sideways glance. I guess she'd been right about everybody getting comfortable being in the nude by the third day.

As she explained to me what to expect at the climbing wall, my eyes widened in anticipation. It sounded terrifying and exciting at the same time.

"Do people ever *fall*?" I asked.

"Everyone's strapped into a harness and they have spotters to maintain tension on the rope holding you up, so even if you do slip, it's perfectly safe."

I frowned at the thought of other people watching my naked body from below.

"So I'll have some stranger watching my bare ass as I stretch my legs and move up the wall?"

"Yes, but that's part of the fun of it. Knowing other people are watching you as you get higher and higher is quite titillating, for both you and the observers. Plus, the staff doing the rope work are usually pretty buff, so it's kind of hot."

The idea of exposing my body while I stimulated myself on the wall reminded me of my Dinner Party experience. I squirmed in my seat reflecting back on the memory of Jasmine playing with me under the table while my fellow diners looked on.

"Tell me more about the unique 'features' on the wall."

"Besides the usual cup and lip-shaped ledges for gaining a comfortable hand and foot hold, there are other more *erotic* holds to clasp onto along the way."

"Such as?"

"For starters, some of the lips vibrate, so you can pause and get a little extra stimulation whenever you're feeling in the mood."

I pictured the idea of being in a harness clinging to a wall while sex toys stimulated my private parts.

"Now I see why they strap you in," I said. "I could barely maintain my balance on solid ground at the fountain yesterday, the more worked up I got. I can imagine how weak in the knees people might get, stimulated in a similar manner while climbing a challenging wall."

"Exactly," Heather said. "Especially the higher you go. The stimulation gets more and more intense the higher you climb."

"How so?"

"The features start out pretty tame at the bottom, just little nodules to rub against. But then they start vibrating, like little magic bullets. They get progressively larger and more animated the higher you go. If you make it all the way to the top, they've got some full-size dildos that twist and rotate to really give you a ride."

"Mmm," I said, feeling the moisture beginning to build inside my pussy. "Just like my favorite rabbit vibrator."

"Kind of like that. Except this time, you're suspended twenty-five feet off the ground in full view of your spotter and any other spectators while you get off."

Suddenly I had a burning need to have something inside me.

"That sounds pretty hot."

Heather raised her eyebrows and nodded.

"There's something about the whole idea that's very arousing. I think you'll find it's quite a different experience."

I wrinkled my forehead as I pondered the possibilities.

"What about the guys? Are there similar erotic features for *them* to enjoy on the wall?"

"Definitely. The wall holds alternate between 'innies' and 'outies', so everybody has a chance to enjoy. Many of them are fashioned in the form of flexible lips, pussies, and anuses, where men can insert their dongs along the way and get a similar thrill. Near the top, they become animated with internal vibrators, just like the bullets and dildos for the ladies. It's quite arousing to watch the men and women stop and fuck the life-like features along the way."

I shook my head and grimaced at a new thought.

"What about all the...*by-products* deposited along the way? It must get pretty slippery and gross before long. I wouldn't want to place my hands or my pussy anywhere near some dude's day-old cum."

Heather scrunched her nose and laughed.

"Not to worry. The ship operators have got it all figured out. After every new climber comes down from the wall, they cover the wall in a tarp and wash it down with high-powered steam water jets. They keep it all very antiseptic."

I clenched my legs together, trying to stimulate my burning clit. I couldn't wait to give it a try.

"What do you say?" Heather said. "Are you up for it?"

"Definitely. My pussy's ready to climb on just about anything right now!"

When we got to the wall, I was surprised by how tall it was. It towered at least thirty feet straight up, with foot and hand holds separated a few feet apart. It was odd but strangely arousing to see the artificial vulvas and dildos sticking out from its surface. Two naked people were already strapped into hip harnesses at the base of the wall, a man and a woman both appearing to be in their mid-20s.

They spoke with familiarity to one another, so I assumed they were a couple. What a thrill I thought it must be for the pair to experience this together. A small crowd of friends and onlookers were gathered a few feet further back from the wall, egging the couple on. As Heather had described, two buff staff members held thick ropes in their hands, which looped up over an extended wheel at the top of the structure. The other end dangled down the front of the facade and clasped securely to the front of their harnesses.

"Are you ready?" the man said, looking at his partner.

She nodded silently, then reached up for the first handhold and placed her foot onto a lip at the base of the wall. Heather looked at me and smiled. The idea of doing this in tandem appealed to me, and I hoped that the two of us would have our turn soon. It was strange watching the climbers spread their legs and bend their asses as they stretched to reach the next higher holds. I could see the man's balls hanging between his thighs and his penis wobbling back and forth as he swung from one placement to the other. They both seemed so focused on figuring out their path of ascent that they barely paused to rest.

But about half way up, the woman suddenly paused and pushed her hips against the wall. I could see a small ball-shaped object resting between her thighs, nestled against her vulva. A gentle vibrating noise emanated from the area. She looked over at her partner and smiled, encouraging him to find a similar place to rest.

He glanced to his left and saw an orange ring protruding from the wall. He stepped up and over until his cock was level with the ring then he positioned his flaccid member inside the hole. Suddenly the ring started vibrating, and the man threw his head back. I could see his cock hardening and lengthening as he positioned the vibrating ring around the glans of his penis. He turned toward his partner and they giggled while they gently humped the wall together.

"Higher! Higher!" their friends urged them on from the bottom of the wall.

The two reluctantly disengaged from their fixed positions and resumed their climb up the wall. About five feet higher up, the woman came upon a curved rubber dildo protruding about three inches from the surface, and she paused over it then lowered her pussy until it disappeared inside her hole. She started humping the small dildo to cheers from the crowd. I was glad everybody's attention was focused on the wall, because my fingers had already begun circling my clit as I matched the woman's hip movements.

The man noticed a new feature on his side of the wall, this time mimicking the lips and tongue of a woman. He didn't hesitate to slip his now fully erect cock inside the orifice and begin to moan as he deep-throated his artificial lover. Both he and his partner began speeding up the movement of their hips and it looked like one or both of them might come soon. But the crowd at the base of the wall weren't quite ready.

"Get to the pussy and the dick at the top!" someone shouted. "You're almost there!"

The couple glanced at one another then looked down and shook their heads in mock frustration. Then they peered up the wall and resumed their climb. All the while, the two staff members holding the ropes held the lines taut while pretending to be uninterested in the actions of the climbers. But I noticed the telltale bulge in their pants that belied their disinterest. I looked over at Heather and saw that her hand had slipped between her legs too.

The couple picked up their climbing speed with new determination, and it didn't take long for them to near the top of the wall, where the woman was presented with a large purple dildo and the man with a gaping artificial pussy. The woman placed her lips around the dildo and pretended to give it blowjob while the man pushed his face into the artificial vulva and shook his head playfully. The crowd below erupted in a loud cheer.

"Fuck it! Fuck it! Fuck it!" they chanted in unison.

The woman climbed a few feet higher, then placed the big dildo inside her pussy, and relaxed her legs. The staff member holding her rope bent his knees, clasping the end of the rope tightly with two hands. He'd obviously been in this situation before, and he braced himself for the shifting load. Just a few feet away on the other side of the wall, the man positioned himself adjacent to the artificial vulva and inserted his dick into the hole.

"Whomp! Whomp! Whomp!" chanted their friends down below, in encouragement.

With everybody's attention focused on the wall, Heather suddenly moved behind me and squeezed my breast with one hand, while she slipped her fingers inside my cunny from behind. I could hear vibrating sounds emanating from the artificial pussy and dildo, and the man and the woman clenched their buttocks as they began to fuck their sex toys more vigorously. They peered over at one another and mouthed something, and I could hear their breathing escalating in urgency.

Heather began to speed up the pace of her ministrations, and I fucked her fingers as I pretended it was me on the wall. Within a minute or so, the couple's bodies began convulsing, and their arms and legs suddenly became rigid. Heather held me tightly while I clamped down hard on her hand as I came at the same time with the couple on the wall.

The handlers held the couple's lines firmly until they pushed away from the edifice and were gently lowered. When they got to the bottom and removed their harnesses, their friends surrounded them in a group hug, jumping up and down in celebration. The staff ordered everybody to step ten feet back from the wall, then a canvas tarp descended from the top and hot jets began cleaning the surface.

I could feel the steam rising above the tarp as a rivulet of water began pooling at the base of the structure, draining into a grated hole beside the podium.

I turned around and looked at Heather. She raised her eyebrows to signal if I was game to try it next. I simply nodded my head and smiled. I could feel my own rivulet of warm liquid running down my legs.

7

HOUSE OF HOLES

After they finished sanitizing the wall, Heather and I took our turn on it. Most of the spectators had moved on after the previous couple came down, but it was still unnerving being watched so closely by our rope handlers. As usual, Heather took the lead sitting over the erotic extrusions, and the look of delight on her face soon encouraged me to do the same. We came multiple times grinding our pussies into the various devices, culminating with two powerful orgasms on the large dildos at the top of the wall.

We spent a few more hours lounging around the pool, then Heather encouraged me to strike out on my own. I protested briefly, still not entirely comfortable with the idea of engaging in public sex by myself, but she suggested a few venues that might provide an opportunity for more privacy. After a quick lunch, I reluctantly began exploring the ship.

My first stop was the Sexy Games Room. It was filled with various contraptions, where solo men and women were getting fucked by automated machines. At one station, a woman bent over on all fours, while a large plastic dildo pounded in and out of her pussy. At another one, a man sat on a chair humping a life-like silicone doll, while he squeezed her fake tits and thrust his tongue into her fellatio-shaped mouth. In the corner of the room, a pretty co-ed straddled a device that looked like a pommel horse, as she bucked and writhed atop its vibrating saddle.

It all seemed so surreal and impersonal for me. I wanted a *human* connection, like the one Heather and I shared at the fantasy fountain. I scanned the activity menu and considered going for an Intimate Massage, thinking at least this way I'd have some human touch, and then I remembered one of Heather's recommendations. The description for the House of Holes sounded intriguing:

Hook up with a stranger on the other side of a wall through your own personal intimate portal. You can choose to 'give', 'receive', or 'merge' with a partner of either sex in an erotic and completely anonymous connection. Or you can choose to simply watch, as other couples get their groove on in this sensuous and erotic 'House of Holes'.

Yes, I thought, *'merging' with a partner is exactly what I need.* The notion of engaging with someone through my own personal 'glory hole', reminded me of the fun I'd had playing with hidden strangers in the Dark Room.

When I got to the venue and opened the door, the first thing I noticed was the sound. A cacophony of moans and grunts greeted me, as a variety of naked men and women shimmied their hips, asses, and mouths against the vinyl-coated walls. The lights were dimmed, but I could see the unmistakable shape of erect penises and vulvas poking through various small holes scattered around the room.

People on the other side were shaking their hips trying to get the attention of someone from inside the room, but everybody was already engaged in some form of coupling. One man was humping the wall, being serviced by someone from the other side. Another one kneeled on the floor giving head to a well-endowed fellow who thrust his cock vigorously into his consort's eager mouth. Not far away, a woman bent over rubbing her ass against the wall, where another man plunged his cock through the hole into her pussy.

But the whole scene somehow left me cold. It struck me as cheap and dirty. Medical clearance or not, I couldn't get on board with the idea of connecting with some other stranger's private parts in such an impersonal way. Just as I was about to leave the room, I noticed a neon sign in the corner reading 'Private View Rooms'.

Private definitely sounded more appealing. And being able to *see* my partner was more along my lines.

I opened the door and entered a dimmed hall with closed doors lining both sides. Most of them were locked with a sign reading 'Occupied', but a little further down the hall I found one marked 'Vacant'. I turned the handle and stepped into a small room. It had a single vinyl chair facing a floor-to-ceiling glass wall with a one-foot diameter hole cut in the middle. On the other side of the glass was a similar room with an empty chair.

I turned and locked my door, then checked the chair to see if it was clean. There were no visible marks or residue, but I ran my hand over its smooth surface just to be sure. Even the vinyl floor looked like it had just been cleaned, reflecting the light from the single overhead incandescent lamp.

At least they clean up after themselves pretty well, I nodded, as I sat down on the chair and waited for someone to enter the adjacent room.

I expected a man looking for a simulated adult video store glory hole experience, but I was pleasantly surprised when a slim young Asian girl opened the door. She paused for a moment and appraised me seated in my chair with my legs slightly ajar, then she turned around and locked her door from the inside. She was carrying something but she kept it hidden from my view as she turned around.

We could have easily talked if we'd wanted to, with a large enough hole in the glass to carry on a private conversation. But we both seemed to want to just *look* for the time being. She sat down on her chair and placed the hidden object behind her, then spread her legs apart. She had a petite figure with firm B-cup breasts and a small V-shaped patch of pubic hair on her mound that pointed toward a protruding nub at the top of her labia. She had large eyes with long lashes, and she smiled at me as she began to run her hands over her body.

I watched her for a moment, as I felt the juices from my pussy puddle on the chair in front of me. She placed her hands on the inside of her thighs and pulled them slowly toward her apex, then continued moving them up toward her chest. She squeezed her tits then pushed them up and tilted her head down, sucking each of her nipples.

I wanted a piece of her so badly, but I was enjoying her little strip-tease. I cupped my left breast with one hand and I began to play with my clit with my other, spreading my legs further apart. She did the same and pointed her toes, as she opened her mouth, signaling her pleasure. I could hear a soft moan emanating through the hole in the glass as she flitted her eyes and began to rock her hips on her chair.

By now I was thoroughly soaked, feeling the intensity rising in my loins. I slipped the fingers from my other hand into my pussy as I rubbed my clit more forcefully. The Asian girl suddenly thrust both of her hands into her love box and began fucking herself with a two-handed motion, rocking her chest in tandem with her hips. The sound of her juices sloshing around as she finger-fucked herself with both hands ratcheted my excitement up another level.

I could feel my orgasm beginning to build as I let out a low moan. The girl spread her legs wider until they were virtually straight out to her sides. I marveled at her flexibility, reminding me of my naked yoga experience with Kayla and Neve. We were groaning in tandem as we each fucked our own pussies, alternating our line of sight between our sopping pussies and our glazed-over eyes. Suddenly the girl's chest began to heave, and she grunted a staccato burst of moans as she hunched over in orgasmic spasms. That was enough to put me over the edge, and I growled like a wild animal as I gushed all over the chair in front of me. It was incredibly erotic watching each other come with only a few feet separating us between the clear pane of glass.

But now I was ready for a more personal connection. After I came down from my high, I stood up and walked toward the glass and motioned for her to do the same. She walked slowly toward the hole in the partition, then placed her palms flat against the glass at shoulder height. She was even prettier up close, with big brown eyes, high cheekbones, and full pouty lips. I placed my hands over hers and we moved our faces toward the glass until our lips touched on the cool surface. There was something about being this close to another naked woman and not being able to touch her that I found highly arousing.

Our opposite hands traced a path down the side of the glass and we reached through the hole to touch each other's pussies. I groaned when I felt the heat of her box and her fingers touching my clit. We lowered our bodies a few more inches to gain better access to our midsections while still peering into one another's eyes. I stuck out my tongue and began to lick the glass, showing that I was ready for a more personal touch.

I bent my knees a little further and her fingers slipped out of me as I squatted down over the hole in front of her pussy. She pushed her hips into the glass to try to give me better access, but it felt awkward tilting my head through the hole trying to get to her clit with my tongue. Sensing my frustration, she suddenly stepped back from the glass then lifted her right leg straight up and placed her heel against the glass beside her shoulder. Then she pushed her body forward until her legs were pressed flat against the glass in a perfect split.

Her open vulva was now pushing through the hole directly toward my face. I didn't hesitate to take her little button into my mouth and roll it around my tongue like a peppermint candy. Her lubrication coated my face as she ground her pussy against my cheeks. I reached through the hole and wrapped my arm around her hips, pulling her harder toward me. She moaned softly and whimpered as she fucked my face. I inserted two fingers into her love canal as I sucked and flicked her little cocklet in my mouth. Then I curled my fingers in a come-hither motion against her G-spot and she bent her knees, pressing her pussy harder against my face and fingers. Her moans were growing in intensity and my heart raced at the idea of her coming on my face. I pushed my fingers deeper inside and circled her clit more quickly with my tongue. Suddenly, she howled as her pussy clamped over my fingers in a long series of hard contractions. I held my face still while she gushed all over me.

If I could have squeezed my whole body through the narrow opening in the glass, I would have pounced on her right then and there and tribbed her hard until we both came together. Instead, I slowly raised myself up until my face was at the same level as hers and kissed her gently against the glass. She smiled at me and blinked twice as if to say 'thank you'. Then she turned around and walked toward the chair and picked up the object which she'd gone to such pains to hide from me. She held it up in the dim light and smiled. It was a long two-sided flexible dildo, anatomically correct on both ends, shaped like a two-headed penis.

Fuck, yes, I thought. *That's what I'm talking about.*

I wanted to fuck this girl so badly, and the two-sided dildo was just what the doctor ordered. She walked up to the glass and held it up in front of me, then licked it up and down the shaft. Then she placed one end in her mouth and simulated fellatio over the silicone glans.

Please, I mouthed through the glass. *I need it inside of me now.*

Demonstrating my urgency, I turned around and placed my ass against the open hole, then bent over to present my open pussy to her. She pushed the dildo through the hole and rubbed it back and forth across my vulva, and I shuddered in pleasure. I bucked my hips against the phallus and pressed my ass harder against the glass, signaling that I wanted her to place it inside me.

When she finally did, I almost fainted in pleasure. The feeling of the thick dildo pushing inside me from behind was exquisite. She pushed it as far as it would go, then I felt some slack on the device as she turned around and faced her ass toward me. I didn't need to look to know what she was doing, as I felt the pressure of the dildo when she pushed the other end inside her own pussy.

When our buttocks touched through the open glass, we groaned as we began to simultaneously fuck the giant phallus. I could feel her juices coating the dildo on the other end as our pussies sloshed and bucked against our imaginary partner. The girl began to whimper as we ground our asses together, trying to come over the thick joystick between our legs. It didn't take long for us to reach our peak as we screamed and shook in simultaneous orgasms on the writhing snake embedded inside us.

It took us over a minute before we were ready to disengage, when the girl finally separated herself from the two-headed dildo and pulled it out of my throbbing pussy. I turned around and placed my lips against the glass, and we kissed one last time before she silently picked up the dildo and exited the room. No words had been necessary the entire time we shared our intimate connection.

Just as I was turning to leave, a buff young man entered the room the girl had just left. I took one look at his large swinging cock and shook my head.

I wouldn't mind a taste of the real thing, I thought.

8

STRAIGHT FLUSH

After I had another go with my new partner in the private view room, I staggered back to my room, sore and exhausted. I slept like a log that night, dreaming of animated cocks and pussies attached to life-like trees, as I walked through a magical forest. When I woke up in the morning, I lay in a giant wet spot atop my leaking cunny and rubbed another one out before showering and heading upstairs to meet Heather for breakfast.

She laughed when I told her about my strange dream, and we entertained each other over lox and pineapple with stories of our experiences from the previous day. She seemed interested in my private view room encounter, but when I told her about my disappointment with the games room, her ears perked up.

"You didn't explore the *other* games rooms?" she said.

"What other games rooms? I only found the one with the holes in the wall."

"There are lots of others that you might find interesting. One of my favorites is the Card Lounge."

"What happens there?"

"It's where groups of people meet to play card games."

"That doesn't sound very interesting."

"It *is* when everybody's naked and they play by different rules."

Heather noticed Marc heading back from the buffet and motioned for him to join them. Virtually everybody was now walking around the ship completely naked, paying little mind to the jiggling breasts and penises as people went about their daily routines.

"Good morning, ladies," Marc said, as he approached our table. "How have you found your shipboard experience so far?"

I took a good long look at Marc's body before he sat down, refreshing my memory from our first night together. Standing well over six feet tall, his well-muscled torso and arms rippled in the bright light streaming through the windows on the top deck. His penis was flaccid, but still hanging a healthy five to six inches as it swung gently above his nicely shaved balls. I picked a thick piece of pineapple from my plate, remembering what his dick felt like standing straight up.

"I think the word is...*eclectic*," I said, sucking the dripping fruit between my lips.

Marc sat down quickly on the other side of our booth to hide his growing erection and smiled.

"There's certainly no shortage of diversions," he said, scooping a large forkful of scrambled eggs into his mouth. "Have you had a favorite experience?"

"You mean besides our little tryst with you?" Heather said, grabbing a sausage from his plate and biting it in half.

"Of course I knew that would be your highlight," Marc said, continued the tease. "I was referring to the venues."

"The climbing wall was fun," Heather said. "But I think Jade may have experienced a different kind of high in one of the private view rooms yesterday."

"Oh? You like those sexy holes, do you?"

"Some holes were a little sexier than others," I said.

"Jade found the rest of the games room a bit underwhelming. I was suggesting she try her hand at a little strip poker. Care to join us after breakfast?"

"Just the three of us?" Marc said.

"I think we need a plus-one to balance things out. Maybe we can persuade one of the guys from the House of Holes to take his dick out of the wall and find a more interesting use for it."

Marc stretched his lips and nodded.

"Game on," he said, finishing his sausage and eggs.

When we got to the card room, we saw an empty round glass table with a pack of playing cards and four trays of betting chips. Heather excused herself for a moment, then returned a few minutes later holding a college-age boy's hand. He looked a little perplexed as he stared at the three of us and the empty table.

"*Three's* a lot more fun than one, don't you think?" she said to the young man. "Plus, there's no barriers here to limit your engagement. Are you ready to play some sexy games?"

He paused for a moment, then stuck out his hand.

"I'm Liam," he said, signaling his assent.

After we all introduced ourselves, we took alternating seats at the table and Heather cracked open the pack of cards.

"What are we playing?" Liam enquired.

"Five card stud," Heather said, winking at me. "With two *real* studs. You *do* know how to play poker, Liam?"

"Yes, but what are the stakes? I didn't bring any money..."

"You're so cute," Heather said. "We're not playing for money. We're playing for *favors*. The rule is that whoever wins each hand, gets to command one or more of us to perform some kind of act. Whoever ends up with the most chips at the end of the hour gets to propose a special group activity. The only limitation is that no one is allowed to come until the very end."

"That makes it a little more interesting," Marc said.

"And challenging," Liam said, crossing his legs to hide his growing erection under the table.

"Right then," Heather said, pulling two red chips from her tray. "The ante is ten dinars."

"Dinars?" Liam said.

"It's just *play* money, remember? They gain *real* value a little later."

Heather dealt one card face down to each player then one more face up. We each looked at our hole cards and placed our bets. Liam placed the largest stake in the pile, then Heather dealt another set of cards face up. Liam showed two Kings and threw in one of his three black chips.

"Too steep for me," Marc huffed, pushing his cards into the waste pile.

Heather displayed two tens, and I had a Jack-high.

Heather matched Liam's bet, and I decided to fold. She dealt the fourth card to herself and Liam. Heather got a Queen, while Liam showed an Ace.

"Hooo!" Marc cheered, as he rubbed his hands together. "Now it's getting interesting. Think hard about what you want the ladies to do for you, Liam."

"I'm *already* hard," Liam said.

I looked through the table top between his legs and saw his good-sized cock pointing straight up on his belly.

Marc reached into his tray and tossed another black marker on the table. Heather paused trying to read his face, then she glanced beneath the table at his throbbing cock.

"I think he's bluffing," she said. "I'll match your bet and raise you one hundred." She threw down her last two black chips then dealt the last card face up. She got another ten and Liam got a six.

Liam didn't hesitate to throw his last black chip in the pot.

"I call," he said, then he turned over his hole card and revealed three Kings.

"Whoa," Heather said, opening her eyes wide in surprise. She turned over her card and revealed a two. Liam had won the hand.

"Well played, young man," Heather said. "Your wish is our command. What would you like us to do?"

Liam ran his eyes up and down Heather's figure and smiled.

"I want you to spread your legs and play with yourself."

Heather pushed her chair back from the table to give everyone a commanding view of her crotch, then she spread her legs apart. She began to circle her clit, while she stared Liam directly in the eyes. His breathing increased as his gaze wandered between her legs. She began to move her hips on the chair, and Liam's hand dropped down to his lap where he began rubbing his cock.

"Hey!" Heather admonished. "That's not allowed. You get to watch only."

"But you said as long as we don't cum—"

"There'll be plenty of time for that later. I want you boys to save those nice big hard-ons for the main event."

Heather sat back up and handed the remaining pack of cards to Liam.

"Your turn to deal," she said.

"That's it?" Liam said. "That was hardly worth three hundred dinars!"

Heather placed her moist fingers in her mouth and licked off her juices.

"You better play your hand wisely the rest of the way, then. Now you've got some extra cash to up the ante. We're just getting started."

Liam collected the pot from the middle of the table, then we all threw in two blue chips for the next round. Liam dealt the cards, and I won the next round with a full house.

I looked at Marc and Liam and licked my lips. I noticed that Liam's dick had lost some of its firmness, but Marc's was rapidly elongating under the table. I wondered how far he'd be willing to go with this game.

"I want Liam to suck Marc's cock," I said.

"What?" Liam said, his eyes flying open. "But I'm not...*gay*."

"It's just a game," Heather said. "No one's going to cum in your mouth, right Marc? At least not yet. Besides, how do you know if you don't like it until you try? Now get down there and suck that bratwurst."

Marc swung his chair out, and I noticed his cock was standing at full mast. Apparently at least *one* of the boys liked the idea of sucking another guy. Liam walked around the table and kneeled down in front of Marc. He stared at the tip of Marc's manhood, unsure what to do.

"Go on," Heather said. "It won't bite you. Just think of it as a popsicle. A very large warm popsicle."

Marc pulled his arms around behind his chair and clasped his hands together to give Liam freer access.

Liam opened his mouth and slowly lowered himself over the head of Marc's joystick. At first he just held it there, but after a few seconds he began to bob his head as Marc slowly swung his hips. They both seemed to be enjoying it, and I had to fight hard to keep my hands away from my steaming pussy. The sight of seeing two hetero men going at it was incredibly erotic. I wanted to see if I could push it a little further.

"Now play with his balls," I ordered.

Liam paused and peered up at me out of the corner of his eyes, and I simply nodded. Marc pushed his hips toward the end of his seat until his tight balls poked over the edge. Liam reached up and cupped them then rolled them gently between his fingers. His own cock had resumed its full length and was bobbing against his flat stomach. It was obvious that he was getting turned on by the experience, and I saw his tongue begin to roll around in his mouth as he circled the head of Marc's cock. Marc let out a groan and lifted his hips higher. I would have happily forfeited the game at that moment to watch Marc cum in Liam's mouth, but Heather interjected to remind us of the rules.

"Okay, I think that's enough for this round," she said. "You boys seem to be having a little bit too much fun."

Liam sheepishly disengaged from Marc and returned to his seat at the other side of the table. We resumed the game, with each round ratcheted up the degree of engagement between the players. Marc won the next round and asked Heather to sit in my lap while we tribbed each other for a couple of minutes. Then Heather won the next round and asked the men to do the same as we watched them jack their two cocks together between their bellies. By the time our hour was up, all four of us were worked up enough to jump each other bones. When we counted our chips, Heather had eked out Liam for the largest residual.

"What now?" Liam said, his cock bobbing on his stomach, already leaking pre-cum.

"I ended up with the highest winnings," Heather said, "so I get to decide on the final group activity. And I think we should all come back to my cabin."

We didn't bother to clean up the table as we quickly found the nearest exit. Unlike our first night together when we'd scurried down the stairs to her stateroom, this time we took the elevator down the three levels to her floor. But the tension in the lift was palpable as none of us said a word to one another, holding our collective breath in anticipation of what would come next.

9

FOUR PLAY

When we got to Heather's room, nobody was sure who should make the first move. When it was just the three of us, Heather hadn't hesitated to jump the only man in the room, but this time we had to figure out what to do with Liam. The obvious thing would have been for us to pair up as two hetero couples, but Heather had seen enough in the games room to have other ideas.

"You boys lie down on the bed with your feet facing each other," she ordered.

Marc and Liam dutifully lay on the mattress as Heather instructed.

"Now bend your knees and move together until your cock and balls are touching one another."

I looked at Heather inquisitively, wondering what she had planned. We'd already seen the men frotting their cocks together in the games room, and I was eager for some of my own touching.

She glanced at Marc and Liam's glistening cocks throbbing against each other and smiled at me.

"Do you want to go first or me?"

I pinched my eyebrows for a second, then gasped when I understood her intention. The idea of having two cocks inside me was something I hadn't yet experienced. I moved toward the bed and kneeled on the mattress straddling the two men, facing Liam. I'd already watched Marc come inside me, this time I wanted to picture a younger man's reaction.

The men paused for a moment, unsure what I wanted. They were probably thinking of the classic DP maneuver, where one would fuck me in my pussy while the other fucked me up the ass. But I had a better idea. Ever since I saw them rubbing their cocks together in the game room, I'd fantasized about grasping them both inside my pussy. Both men were well hung, measuring together at least three times the girth of an average man's erect penis, but I figured if my anatomy could accommodate a baby's head during childbirth, surely it could take the equivalent of two good sized English cucumbers.

I reached around behind my ass and clasped their two penises together then slowly lowered my pussy until it touched the wet heads of their joined hard-ons. Marc's was a little bit longer, so it pushed its way through first, as I felt my lips widen to accommodate his large organ. Slowly sitting down another inch, I could feel Liam's cockhead pressing me apart still further, and I moaned as I felt my pussy stretch to take them both inside me. With both of them lying flat on their backs on the mattress, there was little they could do with the full weight of my body pressing down over their hips. I relished the feeling of control, watching Liam's face contorting in pleasure as my love tunnel squeezed over their joined cocks.

I slowly lowered myself until I felt my vulva resting on Liam's stubbly pubis. I was glad I'd placed Marc in the posterior position, where he had a little more room to sheath his larger cock. I began to use my thigh muscles to move up and down over their connected meat and reflected back on the Asian girl's two-headed cock from the view room the previous day. Two double pricks in as many days was a new milestone for me.

It seemed as if every nook and crevice of my pussy was filled up by the hot, throbbing manhood of these two virile men. I humped them faster, knowing it wouldn't to take long for all of us to come after the long buildup in the game room. Before long, Heather decided she wanted a piece of the action, and I could hear Marc's muffled moans behind me as she sat over his face. The look on Liam's face was priceless. I wasn't sure which he was enjoying more—the feeling of having his cock deeply embedded in my wet pussy, or the feeling of having Marc's throbbing member next to his.

His mouth was wide open as he moaned loudly in pleasure, and I knew he wouldn't be long to this world. I placed my hands over his tight pecs and squeezed the two-headed python inside me as I felt a powerful urge welling inside me. Heather suddenly reached around my back and squeezed my tits and we all howled in unison. When I came, I bucked wildly over the two men as I felt their cocks pulsing together, flooding me inside with their honey.

I sat there for a minute savoring the feeling of having two hard dicks inside me, as I peered out Heather's balcony window at the sun setting over the ocean. This cruise had been one hell of an adventure, and I didn't know if or when I'd have another chance like this again. I wanted to make it last as long as possible.

VOLUME TWO

THE COSTUME PARTY

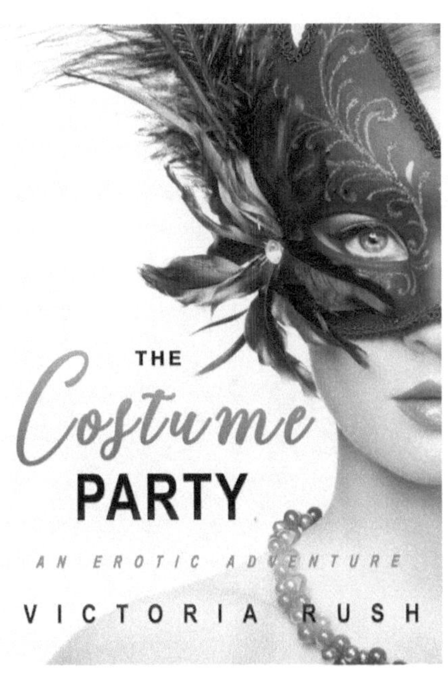

1

———————

I woke up to the sound of my best friend Hannah calling me from the other end of my house. She'd let herself in early on a Saturday morning and for some reason was yelling at me as she ran up the stairs.

"Jade!" she hollered. "Where are you? I've got some exciting news!"

I rolled over and squinted at my clock on the nightstand. It was a little past eight. Saturdays were the only day of the week I allowed myself to sleep in, and I was more than a little ticked at her rude intrusion.

"Aren't you up yet?" she called. "Get up—you're not going to believe what I just heard."

I rolled over and wrapped my pillow around my ears as she dashed into my bedroom. She paused for a minute smiling at my feeble attempt to block her out of my morning daze, then she pounced on the bed below my curled-up knees.

"Wake up, sleepyhead!" she squealed, pushing my shoulders to rouse me from my slumber.

"This better be good," I said, raising my pillow a few inches and peering at her through thin eyes. "You know how much I worship my weekend sleep-ins."

"You'll be glad I woke you when you hear what I have to tell you," she said. "Besides, you're gonna want to get up and begin planning your day right away. We're going to need a few extra hours to go shopping."

I pulled my duvet cover over my shoulders and huffed.

"What could possibly be so important to drag me out of my soft and cozy bed this early in the morning?"

I peered outside, looking at the gray clouds hanging low in the late October skies. I was in no hurry to venture out into the chilly autumn air.

"Only the biggest private shindig of the year. Steve Bannon is hosting his annual Halloween party at his mansion on the lake, and we're invited!"

"Isn't that the party with all the A-list celebrities? How did you score an invitation?"

Hannah peered at me with a wicked look in her eyes.

"Let's just say I know somebody who knows somebody. Someone with whom I may have pulled a few strings to earn some special favors."

"I bet that's not the *only* thing you were pulling to earn those favors," I said, raising an eyebrow.

"Possibly," she smirked. "But I apparently impressed him enough with my naked gymnastics to land an invitation to this special event. Except this year, it's got an extra twist. This time it's going to be a *nude* costume party."

I lifted my head and propped the side of my face on a crooked elbow, suddenly intrigued.

"Isn't that an oxymoron? How can you be in costume and naked at the same time?"

Hannah smiled and handed me a gold-embossed card inscribed with fancy calligraphy writing. I felt the raised surface of the script on the tips of fingers, rubbing it gently trying to divine its meaning through my still bleary eyes. Somebody had gone to a great deal of effort to create an invitation card on par with the most extravagant wedding.

I pulled myself up and leaned against my headboard, slowly reading the message.

You are cordially invited to attend my annual Halloween costume ball at my estate overlooking Lake Michigan.

This year I've added a special twist to make it even more interesting. You're encouraged to wear as little or as much trappings as you feel comfortable—including nothing at all beyond a simple mask. With everyone baring a little more than usual, who knows what kind of shenanigans might break out, and we're always mindful of protecting the anonymity of our special guests.

Of course, I encourage everyone to be playful and creative with their choice of costumes, as this is always the highlight of the event. As in previous years, there will be a special prize for the best costume of the evening and we hope you'll be suitably daring and inventive.

Feel free to bring a partner and let down your britches! As always, what happens at the Bannon residence stays at the Bannon residence. I look forward to seeing you this Saturday, starting at midnight. We'll all have a ghoulish good time!

I peered up at Hannah and grinned.

"No RSVP?"

"There's no need with a Steve Bannon invitation," she said. Everyone who's invited always goes. It's the go-to event of the year in the Chicago area. Models, actresses, rock stars, billionaires—everybody who's anybody in this town will be there. There's even a rumor that the Governor and his wife will attend this year's event."

I looked down at the card, rubbing my fingers over the embossed script.

"The invitation says you're allowed to bring a partner. Was that a condition of your little tryst with your friend—that you accompany him as his plus-one?"

Hannah peered at me devilishly as a tiny curl formed on the sides of her mouth.

"When I told him I had a friend who was even prettier than me and had a body to die for, he didn't hesitate to hand me an extra invitation. *You're* my plus-one, girl." She pulled another card out of her purse and handed it to me. "You know I'd never pass up an opportunity like this without bringing my bestie along to share in the fun."

I looked at Hannah with a quizzical look and shook my head in confusion.

"How are we ever going to find a decent Halloween costume on the Saturday before the end of the month? All the costume stores will be sold out of the best stuff."

Hannah kicked off her shoes and lifted the covers, then scooched in excitedly next to me against the headboard.

"I've been searching online for some ideas. We don't have to wear anything too elaborate, and there's no reason why we have to stick to a Halloween theme. Remember, this is a *nude* costume party. We already look pretty hot for a couple of girls nearing middle age. The less we wear, the better. Let's flaunt it while we've still got it!"

She pulled an iPad out of her purse and tapped the screen. A website opened showing a collection of sexy models wearing risqué costumes. She scrolled through the images, commenting on the various themes.

"Just look at some of these possibilities. We can play any role we like, wearing as much or as little as we please. Most of these costumes can be put together with a simple trip to Walmart and maybe a bit of needle and thread. Plus, we can easily remove one of two pieces from each outfit to reveal a bit more skin. The most important element is the headpiece. We just need something to conceal our identity and highlight our girly figures with a bit of flair."

Hannah paused at a picture of a sexy blonde wearing a Playboy bunny costume. She wore a tight corset and a rubber mask that covered the top half of her face with tall ears pointing up in the air.

"What about this one? You have to admit, it's pretty hot. You'd could even dispense with the bodice altogether and just keep the bunny tail on your naked ass. Imagine the looks you'd get prancing around his mansion in that costume!"

The images of sexy half-nude models wearing unusual masks

reminded me of my encounter at the Fantasy Feast naked dinner party. Suddenly, I became mindful of the wetness that had begun building between my legs.

"Not bad," I said, shifting my weight uncomfortably off the wet spot on my sheets. "Show me some more."

Hannah flipped through a few more images and stopped at a picture of a sexy maid wearing a lacy dress, holding a feather duster in her hand. Her firm tits pressed against the flimsy fabric, creating an irresistible focal point from the sensuous shadows on her bosom.

"How about this?" she said. "You'd look stunning in this outfit. You'd be covering up just enough to drive every man and woman at that party absolutely crazy. And imagine all the fun you could have teasing the naked guests with your little duster!"

"*Intriguing...*" I said as I squeezed my thighs together, trying to quiet my burning clit.

The more images Hannah showed me, the more turned on I got. Whether it was from me imagining myself in the costumes or imagining myself playing with the guests dressed up in the provocative outfits, was unclear. Either way, the more my mind began to ponder the possibilities, the more excited I became about going to this event.

"The only problem is, it will be difficult to cover my face without looking unnatural in that outfit," I frowned. "Show me more costumes with masks."

Hannah refined her search by typing in the words *sexy mask costumes* and the screen refreshed showing a new set of models in racy outfits. Many of the themes revolved around superheroes, with the male models sporting Batman and Superman motifs and the female models wearing Wonder Woman and Batgirl-type costumes.

"Not very original," I frowned. "I bet there'll be a ton of superhero costumes among all those egotistical celebrities. I'm looking for something a little different."

Hannah paused for a moment, then tapped on her photo library pulling up an image of me wearing a business suit painted on my naked body.

"Remember that time you went to the nude bodypainting workshop? You're a graphic artist. You can be virtually anything you want and show off all you wish with a little bit of well-disguised paint. Whether it's Catwoman, Black Widow, or Wonder Woman—all these characters wear is a mask and tight outfits to show off their beautiful physiques. You could even dress up like Mystique in the X-Men movie and wear absolutely nothing other than a full coat of body paint."

"Been there, done that," I said. "If I'm going to really enjoy myself, I want to wear something I've never worn before that will absolutely blow everyone away."

"You sure are a tough customer," Hannah said, shaking her head. "Let's try something a little different..."

She reopened her browser and typed in the words *naked masquerade costumes*. A gallery of Google images popped up with a collection of half-naked men and women.

"*Now* we're talking," I said, squirming on the bed as I scanned the toned bodies of the sexy models.

"Look at that one," Hannah said, pointing at the screen. "It's a picture of Rihanna at last year's Met Gala dressed as Nefertiti. With her sheer lace dress and silver headdress, it doesn't leave much to the imagination. A bit more makeup around the eyes, and you'd be able to mask your identity quite easily."

"That's pretty hot," I said, beginning to feel the sheets getting wetter and wetter between my legs. "She definitely looks fuckable. But it's been done before. I don't want to wear something half of these people will have already seen."

"Damn, girl, you're *impossible!* Remember, less is more. The idea is to show as much of our bodies as possible to attract the attention of all these beautiful people. You could get away with a simple mask, a painted emblem on your chest, and a shiny belt. Who really cares what you're wearing as long as you get the attention of the guests?"

"Humor me for a little longer," I said, squeezing Hannah's leg. "I'm starting to get a few ideas. I just need a bit more inspiration."

Hannah began flipping through the images more quickly until one picture suddenly caught my attention.

"Wait!" I said. "Go back a few frames. I saw something

interesting..."

She scrolled back until an image of six men dressed in contrasting costumes popped up.

"That's the one," I said, scanning the image slowly.

"*The Village People*?" Hannah said. "That might be okay for a gay guy, but how could you possibly look sexy wearing any one of those cheesy costumes?"

My eyes darted back and forth between the sexy cowboy wearing chaps and the indian warrior wearing a feathered headdress and a skimpy loincloth. Suddenly I nodded as a mischievous smile formed on my face.

"What?" Hannah said. "What could you possibly be thinking?"

She glanced down at my breasts peeking above the covers, noticing my hardening nipples.

"Because I know gay dudes—even ones with hard bodies like these guys—don't do it for you. Where is your mind going with this idea?"

"I've decided what I'm going to wear," I said, crossing my arms over my chest. "But I'm going to keep it a secret until we get to the party. It'll be all the more fun and surprising if I reveal it at the last second. But I promise you, it'll be one-of-a-kind and extremely provocative."

Hannah's eyes darted across my face, trying to imagine what I had in mind.

"Now you've got *me* all excited thinking what you're going to do. Judging by your obvious state of arousal, your head is already at the party. Can I crawl under the covers with you and have some fun fantasizing which one of those costumes you're going to wear?"

"By all means," I said, disappearing under the covers with her. "Just imagine me as one of those hot dudes with his clothes off."

"Mmm," Hannah purred, slithering between my slippery thighs. "I'd rather imagine you as a hot *chick* with her clothes off."

"In a couple of days," I said, spreading my legs further apart and pulling her face into my steaming crotch. "You might be able to have it both ways."

2

Just after midnight on the day of the party, I pulled my car up beside a call box in front of a large wrought-iron gate protecting the entrance to Steve Bannon's estate. After providing our names and the identification numbers on the front of our invitation cards, the gates opened and we followed the curved driveway up to the front of a giant French-styled chateau. As a parking attendant approached our car, I turned to Hannah seated next to me and smiled.

"It's show time," I said.

"Not a moment too soon," she huffed. "I've been dying to see what you're wearing under that coat ever since you picked me up."

I'd intentionally worn a long western duster to cover my body all the way from my shoulders to my ankles. Part of it was meant to surprise Hannah when I finally reached the event, but it had much more to do with my desire to shock everyone else once I got in the front door. I reached behind my seat and pulled a thin black mask out of a bag on the floor and wrapped it around the top of my face.

Hannah's forehead wrinkled as she looked at me, still confused.

"Let me guess: Kato, Zorro, Nightshade?"

"You're moving in the right direction with the first two," I smiled, reaching back into the bag and pulling out a pair of western boots.

"Cowboy boots?" Hannah squinted. "I don't know my cowboy characters quite as well—"

"Maybe this will help," I said, donning a white Stetson.

Hannah looked at me blankly for a moment, then her eyes lit up, recognizing the familiar image of the famous cowboy with the white hat and black mask.

"The Lone Ranger?"

"Yes, but with a little twist. You'll have to wait for the full reveal until we get inside."

"You're such a tease," she said as I handed the attendant my keys and we stepped out of the car.

We paused for a moment, taking in the full scale of the Bannon estate close-up. The four-story mansion extended almost a hundred feet in either direction, with tall arched windows and ornate brick-work. The bright spotlights illuminating the front of the house lit up the entire courtyard, reflecting off Hannah's shiny Batgirl outfit.

"Holy shit!" she exclaimed. "This place is gigantic. We're going to have to drop *breadcrumbs* to not get lost in there."

"More like *caviar* or *foie gras*," I chuckled. "Something tells me everything about this affair is going to be top shelf."

"What are we waiting for?" Hannah giggled, rushing ahead of me toward the front door.

My gaze drifted down while I soaked up her tight ass in her black latex outfit. She had a beautiful hourglass figure, and the tight Batgirl costume highlighted every curve of her sexy body. I smiled as I imagined the two of us mingling among the high rollers. But I had a feeling they'd be focused on someone *else's* ass tonight.

With the large double entrance doors pulled back, we peered into the bright marble-floored foyer as we approached the front steps. A large crowd of costumed guests had already begun to gather in the main ballroom, and we could hear soft jazz music wafting out into the courtyard.

"Good evening ladies," a man wearing a crisply tailored tailcoat and black tie said as we stepped into the entrance hall.

He looked at my long shawl and smiled.

"May I check your coat, Madam?"

"Yes, thank you," I said, turning my back to assist him in its removal.

When he pulled the cape off my back and viewed my naked backside, I heard him gasp. To complement my Lone Ranger disguise, I'd chosen to wear a tight-fitting black leather vest and long black chaps with nothing underneath. My tight ass poked out the back of the open leggings, and I could feel him running his eyes up and down my body as he hesitated hanging my coat in the closet.

But when I turned around, both Hannah and the doorman took a step back in shock. On the front of my open pants, I wore a large dildo fashioned in the shape of a man's cock and balls, framed by two silver pistols on either side of my hips. The long phallus slapped against the sides of my naked thighs as it swung from side to side.

"Holy *fuck*, Jade!" Hannah squealed. "That's *outrageous*! Where did you ever come up with that idea?"

"Remember the Village People picture you showed me a few days ago? I decided to borrow elements of both the cowboy and the indian characters to create my own design." I shook my hips to juggle my equipment and smiled. "I thought it would be kind of fun playing *both* sides of coin, so to speak."

"Uh—*yeah*," she said, flicking her eyes between my tight bosom spilling over the top of my vest and my faux genitals. "I'd have to say you pulled it off. With that getup, I expect you'll be the center of attention all night long."

"Um," the doorman said, shyly interrupting. "May I have your tickets, please?"

"Of course," I said, rustling my rubber balls as I fished in the pocket of my chaps for my ticket. When the butler turned to collect Hannah's ticket, I could see the front of his pants tenting in obvious arousal.

"Enjoy your evening," he said, motioning for us to enter the ballroom.

"Oh, I have a feeling we will," Hannah winked, as she nodded toward the lengthening pole pushing down his pant leg.

A waiter approached us with tall glasses of champagne on a silver tray and did a double-take when he noticed the swinging package between my legs.

"Whoa boy," Hannah said to the server, taking two glasses off his unsteady tray. "We wouldn't want you to spill your load before we've sampled the goods."

As we moved into the main entrance hall, the patrons milling in small groups began to turn around to view the newly arriving guests. Suddenly, the gentle buzz of group conversation receded until the only sound we could hear was the hum of the background music. Everyone was so stunned taking in my outfit, they were literally dumbstruck with their mouths agape.

Many of the guests had chosen to wear predictable Halloween costumes with little bits of flesh showing here and there, but nobody was letting it all hang out quite as brazenly as I had. Amid the predictable sprinkling of ghosts and goblins, there was a profusion of superhero figures and Disney characters bedecked in various stages of undress. I shook my head at the lack of imagination of the high-powered group and began to wonder if the event was going to live up to Hannah's hyperbole.

"Damn, girl," she said. "It looks like you're going to be this evening's scene-stealer. You've already stopped the show. I don't know what everybody's thinking right now, but that thing looks so realistic, they must be wondering if you're a legit tranny wearing that impressive package."

I smiled a crooked grin, suddenly feeling self-conscious with all of the eyes in the room surveying my exposed body. Fortunately, a handsome couple dressed as Anthony and Cleopatra began to approach us, providing some distraction.

"Welcome to our little costume party," the man said, extending his hand to Hannah and me. "I'm Steve Bannon and this is my wife

Genevieve. You'll have to excuse me, but I don't recognize either of you under your—*interesting* disguises."

I was taken aback by how handsome the eccentric billionaire looked close up. With his square jaw, dimpled cheeks and thick head of salt-and-pepper hair swept back in a dense poof, he looked like a slightly older version of the famous actor Patrick Dempsey. He wore a loose toga draped over his well-muscled chest, and I could see his pecs flexing as he shook my hand.

But I found his wife even more beguiling. Wearing a tight-fitting gold-lamé dress slitted at one side of her hips and a pretty beaded headdress, she looked like a dead-ringer for a young Elizabeth Taylor. As I ran my eyes shamelessly over her luscious figure, I felt a sudden dampness building under the weight of my latex balls pressing against my flaring clit.

"Jade," I introduced myself, not yet wanting to reveal my full identity.

"Hannah," my partner responded, politely shaking their hands.

"It appears that you two have already captured the attention of my guests," Bannon said, turning to appraise the congregation still gazing awkwardly in our direction. He extended his arm in the direction of the main hall and nodded. "Please, come in and mingle. There are so many fascinating people to meet. I'm sure we'll catch up with the two of you a little later this evening."

"I'll look forward to that," I said, smiling at Genevieve, lingering for a moment longer at her dazzling figure. She returned the gesture, widening her eyes as my member twitched while I held my palm over the handle of one of my six-shooters.

"Holy shit," Hannah said, as Bannon and his wife melted back into the crowd. "Did you see the way he was looking at you? He was practically *raping* you with his eyes. Something tells me this is going to be a very interesting night. It seems the men are even more enamored with your disguise than the women. Either there's a lot of bi-curious guys in here, or they're attracted to that whole futa thing."

"I dunno," I said. "I'm showing off a lot of *girl* parts too. Who's to say what they're more attracted to? But did you notice his wife? I'd far rather get into *her* pants."

"It's too bad that thing isn't animated," Hannah chuckled, glancing at my pendulous dick. "If you could actually get it up, you could probably have your way with just about everybody in this place."

"Who knows?" I said, winking at Hannah. "In my current state of arousal, I wouldn't be surprised if this thing had a life of its own."

Little did she know how much truth in this statement I was about to reveal before the evening was over.

3

———————

After Bannon and his wife resumed mingling with the rest of the crowd, Hannah and I wandered into the main ballroom. At first, most of the assembled groups gave us a wide berth, unsure what to make of the two girls dressed in such revealing costumes. Hannah's latex Batgirl outfit clung to her naked body like a second skin, the shiny fabric accentuating every crease and curve like it was painted on her. And the cutouts on both sides of my leather chaps left little to the imagination, even with the modicum of cover provided by my fake genitals covering my bare mound.

I was glad to have the freedom to mill about the room for a while, surveying the faces and costumes of the high-powered gathering. I recognized a fair number of public figures from the senior ranks of the local political, business, and media fields. The mayor was there with his wife, dressed as Little Red Riding Hood and the Big Bad Wolf, which seemed fitting given the ongoing level of corruption at City Hall. Bannon's business partner and fellow billionaire Kent Schiffer circled the room with a familiar supermodel, outfitted in matching red tights as Mr. Incredible and Elastagirl. And our local news anchorman was paired with his pretty sidekick, dressed as Woody and Bo Peep from the movie Toy Story.

Many of the guests were dressed as famous characters from superhero movies or nursery rhyme stories, with most of the men playing the more dominant role. *Typical display of macho-entitled privilege*, I thought. *Why does it seem every man who achieves a certain degree of power have to lord it over everyone else, thinking they're better than the rest of us?* My cheeky cowboy costume seemed a perfect counterpoint to the heavy dose of testosterone permeating the room, mocking their oversize male egos as I swung my big dick around like I owned it.

As Hannah and I began mingling with the small cliques scattered around the room, I found it amusing that while most of the women praised my cocky outfit, their male partners seemed threatened by it, silently stealing glances at my huge dong while their wives and girlfriends chatted with me comfortably. I wasn't sure if it was because they felt intimidated by my outsize genitals, or because they were secretly fantasizing about fucking me.

As more and more people began gravitating toward us, intrigued by my outrageous costume, Hannah slowly drifted off to the other side of the room. I couldn't blame her, with everyone asking me silly questions like what it felt like to be a woman carrying a man's dick. For a while I amused them, swinging my hips from side to side and playfully grabbing my balls, flaunting my male persona.

But I soon tired of the incessant stares and never-ending quips about my tranny disguise, and began looking for an excuse to break away. Just as I was about to excuse myself to go to the ladies' room, the governor and his wife approached our group and introduced themselves. They were dressed in matching his and hers chef outfits, the only difference being that his wife wore a less poofy hat and a backless apron that showed off her sexy ass and legs.

"That's quite a provocative costume," the governor said, extending his hand to me. "I'm Jack Scanlon and this is my wife, Alicia."

"Pleased to meet you, Mr. Governor," I said, quickly seeing through his thin disguise. "But no less daring than your wife's, which I dare say is even *more* revealing."

"In some respects, possibly," he said. "Except you're revealing both sides of the coin."

"Heads *and* tails, you mean?" I smiled.

"In a manner of speaking," he said, temporarily at a loss for words by my sassy attitude. "Are you here alone tonight?"

I scanned the room and noticed Hannah chatting it up with a hunky guest dressed in a Tarzan outfit.

"It seems my partner is out looking for greener pastures. I guess she felt this one had been fully tilled."

"Oh?" the governor said, glancing at my pendulous prick. "Who's been doing most of the figurative plowing—you, or all these other farm animals?"

"At this point, I'd say everybody's just getting the lay of the land," I said, dragging out the metaphor. "Surveying the landscape, deciding the best place to position their hoes."

"I see what you mean," the governor said, his eyes widening from my double entendre. "You seem to be particularly–*ambidextrous* in that respect."

"I'm just having fun pretending what it might be like to cultivate both sides of the field," I said, running my eyes up and down his wife's sexy body before locking eyes with her. "You never know when a particularly fertile plot might need tending."

"Well put, my lady."

"Please—call me Jade," I said, turning my attention to his wife, who'd been staring at my outfit the entire time. "What about you, Alicia? Have you been enjoying the evening so far?"

"Yes," she said, happy to deflect attention away from her overbearing husband for a moment. "So many interesting people and costumes."

"I find yours very alluring also," I said, staring at her plump breasts pressing against the front of her skimpy apron. "But it seems that all your fun parts are hidden from view, at least while we're talking face-to-face. It's only when you turn around that you reveal your adventurous side."

"I guess you'll just have to catch me when my back is turned then," she said, winking at me sexily.

"I'll definitely be keeping a lookout. Hopefully we can catch up later."

As much as I wanted to continue our playful flirtation, I knew I'd never have a chance for some alone time with her as long as I continued to engage them as a couple. Besides, I was getting tired of her husband's thinly veiled sexist comments.

"Will you excuse me for a moment while I use the restroom?"

"Of course," she said. "But be careful in there. It's not as simple for us ladies to pee standing up as it is for the men."

"Not to worry," I smiled. "Fortunately, this thing is easily removed. Though it might be kind of fun to try it just once."

"Will you be using the men's or the ladies' room?" the governor smirked.

"I'm pretty sure the toilets are unisex in this place," I said, gently admonishing him for another chauvinist remark. "Which will be a refreshing change from the usually cramped ladies' rooms we have to endure in other public places. Enjoy your evening. Perhaps we'll see each other a little later."

"We'll look forward to that," the governor smiled.

As I pulled away from the crowd, I shook my head at the impudent tone of the governor, ignoring his beautiful wife while he shamelessly flirted with me. Little did he know that I was far more impressed with Alicia than by the trappings of his high political office. I felt like I needed to wash myself off after dealing with his sexist attitude and while looking for a place to freshen up, I recognized the familiar red and white uniform of the mayor's wife as she waited outside the closed door of an adjacent anteroom. As I approached her from the side, I admired her shapely legs and full bosom pressing against her tight bodice. Her Little Red Riding Hood costume seemed the perfect outfit to highlight her youthful face and figure.

"You'd think we wouldn't have to wait to use a toilet in this place," I said, sauntering up next to her. "There must be at least twenty washrooms in this mansion."

"No doubt," she laughed. "But even in a place like this, with this many guests, unfortunately we ladies still have to wait to use the lavatory." She glanced down at my faux genitalia and smiled. "It's too bad they don't have his and hers toilets like in most public settings. With that getup, you'd probably get away with slipping into the men's room."

"Maybe," I said. "But I'd still have to pee sitting down. I'm just looking to freshen up anyway. I was hoping for a respite from all the overcharged testosterone out there."

"Tell me about it," she nodded. "I've been dealing with city politics from the other side for almost twenty years now. It's still very much an old-boys network in this business. Women are just treated as chattel, to be trotted out as eye candy whenever there's a public relations opportunity like this."

"That's partly why I wore this outfit," I admitted. "I thought it would be kind of fun to swing my own dick around all these heavy hitters at this posh event."

The washroom door suddenly swung open and a woman wearing a Victorian costume brushed past us, sneering at our haughty outfits.

"Judging by the heft of that thing," she said, "I'd say yours is the biggest one here by a large margin. Do you want to join me while I freshen up inside? It looks like the last thing you need right now is to stand outside alone while everybody wags their tongues at you."

"Thanks," I said. scurrying in behind her as we locked the door, giggling like two schoolgirls. "I'm Jade, by the way," I said stretching out my hand.

"Haley," she said, grasping my hand firmly as she smiled into my eyes.

As we leaned in to the doublewide mirror over the marble vanity to check our lipstick and mascara, I noticed Haley's gaze drifting lower to check out my package.

"You know, if it weren't for the straps holding that apparatus onto your hips, I'd swear that thing was real," she said. "It's so life-like. Even your *testicles* look authentic."

"The whole thing is made out of a special latex engineered to mimic real skin. With all the advances in artificial dolls these days, it's amazing what they can do with sex toys."

"Do you mind if I—*touch* it?" she asked.

"I thought you'd never ask."

As I stepped back from the vanity, Haley turned to face me, reaching her hand down to touch my artificial cock.

"My God," she said, squeezing it firmly. "It even *feels* like a real dick. If only it could get hard, I shudder to think how big it would be angry."

As she reached further down to cup my balls, her face came closer to mine, and we kissed. I pressed my tongue into her mouth and she reached lower still, running her fingers over my moist labia. I purred in pleasure, pressing my crotch harder into her hips. She hiked up her skirt, and I was pleasantly surprised to see that she was completely naked underneath. Recognizing my opportunity to have a little fun, I positioned my hand over my right pistol, gently pumping the trigger. Slowly, my synthetic cock began to fill with air and inflate between her legs.

"What the—" Haley gasped, pulling back to see what was happening. "You've got to be kidding me. You can *animate* that thing?"

"In a manner of speaking," I said. "You want to give it a try?"

"*Hell* yes!" she said. "I'm so horny right now, I could fuck just about anything. But first, let me take a closer look at what I'm working with."

As I smiled at her wickedly, I pumped my trigger harder until my organ rose to a full ten inches of erect flesh. Haley couldn't help herself as she fell to the floor and took my member into her mouth while she proceeded to give me a pretend blowjob. As I watched her stretch her lips around my thick pole, I placed my hands behind her head and imagined fucking her face like a man. Although I was being far gentler than most, it was fun fantasizing being in the man's role for a change, having my way with my muse.

"That's it," I purred. "Suck my big cock, baby. Squeeze my balls while I fuck your pretty face."

Without hesitating, Haley reached underneath me and began

rubbing my balls against my raging clit. The sensation was not unlike what I imagined a real man would be feeling as she stimulated my sex organ.

"Fuck, yes," I panted. "That feels good, Haley. I want to fuck you so bad."

Suddenly, she stood up and smiled at me.

"That makes *two* of us. I'm so turned-on, I could pop off any second."

She reached behind her, placing her hands on top of the vanity and lifted herself up onto the counter, hiking her skirt all the way up. I took one look at her glistening pussy and leaned in to kiss her passionately. She reached down and pointed my hard pecker toward her opening and when I pressed it into her, she gasped.

"Oh God, Jade," she groaned. "Your cock feels so good. Fill me up with your big dick. I want to feel your balls slapping against my pussy."

Her dirty talk got me even more worked up, and as I pressed my hips forward, she moaned loudly. As we began to grind our hips together, our tongues danced in each other's mouths. Haley flapped her thighs against me as I plowed in and out of her, grinding my clit against the underside of my rubbery balls. While we grunted and moaned with abandon, anybody who might have been waiting to use the restroom must have surely known what was going on inside. But neither one of us cared, lost in the moment by the rising feeling of ecstasy engulfing our joined bodies.

Suddenly, Haley wrapped her legs around my ass and pulled me even deeper inside her pussy.

"*Damn*, girl," she panted. "You're going to make me come with that big thumper of yours. Fill me up while I come all over your pretty pussy."

"Yes," I groaned. "I'm close too. I'm going to cum with you. God damn, I like fucking you."

"Here it comes," Haley moaned. "Take me over the edge."

I grabbed Haley's hips by both sides and pulled her strongly toward me, grinding my cock and balls as hard as I could against her while ramming my cock in and out of her sloshing pussy. Suddenly, a wave of passion rolled over me as my clit began pulsating against the underside of my faux balls.

"Oh God, Haley," I groaned. "Cum with me baby. Come all over my big dick."

"Yes!" Haley howled. "I can feel you pounding my G-spot. It feels soooo good!"

Suddenly, I felt Haley spraying all over my balls and mound as her pussy clenched down over my phallus while we ground our hips against one another. We moaned inside each other's mouths as we locked lips in a tight and passionate kiss. After what seemed like a full minute of shaking and convulsing in each other's arms, our breathing finally returned to normal, while we kissed with me still inside her.

"*Ahem*," a woman's voice called impatiently from outside the door, from someone waiting to use the facilities.

"I guess we'll have to vacate the premises," Haley smiled. "Though I could make love to you all night long."

"Same here," I said. "Let's clean up and get out of here. Maybe we can find a more private place to continue our fun."

While Haley pulled down her skirt and reapplied her smudged lipstick, I unfastened my appendage and washed it under the tap before reattaching it to my mound. When we finally got ourselves put back together, we opened the door and walked past a long line of stunned onlookers as their eyes widened in shock ogling my still-dripping, semi-hard cock.

4

———————

It didn't take long after Haley and I returned to the main ballroom for her husband to spot us. While we giggled amongst ourselves about the pretentious costumes of all the men in the room masking their tiny peckers, the mayor approached us with an angry scowl on his face.

"Where've you been?" he barked at Haley, his ruddy, pockmarked face making his wolf costume look all the more ridiculous. "I've been looking all over for you. There are a lot of prominent people I wanted to introduce you to."

"Jade and I were just freshening up. No need to get your knickers in a twist, dear."

"*Freshening up*?" he said, darting his eyes back and forth between Haley's face and my tumescent cock. "How long does that take? You must have been gone for at least a half hour!"

"Well, you know how we women are when we hang out in the ladies' room," she replied with a straight face. "There's no telling how long it might take to get ourselves put together in front of the mirror. You *do* want me to look pretty and proper for all your important friends, don't you?"

"I—suppose so," he stammered, distracted by my glistening

joystick. He grabbed Haley's hand, trying to drag her away from me. "Come, I want you to meet one of my biggest fundraisers, Kent Schiffer."

As he steered Haley toward a gathering in the center of the room, she looked back at me with an apologetic expression, mouthing the words *later*. Soon after, Hannah came up behind me and cupped one of my bare cheeks with her hand.

"What was *that* all about?" she said. "It looked like the Big Bad Wolf was about to bite off his wife's head."

"He might as well have," I huffed. "The way he was acting as if he owned her. All these upper-class snobs seem interested in is congratulating themselves around their buddies while showing off their arm candy."

"He did seem a little distracted by you," Hannah said, noticing Haley peering in my direction with a flushed face. "And he wasn't the *only* one. What kind of trouble did you get into with his wife? You've got a strange glow about you."

"Nothing much," I lied. "We were just freshening up in the ladies' room, looking for an escape from all the overbearing egos in this place."

Hannah looked at me suspiciously, pinching her eyebrows as she peered at my puffy appendage.

"Well, judging by the flush on your chest and the sweat dripping down your ass, I'd say you were up to a little more than just fixing your makeup. If I didn't know better, I'd swear even your *dick* looks more excited than usual."

"We may have been touching up a bit more than just our *faces*," I admitted. "We started admiring each other's costumes and one thing led to another..."

Hannah reached down and squeezed my tumescent dildo, then her eyes widened as her lips curled up into a knowing smile.

"Is it just my imagination, or does it seem a little *bigger* than when we first came in? You better be careful—you could poke somebody's eye out with that thing."

"That's not the only thing it's good for poking," I grinned.

"No way!" she said, stepping back in mock indignation. "You were *fucking* the mayor's wife in the washroom? Did he have any inkling?"

"I don't think so. But judging by how much noise we were making in there, I imagine it won't take long for word to spread around the room."

"Not to worry–just stick with me, girl," Hannah said, moving closer to protect me from everyone's disapproving glares. "If any of these jokers cause you any trouble, I'll give them a batkick to the groin."

"I doubt that'll be necessary," I sighed, catching Hannah's Tarzan friend stealing glances at me from the open bar on the other side of the room. "Most of the men in here seem reluctant to engage me in any kind of conversation, let alone actually approach me in this getup. I don't know if they're more threatened by my provocative outfit or they're just afraid to admit they're attracted to a pretty girl with a big cock."

I noticed Tarzan moving to the other side of the bar to get a clearer look at me. I found it strange that he seemed so focused on me after Hannah had spent so much time with him earlier. Unlike me, I knew she had a preference for men, and I suspected she was hoping to land a wealthy boyfriend at this event.

"What about you?" I said, shifting my position to deflect Tarzan's gaze. "What kind of trouble have you been getting up to around all these society types?"

"Not as much as I'd like," Hannah frowned. "I've found a few interesting candidates, but so far everybody's been politely keeping their dicks in their pants."

"Well, you know how it is. With all their extra ornamentation, it might be kind of hard to just whip it out. Most of these guys seem to have gone to great lengths to gussy themselves up with all this embellishment."

"I know what you mean," Hannah said, pulling her tight latex skin down uncomfortably under her crotch. "I guess I didn't give this costume as much forethought as I should have. I'm sweating like a pig under here. I have to dismantle the whole thing just to go pee."

"Not exactly conducive to pulling off a quickie in this place," I chuckled.

"Not as easily as you," she grumbled. "You don't have to remove a single stitch of clothing to get your freak on. All you have to do is find a willing accomplice and insert your magic wand."

With Hannah's back turned away from the bar, I saw Tarzan adjusting his equipment under the counter. His loincloth had begun pouching in front of his penis, and he seemed to be getting more and more aroused watching me.

"What about that hunky Tarzan character I saw you flirting with earlier?" I said, hoping to redirect his attention. "He seems worthy of a little deconstruction."

"It crossed my mind, believe me," Hannah said. "But he seemed more interested in talking about everyone else in the room. Either he's just here for the people watching, or he's gay. I mean, I'm still a *catch*, right? Who can resist a sexy chick in this tight outfit? I was practically throwing myself at him."

Tarzan turned away from me holding his hands in front of his crotch, trying to keep his rising member from making too obvious an appearance. Then he suddenly stood up and exited through a door next to the bar.

"He's probably just trying to keep up appearances," I said. "It's a pretty snooty affair, you have to admit. People would likely get their nose out of joint if they caught a couple getting too carried away in public."

"That's what *powder rooms* are for, right?" Hannah grinned.

"Speaking of, I gotta go pee for real this time. Catch up with you in a bit?"

"Sure," Hannah said. "Just try not to dip your dick anywhere it doesn't belong this time. There's no telling what kind of hullabaloo it might generate if one of these heavy hitters caught you getting it on again with another one of their wives."

"Don't worry," I smiled. "I'll be staying far away from the ladies this time."

As soon as I left Hannah, a flock of men suddenly converged on her, no longer threatened by the presence of her sexy androgynous partner. But I was happy for the distraction, because there was something about this Tarzan hunk I needed to check out. He was the first man I'd met at the ball who'd demonstrated any genuine interest in me, and I wanted to see which persona he was more attracted to.

I meandered through the crowd making small talk with some of the guests then I ordered a cocktail at the bar and slipped quietly out the same door I'd seen Tarzan use. It led to a large wine cellar, darkened and chilled to a frigid fifty degrees. I looked around the room, catching sight of Tarzan huddled between two kegs with his hand moving suspiciously between his legs.

I strolled over in his direction and smiled when I noticed his predicament. His cock was at full mast, flapping up over his flimsy loincloth, high up against his belly. I nodded when I saw how well hung he was, his organ standing a good eight inches in length and at least two inches thick.

"Aren't you a bit underdressed for this place?" I asked.

"I suppose so," he said in a shaky voice. "But I didn't know where else to go." He looked down at his crotch with a sheepish expression, vainly trying to cover up his erection. "It seems I'm having a bit of a wardrobe malfunction."

"Is *that* what you call it?" I said. "Can I offer some help? Provide a little body heat at least? You're shivering in that skimpy outfit."

"Maybe," he hesitated, peering down at my even bigger cock hanging down over my naked belly. "At least you can provide some cover if anyone else comes in here."

As if on cue, the door on the other side of the wine cellar opened, and a uniformed waiter entered the room, walking in our direction. He appeared to be looking for a particular bottle, but when he caught sight of the two of us, he stopped and did a double-take. Without pausing, I stepped closer to Tarzan and flung my arms around him, pretending to make out. It was just the cover he needed, and this was the perfect excuse to get a little closer. The waiter smiled as he nodded toward us, then collected his items and exited the room.

"Thanks," Tarzan said, pulling away awkwardly. "This is beyond embarrassing. I can't seem to make this thing go down and I have nothing to cover up with."

"I can't imagine why you'd *want* to," I said, running my fingers over his hard chest muscles. "With a body like this, you should be showing off as much of it as you can."

He glanced down at my full breasts pressing up against him in my tight leather vest.

"I hadn't counted on getting quite so—*aroused* at this event," he stuttered. "I thought I'd be able to keep it together around all these stiff necks. This has never happened to me before in a public place..."

"Not to worry," I said. "This little accident will stay between us. But if you don't mind my asking, may I ask what's gotten you so worked up? I saw you looking in my direction, and all of a sudden you wanted to hide."

"I'm sorry," he said, his face flushing like a teenager. "I just couldn't help staring at you. I find you incredibly sexy, and with so much of you hanging out for everyone to see, I guess I just had a visceral reaction."

"I understand," I said, darting my eyes over his handsome face, finding myself getting surprisingly turned by his shy demeanor. "But which *part* of me were you most attracted to? I'm hanging out on both sides."

"Both," he said, without hesitation. "You have a sexy body and you're absolutely stunning. But there's something especially alluring about a woman flaunting a man's genitals overtop their naked body. It's very—*ballsy* of you."

"You like *cocky* women, do you?" I said, leaning in towards him as I brushed my thick cock against his tight balls.

"In a manner of speaking," he huffed.

"Did you want to play with it?"

"May I?" he said. "I've never really touched another penis before..."

"You mean besides your *own*?" I kidded. "Is that what you were doing in here? Stroking it trying to make it go down before you went back into the ballroom?"

"I was so turned on, I didn't think there was any other way to get myself back together."

"Maybe I can help you with that," I smiled, reaching down and grasping his throbbing cock with my left hand. "Is this warming you up a little bit?"

"Yes," he panted, clutching my ass while he rocked his hips toward me, trying to create some much-needed friction against his throbbing hard-on. "But you've got goosebumps too. How can I help warm you up?"

I wasn't sure what he had in mind, but I wasn't interested in him fucking me in the usual manner. I'd long been fascinated seeing gay men play with themselves. I found one of the most erotic things was when they rubbed their erect cocks together. Something about the playful jousting of their erogenous parts always got me turned on.

"Well, we're both equipped with similar equipment," I said, raising an eyebrow. "I've always wondered what it would feel like to rub two cocks together..."

"Oh my God," Tarzan said. "I've fantasized about that too. But you're not exactly *functional* in the way most men are—"

"You might be surprised what this ladyboy is capable of," I grinned. "This little package comes equipped with a few extra features."

As I began stroking his hard-on, I squeezed the trigger of the pistol on my right hip, slowly inflating my rising pecker. Tarzan looked down and widened his eyes, seeing my love muscle inflating to its full ten inches. When it reached its maximum length, I placed it against the underside of his prick and began rocking my hips in tandem with his. Even though he was better endowed than most men, my giant phallus looked like an anaconda slithering up next to his garden snake. As the rubbery veins of my dildo rolled over the sensitive flesh on the tip of his rod, he shuddered and emitted a drop of dew out of his hole.

"Uhnnn," he groaned. "This is incredibly hot. I've always wondered what this would feel like, but to do it with such a sexy woman is a dream come true."

"You've always wanted to get it on with a *tranny*?" I smirked. "Well now you've got your wish."

I reached down and cupped my hands around both of our cocks and began humping him more vigorously. Tarzan groaned as he placed his hands against my chest, squeezing my breasts over my cowboy vest.

"Open it up," I nodded. "See what it's like to fuck a real ladyboy. I want to feel your hard pecs rubbing against my tits."

He didn't need any more encouragement as he fumbled with my buttons until he freed my boobs from their tight enclosure. When he saw my firm breasts bouncing on my chest, he circled them with his hands and pinched my nipples gently while I continued frotting our cocks together in my hands.

"Fucking hell," he said. "You are so hot. You are truly the woman of my dreams."

"And *man* also?" I smiled.

"Yes," he admitted. "I've long fantasized what it would be like to hold another man's penis in my hands."

"Why don't you take the driver's seat then?" I said, acknowledging his bisexual nature. "Let me admire the scenery for a while."

When I removed my hands, he placed his palms around our joined cocks and squeezed them together firmly. More precum oozed out of the head of his pole, and he moaned as he began to pick up the pace of his rocking motion. Neither one of us seemed interested in kissing, fixated on the appearance of our two big cocks frotting in and out of his hands. As he began to moan more loudly, I slapped my sweaty breasts against his hard chest. I could tell he was getting close to the point of no return, and I was eager to watch him cum with our cocks joined together.

"Yes, baby," I purred. "Let it come. Cum all over my big tits. Let me hear Tarzan's call of the wild."

Suddenly, he arched his back and thrust his dick as hard as he could against my organ, pressing his balls tightly against mine. My clit throbbed as he shot one giant geyser after another between my boobs, cumming all over the underside of his chin and face.

"Fuckkkk!" he growled with each spurt. "I'm cumming all over your cock. *Uhn, uhn, uhn!*"

With each throb and spasm, he grunted like a wild animal until he was fully spent. When he finally recovered his strength, he looked up at me with gratitude.

"Thank you," he said. "I needed that. You were even more magnificent than I imagined."

"Glad I could be of service," I said. "Now you should get yourself back in there. Somewhere out there is your *real* Jane, waiting for you to scoop her up and take her away to your jungle."

"What about you?" he said, looking at me confused.

"I'm still looking for my Jane, too," I smiled.

The whole time neither one of us had so much as touched lips. All either one of us wanted was a quickie in the wine cellar, where we could live out one of our mutual boy-on-boy fantasies. As Tarzan tucked his pecker back under his loincloth and staggered out of the cellar, I smiled.

That's one way to get it on with a man, I thought. I wondered what other fantasies awaited me before the night would be over.

5

After Tarzan left the wine cellar, I found a sink nearby and cleaned myself up, removing all the cum that he'd splattered over my dildo and chest. Feeling flushed and sweaty, I decided to catch some fresh air before going back into the main room. A side door from the cellar led onto an expansive terrace overlooking the lake. Standing alone in a corner of the balcony stood the governor's wife Alicia with her back toward me. Her arms rested on the stone railing as she puffed a cigarette, leaning over with her naked ass jutting out behind her backless apron. My pussy fluttered as I admired her shapely figure, feeling the moisture accumulating on my lips tingling in the cool autumn air.

Alicia had one of the most magnificent backsides I'd ever beheld. Her long, slender legs were taut and shapely like a professional dancer's and her ass was as tight and firm as a teenager. The rising moonlight reflecting off Lake Michigan shimmered between the space in her thighs, illuminating the dark pit under her mound. It was almost as if she were daring me to approach her and fuck her from behind.

I surveyed the rest of balcony and seeing that we were alone, I began tiptoeing toward her. It was a calm and cloudless night and the light of the full moon shone brightly over the Bannon estate, revealing the splendor of its manicured gardens. Amidst autumn-speckled trees and perfectly manicured flower beds, lay a geometric hedge maze accented with stone sculptures and a flowing water fountain.

I paused for a moment to breathe in the floral scent of the breeze wafting in from the shore. I couldn't imagine a more romantic setting for a private encounter with my pretty temptress. As I edged closer toward her, I stepped on a small pebble and it went skittering over the stone tiles in Alicia's direction. She cocked her head and turned slightly in my direction, then bent lower on the handrail, taking another puff of her cigarette. Whoever she imagined approaching her from behind only increased the boldness of her seductive pose.

Maybe being the wife of the most powerful figure in the state gave her the confidence to blow off any would-be interlopers. Or maybe she was just bored and looking for an anonymous fling to mix up her dull political life. Whatever the reason, her self-assured nature turned me on even more and as the glistening slit of her pussy came into focus, I felt the wetness from my own sex beginning to run down the insides of my thighs. When I came within a few feet of her, she stood up with her arms extended on the balustrade and blew a stream of smoke high in the air.

"Beautiful night, isn't it?" she said to no one in particular.

"Spectacular," I said. "The view is truly magnificent in this light."

"Mmm," she replied, oblivious to the identity of her midnight paramour. "Were you admiring the landscaping?"

"Among other things," I said, staring at her bald snatch. "Everything is so perfectly balanced and neatly trimmed. It really makes you want to pause and appreciate Mother Nature."

Alicia took a step back with one of her legs, arching her ass higher.

"It would be a shame just to *look* at it," she said, "Nature is meant to be immersed in, don't you think?"

"Absolutely," I said, taking a step closer, brushing my bare breasts against her chilly back. "You never know what you might find until you make contact."

"Like the way a woman's nipples pucker when it's cold?"

"Or when they brush against a soft surface," I replied.

"Or her lover's skin," she said

She pressed her ass further toward me and touched my protruding organ, then gasped and turned her head in my direction, checking it before we made eye contact.

"And sometimes—" she mused, recognizing the familiar shape of my leather chaps. "Nature has a way of *surprising* us with her wonderful diversity."

"Do like surprises?" I teased.

"In the right circumstances."

I reached under the front of her apron and squeezed her breasts, pressing my cock harder between her legs. She reached underneath and began stroking my dildo against her wet cleft.

"I particularly like the way nature has a way of adapting to its surroundings—" I said, beginning to inflate my rubber penis with my pistol trigger. "Like the way it expands and contracts to fill the void in any particular situation."

"Yes," Alicia panted, running her hand up and down my giant shaft. "I'd like you to fill *my* void."

By now, my inflatable penis had reached its maximum length and Alicia was busy rubbing the bulbous head against her inflamed clit.

"Fuck me, Jade," she said, dispensing with any further pretense. "I've been fantasizing about you banging me with your beautiful dick all night long."

"As have I," I panted, angling the tip into her dripping opening. I've dreamt of pounding your beautiful ass from the moment we met."

"*Fuck* yes," she grunted, as I pressed myself inside her. "Pound me with your big cowboy dick. Let me feel your balls slapping up against me while you ride me."

As I began to hump her, I marveled at how enthralled all the guests seemed to be with my transgender persona—both male and female. Everyone seemed to want a piece of my girl-cock, no matter how they could get it. While I watched my drumstick pounding in and out of her hole, I had to admit it was kind of fun assuming the male role for a change. There was something strangely empowering about being connected to a man's cock, watching all these strangers bow to my made-up masculinity. As I grasped the sides of her hips and pulled her toward me, she moaned and gyrated her hips, holding on to the rail for support.

"God damn, girl," she hissed. "You feel so good inside me. I've never had a man fill me up quite this way before. I only wish you could cum inside me. I want to hear you get off with me."

There was something about the sight of my big phallus plowing into her tight little ass that was getting me especially worked up. Even though she wasn't providing direct stimulation to my lady parts, I could have come just watching the incredibly sexy scene that was unfolding before my eyes. But I'd been saving up one more special secret. I pressed a button on the inside of my handle and suddenly my balls began vibrating from a battery-operated motor embedded inside. As I pressed my scrotum against her underside, I was instantly taken to a whole new level of excitement.

"Holy shit!" she squealed. "That's *definitely* something no man has ever done to me. Grind your nuts against me, Jade. Trib me with your big fat balls."

"Fuck, yes," I growled, feeling the rising tide of ecstasy building within me.

I couldn't help smiling, acknowledging the multipurpose capability of my male equipment. Not too long ago I was frotting a man with my big firehose, and now I was tribbing a sexy woman with my vibrating balls. For a brief moment, I felt envious of a man's equipment, but as my pussy began throbbing and dripping over my strap-on apparatus, I became acutely aware of my true gender. I leaned forward and rubbed my tits against Alicia's back, pinching and rolling her nipples between my fingers.

"Can you feel my wetness, Alicia?" I panted. "Can you feel how much you're turning me on?"

She reached under my vibrating balls and inserted two fingers inside me, stroking the front of my G-spot.

"Yes," she grunted. "You feel exquisite. You're going to make me come soon. I want to feel you come with me."

"With every part of my body actively engaged in fucking her, I didn't need any further encouragement. Within seconds, a surge of energy coursed through me, as my pussy began clamping down over Alicia's fingers. At the same time, she hunched over and began shaking wildly as she gripped the railing with all her strength.

"Fuck, Jade!" she hissed. "I'm cumming! Pound my ass with your big dick. God, I'm cumming so hard!"

As the two of us grunted and shook in simultaneous orgasm with my buttocks clenching as I pressed my cock deep into her, I suddenly became conscious of the extra light that was being cast onto the terrace from the open windows of the ballroom. When we finally came down from our powerful climax, she turned around and gently kissed me.

"It seems we have an audience," she smiled, directing her eyes toward the adjacent wall.

I peered in the direction of the ballroom and noticed a giant crowd of onlookers staring out the windows with their eyes and mouths agape.

"Good," I said. "It's about time some of these snobs got a taste of the real world outside their sheltered cocoons. "Maybe this will open their minds about the natural order of things."

With that, I lifted Alicia up onto the stone abutment and spread her legs far apart, pressing my still buzzing cock back inside her.

"If they want a show, let's really give them a show."

6

———

After Alicia and I came a second time in full view of the crowd, we took a moment to compose ourselves then walked back into the main ballroom as if nothing had happened. Neither one of us seemed to care that virtually everyone was staring at us as they continued gossiping in their little cliques. I didn't even bother to refasten my leather vest or deflate my dildo as my breasts bounced freely on my bare chest in tandem with my turgid hard-on.

The two of us approached the bar and ordered matching margaritas then giggled amongst ourselves about the way everyone was trying not to stare as they talked amongst themselves. In spite of the fact that they pretended to carry on normal conversations, it was obvious that they were still highly aroused by our little tête-a-tête.

"I think Mr. Incredible is regretting his wardrobe choice right about now," Alicia chuckled, motioning toward the billionaire and his supermodel girlfriend.

I stole a glance in their direction and noticed Schiffer had a pronounced erection tenting the front of his tights.

"He's looking more like *Mr. Fantastic* with that cucumber wedged between his legs," I joked.

"And check out our favorite newscaster," she said. "It looks like Woody's popping a little Pinocchio of his own."

I peered at the anchorman and noticed him rearranging the front of his denims as a prominent bulge ran down one side of his pant legs.

"Ha," I chuckled. "I bet he's wishing he wore chaps like me."

I had to admit that I was enjoying the attention of all the powerful people in the room, particularly amongst the men who seemed especially attracted by my naked ladyboy costume.

"I don't know about *Jack* though," she said, furrowing her brow as her husband marched toward us with an angry expression on his face. "I have a feeling that his little willie will be even more shriveled than usual after watching you pound me with your big tool."

The governor stormed up to the bar and grabbed Alicia's hand, trying to ignore the pink pole jutting up from my lap.

"What is it, dear?" Alicia said, feigning surprise at her husband's indignation. "I was just enjoying a quiet drink with my new friend."

"That was hardly *quiet*!" he huffed, dragging her off her barstool. "Come on, it's time for us to go."

"But the party was just getting started," Alicia protested. "I was just starting to get warmed up."

The governor glanced down at my flaring joystick then glared at me.

"It looks like the two of you were getting more than just *warmed up*."

"Oh, come on, Jack," Alicia said, trying to resist his advance. "We were just having a little fun. You said that you wanted me to get more comfortable around your political friends."

"Not *that* way!" he fumed. "You've made a fool out of me and embarrassed me in front of all my colleagues!"

Alicia tried to protest, but the governor pulled her away from the bar and stormed toward the entrance. After collecting their coats from the butler, they soon disappeared out the front door. Alarmed by the commotion, Hannah joined me at the bar and sat on Alicia's stool, taking a sip of her cocktail.

"Jesus, Jade," she said, slapping my dripping dildo. "You sure know how to rock the boat in these genteel affairs."

"That's not the *only* boat I was rocking around here," I said. "Were you watching the show like everybody else?"

"How could I miss it?" Hannah chuckled. "It only took one person to catch you fucking the governor's wife before the entire room joined in the spectacle. Not like they could have *ignored* it, with all the grunting and groaning the two of you were doing."

"I wasn't paying much attention. I was kind of lost in the moment."

"You sure looked like it," Hannah said. "I have to say, It was an incredible turn-on watching you fuck her from behind. I could actually see your buttocks shaking when you came." She glanced down at my swollen cock and shook her head. "How does that work, exactly? I thought you were kind of detached from that thing."

"Not as much as you might imagine," I smiled. "Touch my balls to see for yourself."

Hannah placed her hand over my rubber scrotum and I switched on the vibrator, then her eyes suddenly flung open.

"Holy shit!" she said. "That thing really *is* fully animated. What else can it do? Spurt out fake cum?"

"As much as I wish it could, no. But these two extra tricks seem to be providing all the entertainment I need."

"I'd say so, judging by how loud the two of you were howling out there on the balcony. I fact, I've got a little girly hard-on of my own thinking what that would feel like inside me. I don't suppose we could find our own private alcove for a little fun, could we? I'm so horny right now, this costume is practically glued onto my body."

I glanced around the room and noticed that everybody was staring at us with disapproving expressions.

"Why not?" I said. "After that last escapade, it looks like all bets are off. There's not much to hide any more at this point."

I took Hannah's hand and began heading in the direction of the wine cellar, but Steve Bannon and his wife stepped in front of us, smiling like Cheshire Cats.

"It appears you've been enjoying my party even more than I could have imagined," he smirked, peering at my dripping dildo. "You seem to have gotten a rise out of more than a few of our guests this evening. I'd have to say you win the prize for the most inventive costume."

"I have to admit, it's been far less of a stuffy affair than I imagined." I glanced at Genevieve, noticing the slit in the side of her dress looking even more pronounced than before, revealing her hip bone above her barely concealed pussy. "I've found the conversation very stimulating."

"So it would seem," he said, staring at my tumescent totem. "Would you like to join my wife and me for a little nightcap in our private lounge? We've been admiring you all night long and would love to continue the conversation."

"Hmm," I said, raising an eyebrow toward Hannah. "Do you mind if I bring my friend along? We were just about to explore some private time of our own."

Bannon leered at Hannah's costume then smiled at her.

"I don't see why not," he said. "What do you think dear? Would you like to bring another partner into our little meeting?"

"The more the merrier," she smiled, jumping at the chance to have some more alone time with me. "Besides, now it'll be more evenly balanced. I'm not sure I could manage the two of you all by myself."

"Come then," Bannon said, leading us to a private elevator at the base of his stairs.

As we crossed the ballroom floor, the entire room followed our movement while my protruding penis waggled playfully between my legs. When we got in the elevator and the doors closed behind us, Bannon pressed button number four and smiled at Hannah and me.

"You've already explored many of the rooms in my house," he said. "But I think you'll find the view particularly appealing from the top floor."

I glanced toward Hannah and saw that her pupils were already dilated in excitement. I didn't know if she was more impressed by the fact that Bannon's mansion had four floors and a personal elevator or that she was about to participate in a private orgy with the richest man in the Midwest.

When the lift stopped and the doors opened, we both gasped at the view. The elevator opened to an enormous bedroom with floor-to-ceiling windows providing a panoramic view of Lake Michigan. As impressed as I'd been with the view from his main floor balcony, from this elevation the lake seemed to stretch out in every direction forever. But the view on the *inside* was even more spectacular. Bannon's bedroom was almost as large as most people's houses, with giant expressionist paintings hanging on the walls, a huge wood-burning fireplace next to the bed, and a separate bar beside the sliding glass windows.

"Would you like something to drink?" he said, lifting a crystal decanter off the table. "Perhaps a glass of brandy? I've got a thirty-year-old bottle of Hennessey that I've been meaning to open for a special event."

As much as I admired his impressive collection of personal effects, I was far more attracted to the elaborate trimmings of his beautiful wife.

"That would be lovely," I said, smiling at Genevieve.

Bannon handed each of us a large goblet filled with cognac, then he pressed a remote control device and the large window panes began to separate, bringing in a gust of cool air.

"Would you like to move to the balcony? The view is even more magical at this time of the night."

"Sure," I said, checking with Hannah to make sure she was still feeling comfortable. She simply peered back at me with wide eyes and nodded silently. We stepped out onto the deck and Bannon motioned to a wicker settee encircling a bubbling Jacuzzi.

"It might be a bit warmer next to the hot tub," he said, extending his hand toward the tub. "Please—make yourselves comfortable."

Hannan and I took a spot next to one another, while Bannon and his wife sat kitty-corner to us, a few feet to our left. The view of the lake was magnificent with the light of the full moon reflecting off the ripples like an evening sunset on a secluded beach. A cool breeze wafted in from the shore, and I pulled my vest over my exposed abdomen.

"Feel free to dip your toes in the water," he said. "Or climb right in if you prefer. It's chillier outside than usual tonight."

"I wouldn't mind getting out of these boots," I said, kicking off my footwear and placing my feet in the churning water.

Then I turned to Hannah and smiled.

"This feels heavenly, Han. Why don't you join me?"

She motioned to her all-in-one ensemble and frowned.

"It's not quite as simple for me as it is for you."

"Don't be concerned about *us*," Bannon grinned. "We're all adults here. Besides, I think we've seen just about everything already tonight. No one's watching this time besides Genevieve and me."

Hannah peered at me for a moment and I nodded. I'd never known her to be shy in these kinds of circumstances and it didn't take long for her to shed her clothes and slide under the bubbling water.

"Mmm," she purred, glancing up at me. "It's lovely. You should come in. These jets are good for massaging more than just your feet."

I looked toward Bannon and his wife and they smiled with a knowing grin.

"You said you wanted to find a private spot to continue your engagement," he said. "Don't let us stop you. We'll just finish our brandies while you two make yourselves comfortable."

He glanced down at my bobbing tool then peered back up at me.

"Is your equipment waterproof?"

"It should be," I said, winking toward Hannah. "Would you like me to keep it on?"

"I think we would," Bannon grinned. "I'd love to see how you use that thing close-up. How about you, dear? Are you interested in watching Jade play with her magic wand again?"

"Absolutely," Genevieve said, staring me directly in the eye. "I'd love to see her make another pretty girl come with her big man-cock."

I pulled off my chaps and vest and squeezed the trigger on my pistol to re-inflate my shaft to its full length then pressed the button on the handle to turn on the vibrator. Bannon and Genevieve squinted at the humming device, and I smiled at them as I slipped under the surface next to Hannah.

She scooted up next to me and lowered her hand under the water, stroking my phallus as she caressed the inside of my thighs. I turned toward her and we embraced in a passionate kiss. I could feel the jets of the Jacuzzi shooting between our breasts as we rubbed our tits together while she lifted her leg, straddling my hips. Within seconds, she lowered herself onto my pole and wrapped her arms around my back. As she began to rock her hips together with mine, I glanced up and made eye contact with Bannon and his wife. I noticed the front of his toga was tenting between his legs and Genevieve's hand was moving up and down as he smiled lasciviously toward us.

"Damn, Jade," Hannah groaned as I embedded my rod deep inside her. "That thing feels amazing. Fuck me with your big cock. Rub your balls on my cunt. I can feel it vibrating."

"Mmm," I sighed, as her tits mashed up against mine in the swirling water. "Squeeze my dick, Hannah. Let's put on a nice show for our hosts."

By now, Bannon had dispensed with any form of modesty, flinging his toga to the side where I could see his throbbing erection standing up between his spread legs. Judging by the size of his wife's hand, he appeared to have a decent-sized hard-on, but nowhere near as large as my own. Genevieve had apparently gotten just worked up watching Hannah and me fucking under the swirling water, and before long she kicked off her heels and hiked up her dress, sitting down over her husband's cock while she faced us. As I darted my eyes between her husband's prick thrusting in and out of her pussy and her dark eyes, our mouths began to open in mutual pleasure.

It was an incredible turn-on watching Genevieve's sexy body squirming over her husband's cock as she watched the two of us writhing in the churning water. Whether she was more excited getting fucked by her husband while two pretty girls watched them get it on or by the sight of Hannan and me enjoying ourselves underneath the surface, it didn't matter. Before long, all four of us were moaning loudly as we watched each other fuck our partners with abandon.

Hannah was the first to go off, as she started shaking wildly on my hips.

"Oh God, Jade," she groaned. "I'm cumming! Ram it inside me. Let me feel your balls slap up against me. Uhnnnnnn!"

Seeing Hannah having a powerful orgasm on top of me soon put Bannon over the edge as he grunted with his shaft pulsing inside his wife's pussy. Although he was staring at me, I was more interested in watching the expression on Genevieve's face as she returned my gaze with glassy eyes. I could tell that she was close, but needed a little extra stimulation to reach her goal.

As she locked eyes on me, she placed her hand over the front of her mound and began jerking her protruding nub. As her eyes opened progressively wider, I leaned forward and lifted my ass over one of the jets behind me. While the water gushed against my quivering opening, the vibrating balls pressed against my clit, and I felt a surge of pleasure engulfing my body.

"I'm close," I panted, locking eyes with Bannon's wife. "Come for me, Genevieve. Let me watch you come all over my big dick."

Even though she was planted on her husband's cock, we were both thinking the same thing. In that moment of mutual ecstasy, we were both imagining that it was *my* cock embedded in her pussy instead of her husband's.

"Yes, Jade!" she howled. "I'm cumming! I feel you inside me. I want you so bad. Oh *Gawd...*"

While the four of us panted and groaned in simultaneous climax, I glanced at Bannon, noticing him watching me with a wild look in his eye. Locked on me with laser focus, he had a strange, almost animalistic expression. I wasn't sure what he was channeling at that moment, but I could tell it wasn't his wife he was thinking about.

After we all settled down, Genevieve lifted herself off her husband's cock and slid in the water next to Hannah and me. She cuddled up beside me and her hand disappeared under the water, and soon after I felt her caressing my vibrating dildo. As Hannah leaned over to kiss her, Bannon stood up with his penis dripping a string of cum, motioning with his head inside his bed chamber.

"Why don't we all go back inside?" he said. "There'll be more room for us to play and we can watch each other better on the bed. Something tells me there's still a lot of pent-up energy between you girls."

Genevieve stepped up out of the tub first and led me by the hand into the bedroom as Hannah scampered in behind us, shivering. Bannon returned from his washroom and threw each of us a towel. Then he walked over to the bed and sat on the edge, beckoning for the rest of us to join him.

"Come," he said. "Let's share the wealth. There's plenty to go around."

"What did you have in mind?" I said, raising my eyebrows. After the Tarzan episode, I wasn't sure what part of me he was more interested in.

"There's enough parts between us for us to create an interesting *foursome*, don't you think?" he smirked.

As we all lay down on the bed and began exploring each other's bodies, Bannon seemed immediately drawn to my cock. As he sucked on my nipples, he reached down and began stroking my phallus while he masturbated himself with his other hand. While Hannah and Jenny intertwined their legs and began rubbing their pussies together, Bannon lowered himself down my abdomen until his face was directly in front of my giant pole. Suddenly, he stretched his lips around the head and began sucking it while he jerked his hand over his own dripping dick. Within seconds, he began moaning loudly, as he jetted squirts of cum all over his stomach.

Seeing her husband getting off so quickly again, Genevieve sat up and peered at the two of us with a sly smile.

"You seem quite enamored with Jade's cock, dear. I have an idea, if you're game for a little four-way fun. How would you like a *real* cock inside you this time, Hannah?"

Hannah looked at Genevieve then back at her husband, and smiled. There was little doubt that she'd fantasized about being fucked by the hot billionaire for a long time.

"*Definitely*," she said.

"Lie down face up on the bed," Genevieve instructed. "That way we can *both* have access to you. And *Jade*," she purred, with a gleam in her eye. "Why don't you choose whatever outlet looks most enticing to you among the three of us?"

As Genevieve spread her thighs over Hannah's face and lowered her pussy onto her lips, Bannon pulled Hannah's legs apart and straddled her opening with his dripping dick. As I watched them begin to fuck my best friend like she was a piece of meat, something inside me snapped. There was something about the way Bannon thought he could use her any way he wanted that pissed me off.

Just another self-righteous rich asshole, I thought. *This guy needs to be put in his place.*

As I kneeled behind him watching the two of them grinding their bodies against Hannah, Genevieve looked up at me and smiled. She glanced down toward her husband's ass and nodded. It was almost like she was *begging* me to fuck him from behind.

As the sides of my lips slowly curled up in acknowledgement, I brushed my erect dildo over Bannon's cheeks. Instead of flinching, he leaned further forward until I could see his balls waggling above Hannah's pussy. His asshole puckered as he thrust in and out of her, and for the first time in my life, I sensed the attraction of anal sex. There was something incredibly sexy and empowering about fucking a man up the ass. Now I knew why gay men separated into tops and bottoms. Just as with lesbian couples, one had to be the dominant one and one was meant to be the submissive one.

And *this* time, it was *my* turn to be the dominant one. Only in a way I'd never envisioned.

I lifted the tip of my pole, still glistening with Hannah's juices, and pointed it toward Bannon's opening. As I pressed it against his pucker, he grunted and pushed back gently.

So he likes being fucked by a woman? I thought. *It's time to show him who's really in charge here.*

I grabbed the sides of his hips and slowly pressed my cock deeper inside him. It felt strange and titillating at the same time to be fucking a man with my faux hard-on. As my balls pressed back against my clit, I imagined what it would feel like for a man to fuck another man this way. Suddenly, all the times I'd felt used by men who fucked from behind came flooding back. I thrust my dick as far into Bannon's ass as I could and began pounding my hips against his butt cheeks.

As his hole stretched as far as it could go by my coke-can-width hard-on, I found myself enjoying the feeling of thrusting in and out of him. Strangely, Genevieve seemed to be enjoying the show almost as much as me, as she writhed and moaned on Hannah's face while watching the two of us.

"Yes, Jade," she grunted. "Fuck Jack's ass. Make him your bitch. I want to watch him get off while you have your way with him."

Whether it was the sight of her pretty body twisting over Hannah's face or the sense of power I felt fucking her husband, I soon felt the familiar wall of pleasure beginning to overtake me. As I pressed my balls tight against his ass, creating more friction against my clit, I began to moan approaching my peak.

"Damn this is hot," I grunted. "I'm going to come soon. Watch me cum inside your husband's ass, Genevieve."

"Yes," she groaned, suddenly shifting her gaze to her husband's eyes.

I wasn't sure if she was communing with him at that moment or she just enjoyed seeing him at his most vulnerable moment. Either way, the sight of her convulsing over Hannah's mouth as she reached her own orgasm soon opened my floodgates. I pulled Bannon's ass hard toward me as I thrust my cock one last time deep into him, squirting all over my vibrating balls and Hannah's pussy. Within seconds, all four of us were howling in mutual ecstasy as we pounded and quivered atop one another in a mass of sweaty flesh. When we finally collapsed onto the bed in exhaustion, Genevieve leaned over and kissed me, whispering in my ear.

"Thanks for putting my husband in his rightful place," she mewed. "You have no idea how much both of us needed that."

VOLUME THREE

WEBCAM CHAT

1

CYBERSURFING

After my playdate with the dominatrix, I felt I needed a breather to regain control over my sex life. My little excursion into the world of BDSM had been fun, but being whipped and hog-tied by a domme had its limits. Now it was *my* turn to set the terms of engagement. I wanted to be back in the driver's seat and branch out beyond one dominant partner.

One lonely night at home, I sat down in front of my computer and began searching for some online fun. I wanted something different from the run-of-the-mill porn—something more engaging. I needed something involving a live, two-way interaction. With a real person, someone with whom I could share a genuine, passionate, if only temporary, relationship. A virtual *fuck buddy*, for want of a better word.

I typed in the search words *webcam sex chat* and a bunch of listings popped up for live online chat. I clicked on one labeled *LiveGirls*, and a gallery of videos showing scantily-clad women touching themselves filled the screen. I tapped one of the thumbnails, where a live stream showed a pretty girl lying facedown on a bed, wearing only a thong. As she swayed her hips from side to side, she looked over her shoulder suggestively toward the camera. Beside the video window, a flurry of comments filled the chat box.

Spread your legs, someone named bigjohn said.

Nice ass, hornyjoe commented.

Can I see your tits? guest34 pleaded.

All the while, the pretty brunette ran her hands across her concealed breasts and rolled her hips in the same robotic manner. For a moment, I was hypnotized like everyone else by her lithe and sexy body. But as attractive as she was, I had no interest in joining what amounted to a public strip show. I was just about to exit the screen when I noticed a button for Private Chat.

Let's see if she's any more engaging one-on-one, I thought.

I clicked the button and a Join Now window covered the stream.

Jeesuz, I cursed. They never make this easy.

I filled in the required fields for Username, Password, and E-mail, then clicked the button. The next screen presented me with a choice between selecting ten free credits or buying a package of credits starting at fifty dollars.

So that's how it works, I thought. *It's not much different from a real strip club. As long as you're stuffing their stockings with cash, the girls are happy to put on a show for you.*

I'd never paid for sex of any kind, and I wasn't about to get started now. I didn't want to chat with someone who was only in it for the money. I backtracked to the main search screen and adjusted my search phrase to *free amateur sex chat* and clicked Enter.

A fresh set of listings popped up, including an intriguing one named *SexRoulette — free webcam live chat*. When I clicked on the link, a window came up with two side-by-side blank video screens. I enabled my laptop cam and mic, then I clicked the Start button. Suddenly, a live feed of me sitting half-naked in my bathrobe appeared in the left window, while some naked guy stroking his dick appeared in the right window.

Horrified to see that my face was showing, I quickly tilted my screen down and cursed out loud.

What's the matter? the naked guy typed in the chat box. *You're very pretty. Can I see your face again?*

I paused for a moment, realizing that he could hear me, then I clicked the microphone button to mute my mic. I wasn't prepared to carry on a live audio conversation with some naked guy. For that matter, I wasn't interested in carrying on a sex chat with *any* man.

I clicked the Next button and a different naked guy appeared with his legs spread wide apart, revealing another erect, throbbing cock. Every time I clicked Next, a different naked man appeared, pulling on his pud. As amusing as I found the experience of scrolling through a bunch of men's penises, the thought of chatting with one of these nameless guys turned my stomach.

Where were all the girls? I thought. *Are only guys interested in naughty online chats?*

I scanned the site and noticed some links across the top for different chat rooms. The default setting was for Mixed, but I could also choose between Guys, Girls, and Couples. Intrigued, I clicked on the Couples link, and a new window popped up showing a woman bobbing her head between a man's knees while his hand typed on a computer keyboard beside him on the bed.

Hi, the man typed in the chat window. *Wanna play?*

I paused for a moment, wondering if it might be fun to watch a hetero couple going at it.

Maybe some other time, I typed, before clicking on the Girls tab.

A new window popped up requiring me to verify that I was over eighteen years of age (*only to view girls??*) then I was redirected to a different website showing the familiar gallery of naked girls from the LiveGirls site. When I clicked on one of the images, a similar video and chat screen appeared. Another pretty young girl perched half-naked on a bed, while a bunch of anonymous viewers made lewd comments, 'tipping' her occasionally with tokens. Whenever anybody tipped her enough tokens, she bent over and waved her ass in front of the camera.

What the fuck? I thought. *Is it only professional girls who want to chat online?*

I clicked out of the website and was about to pull my vibrator out of my nightstand for some quiet alone time, when I decided to give it one last try.

There's got to be other lonely girls who are looking for a quick hookup with like-minded women.

I went back to the main search page and typed in *lesbian online chat*. Near the top of the listings, I noticed a site titled *SapphicChat — girls only free online chat*.

That's what I'm talking about, I said out loud, clicking the link.

Another side-by-side video setup appeared on the screen with a chat box underneath. I enabled my cam and carefully positioned my laptop lid so that only my torso was visible, then I pulled my robe tightly around my neck to cover myself up. There'd be no more skin showing until I was able to qualify a suitable candidate.

I clicked the Start button, and within a few seconds the adjacent window flickered with a live stream showing a fat woman lying on her bed with her droopy boobs hanging down by her waist.

Yikes, I said, quickly clicking the Next button. I felt bad judging the visitors so harshly, but it wasn't much different from other dating apps. If you didn't feel the chemistry right away, everybody just moved on.

After a few seconds, a new image filled the sender window. This time an older woman sat in front of her computer with her elbows propped up on her desk. Deep folds of flesh hung from her neck and upper chest as she peered sadly into the screen.

Wow, I thought. *These online forums really bring out the lonely girls.*

I toggled through the list of online visitors until an image appeared showing a younger girl sitting cross-legged on her bed, wearing a tight V-neck sweater. Her breasts were full and plump, and although her face was partially hidden off-screen, I could tell from the downiness of her bare legs in a mid-thigh skirt that she was considerably younger than me. I parted my legs unconsciously as my pussy throbbed in excitement.

Finally. A sexy girl who wants an authentic online chat.

ASL? I typed, wanting to be sure she was of legal age. The last thing I needed was to have the police breaking down my door for engaging a minor in online sex.

19, curious, Houston, she typed. *You?*

Nineteen? She barely looked of age. I'd have to vet her more carefully if things went much further.

I paused for a moment, wondering how I wanted to present myself. I didn't want to scare her away by revealing my true age if she was looking to hook up with someone younger. But she had to lean at least a little bit toward girls if she'd engaged me this far.

28, bi, Milwaukee, I stretched the facts on all three aspects.

She paused for a moment holding her hand over her computer keyboard, then the video screen suddenly went blank and a new visitor came online.

Touché, I thought. *I guess this works both ways. My fellow online surfers can be just as rash and judgmental as me when it comes to who they find attractive.*

Obviously. I hadn't measured up in her eyes. But had I been too old, not the right sexual orientation, or was it my *body* she didn't like?

I peered at my image in my webcam feed and looked at my tightly-bound boobs wrapped up in my bathrobe. I'd been slouching a bit, and the heavy terrycloth robe wasn't doing much justice to the shape of my bosom. I spread the lapels of my robe a few inches apart and lifted my chest. My ample cleavage shone through the opening, revealing the roundness of my breasts.

That looks better, I smiled, nodding at the sexy reflection. *If this doesn't hook them, I'm really losing my mojo.*

The next visitor appeared to be another young girl seated on a chair in front of her computer. She only showed the lower half of her face, but from her tight skin and smooth neck muscles, she looked to be in her late teens or early twenties. Her tight T-shirt had a wishbone-shaped "C" emblem on the front. In the background, two small double beds sat on either side of her small room.

Hi, I typed, deciding to take a more measured approach with this new visitor. *What brings you to this crazy place so late at night?*

Just bored I guess, she responded.

Me too, I said. *This is my first time doing something like this. I'm used to meeting people the old-fashioned way.*

Boys or girls? she typed.

It was obvious that she was fishing. I had no idea what the right answer was, so I decided to play it safe.

Both, I guess. *But I prefer girls. How about you?*

I like boys... she typed. *But lately I've been finding myself unusually attracted to my dorm mate.*

Oh, I said, happy to hear she tilted both ways. *Where do you go to school?*

University of Chicago.

My heart skipped a beat when I realized how close she was to me in the real world.

What are you studying? I said, trying to steady my nervous hand as I typed.

I'm enrolled in the BA program, so right now it's mostly liberal arts. I'm just in my first year, so I haven't really decided on my major yet. I'm thinking maybe Communications...

She's barely eighteen! I thought. *My pussy throbbed at the thought of uncovering more of this pretty co-ed.*

What kind of career were you thinking of?

I dunno. Public relations, marketing, maybe television.

On the production side?

I suppose so. Somewhere behind the camera. I don't think I have prime time face.

You should let other people be the judge of that. From what I can see so far, I think you're very pretty. The combination of good looks and good communication skills will give you quite a leg up in that field.

Thanks, she said, tilting the camera up a little higher on her face. She smiled a broad smile, revealing perfectly-straight, pearly-white teeth. *What about you, what do you do?*

I'm a freelance graphic designer.

So you design websites and stuff like that?

A little bit of that. But I do more corporate work like logos, editorial layouts, that sort of thing.

That sounds interesting, the girl said. *I guess we both have an interest in communications of sorts...*

I paused for a moment, wondering how much longer I wanted to focus on the professional sides of our lives.

It looks like we share an interest in another form of communicating too. ;-)

LOL. This isn't the kind of communications my profs talk about.

I'm a little surprised to hear that, I said. *The world is rapidly adopting new forms of social media every day. Perhaps you can consider this as a type of vocational training.*

Except most people who come to this website are interested in only one thing.

You mean meeting people? I teased.

In a manner of speaking...

Are you testing the waters here because of your roommate?

Maybe. I didn't realize I had such a strong attraction to girls until I met her.

Have you shared your feelings with her?

Gawd no. She has a boyfriend. It could get very uncomfortable around here if I came on to her too strongly. We have to share this small room for the rest of the year and perhaps for the rest of our college residency.

Two charged up bodies in a small space can make for a combustible mixture. Do you think she's attracted to you also?

Not by the way I've seen her and her boyfriend go at it. I can't tell you how many times I've come back to my room to find a sock on the door.

Poor thing, I thought. *It doesn't sound like she's got much of an outlet to express her real feelings. I better tread lightly.*

Maybe you just need to be a little more suggestive when you have some alone time with her. You know, wear skimpier clothes to bed, come back from the shower naked. That sort of thing. If she's interested, she'll soon let you know.

It sounds like you have a little more experience with girls, she said. *Are you lesbian?*

Now we're getting to the crux of it, I thought. It was kind of fun playing the role of the girl's online mentor.

They say everyone's somewhere on the continuum, I said. *I'd say I'm about a nine, but I seem to be moving more to the right with each passing year. Men don't really do it for me any longer.*

The chat window paused for a moment as the girl seemed to process what I said.

What's it like? she said. *You know, being with a woman?*

Crikey, I thought. *How do I answer that without sounding like some kind of stalker?*

That's an interesting question. It's different in so many ways. Woman like different things than men. We're more focused on building the relationship. Men are mostly just interested in sex.

Aren't women interested in that too?

Yes, of course, I laughed. *We just let it happen more—organically.*

Organically?

We let it happen naturally, as our feelings for one another grow stronger. Instead of just jumping on the biscuit, in a manner of speaking.

You mean kind of like what we're doing right now?

I was beginning to feel a strange attraction to this girl. Beyond the pretty outside package, she had a sweet innocence to her.

I suppose, I said. *We lesbians generally like to get to know our partner a little better before jumping into bed with them.*

Do you mind my asking how that works when you do get together? I mean, it's not like regular boy-girl coupling...

All this tip-toeing around the edges of sexy talk was beginning to stir some new feelings inside me. I was enjoying the process of educating this young girl on the nuances of lesbian relationships.

It's not so different, when it comes right down to it. We have the same sensitive parts. We just use them a little differently.

Do you miss the penetration aspect of the relationship?

Maybe it's time to stop being so nuanced, I thought.

Who says we have to forego the penetration aspect?

*Oh, sorry—*the girl said, as I saw a flush roll over her face. *It's just that without a penis involved in the equation...*

There are lots of ways us girls can enjoy penetration without a man.

Strap-on dildos, two-sided phalluses, using sex toys. I'm guessing you've tried one or two of these before?

Well, yes. I have a vibrator I play with when my roommate is away. But I had no idea women used them together like you said.

Oh, yes. There are lots of interesting ways we make our own fun.

You're getting me pretty worked up talking about it. Can you tell me how you use a two-sided phallus?

Suddenly I became acutely aware of the wetness that had been accumulating between my legs. This innocent but sexy banter had been getting *both* of us worked up.

Well, usually it starts with us lying on our backs with our butts facing one another...

Mmm, the girl typed.

Fuck! I thought. *It's happening. I'm actually seducing a young college girl online!*

Then we insert the two ends in each of our pussies and push our bodies together...

The girl's left hand wandered below my line of vision as she began to squirm in her seat while pecking her keyboard with her other hand.

All the way? she asked. *Do you touch your bodies together?*

Usually, if the dildo isn't too long. That's where it really gets fun. There's nothing so electrifying as feeling your lover's peachka pressed up against your own.

God, that's so hot!

And wet. ;-)

You're making me very wet right now.

I spread my legs and began strumming my clit with my fingers at the thought of the pretty co-ed getting turned on by my explanation.

Are you touching yourself? I said.

Yes. Are you?

I am now.

I wish I could touch you the way you're describing right now.

If I could reach out through my screen, believe me, I would. I'd love to show you what it feels like to make love to a woman.

Can I see your breasts? They look very full and sexy.

I thought you'd never ask.

I pulled my robe apart and let the shawl fall around my shoulders.

OMG! the girl typed. *They're gorgeous. Do you mind if I ask how old you are? Because those are the most beautiful tits I think I've ever seen.*

I paused for a moment trying to decide how young I wanted to pretend to be. The last thing I wanted to do in the heat of the action was scare away another online partner because she thought I was too old.

Everybody tells me I look ten years younger than my real age, I thought. *She'll never know.*

That's very kind of you, I said. *I'm twenty-five. But before we go any further, I should probably ask you the same. If you're in your first year of college, you must be barely legal.*

I turned eighteen two months ago.

Like I said. Barely legal.

We're two consenting adults.

Since we're getting to know each other so intimately, can I ask your name? I don't want to have sex with a faceless, nameless person.

I'm Holly.

Pleased to meet you Holly. My name's Jade.

That's a lovely name.

Yours too, I said. *Holly and Jade. I like the way they go together.*

I'm imagining us going together in more ways than one.

Damn, girl, you're making me soaking wet. Can I see a bit more of you too? I want to let my mind run all over your sweet body.

The girl reached up over her shoulders and pulled her T-shirt over her head. Then she reached behind her back and unclasped her bra. When she pulled it off her shoulders and threw it on the floor, I gasped. Her breasts were smaller than mine, but stood firm and erect on her chest. But far more fascinating, was their *shape*. They were far pointier than most, pressing straight out toward me like two fleshy obelisks.

Mmm, I typed. *Those are mighty succulent boobies you have, Holly.*

Not as full and appetizing as yours! she returned.

I love their shape. I could suck on your pointy nipples all day!

I'd like that, Holly said. *You're going to make me cum pretty soon if you keep talking to me like that.*

That's not the only part of you that I want to suck, I said, starting to rub my clit more quickly. *I want to take your sweet nub into my mouth and watch your twist all over my face.*

Yes, Jade. I want you to suck my clit. Make me cum all over your face.

Oh Baby, I said. *Let me see and feel you cum. I'm pressing my fingers inside you now...*

Fuck, Jade. I can feel you inside me. I'm going to cum...

As I watched Holly writhing in her chair, my mouth opened unconsciously, imagining her riding my face.

Yes, baby, I said. *Cum in my mouth. Let it go.*

Suddenly, a deep flush spread over Holly's chest and she began jerking wildly in her chair.

Ohhhhhhh, she typed. *I'm cumming Jade!*

I hadn't been concentrating very much on my own feelings up to this point, but when I saw Holly coming, I thrust my fingers deep into my pussy and gushed all over my hand. While I watched her jerking in her chair, my tits jiggled spastically on my chest as the tremors spread throughout my body.

After a long pause, Holly began to type again.

That was incredible! she said. *I haven't had an orgasm that powerful in a long time.*

You should try this girl thing more often, I typed. *It's even better in real life. Maybe you and your roommate can find a way—*

Suddenly, Holly's face turned to the side and a panicked expression fell over her face.

I think she's here! she typed. *Someone's at the door!*

Oh no—not now, I thought. *Just when we were establishing such a strong connection.* I banged away at my keyboard, fearful of losing her forever.

Can we do this again some—

Holly's video stream suddenly went dark as she signed out of the program. I was sad to see her go, but at the same time I was thrilled to have made such an exhilarating connection my first time online.

I'm going to have to try this again very soon, I thought, closing my laptop with sticky fingers.

2

───────

FULL DISCLOSURE

After my chat with Holly ended so abruptly, I stayed online for more than an hour hoping she'd reconnect and continue our conversation. But I knew that if her roommate had returned to their dorm, she'd be hard-pressed to find any privacy for the rest of the night. Their single room was so tiny that it would be impossible to find any place for a private conversation, let alone an online sex chat.

For the rest of the night, I fantasized about her roommate barging in to find her masturbating in front of her computer, then tearing off her clothes to join the innocent college girl in her lesbian discovery. If anything could persuade a straight girl to stray to the other side, surely it would be the sight of the winsome co-ed getting off watching other naked women. I came many times that night imagining all the fun the two of them might have discovering the joys of lesbian love-making for the first time.

The following night, I was eager to get back online to see if I could reconnect with Holly. Even though I knew my chances were slim, if she found herself alone again and was in a similar frame of mind, I hoped she might have the same idea. Around the same time that evening, I logged back into the SapphicChat site and began toggling through the gallery of online visitors.

I found a few interesting candidates, and for a short time I engaged in some playful banter with a closeted housewife from Texas, then a curious divorcée from California, then a sexy dyke from Delaware. On any other day, I might have been enticed to remove my clothing and begin another erotic online encounter, but after a few minutes of superficial conversation, I found myself clicking the Next button in search of my innocent college girl.

I was just about to reengage with the Texas housewife when a familiar silhouette filled the visitor chat window. She was sitting cross-legged in the middle of her bed wearing a tight T-shirt and shorts with her face out of the frame, but I recognized the contour of her breasts instantly. Her pointy tits pressed against the soft fabric of her shirt, barely concealing the two tubers of mouthwatering flesh. My pussy throbbed at the sight of the familiar swellings.

Holly? I typed on my keyboard.

Who's this? she responded in the chat box. I was wearing a different outfit this evening, and with my face off-camera, it was obvious she didn't recognize me.

It's Jade. I've been thinking about you so much since our chat last night.

She stretched her legs out on opposite sides of her laptop and leaned her body forward to type on her keyboard. This only accentuated the elongated shape of her breasts, highlighting the meaty areolas at their tips.

Me too. I wasn't sure if I'd find you again. Sorry for cutting you off so suddenly last night.

I completely understand. Did your roommate catch you in the act?

I was able to get myself pulled together pretty quickly. But she must have sensed something was up from the look on my face. Plus, I'm sure the room was saturated with the scent of my sex by the time we finished.

The thought of Holly's scent filling the room made my pussy weep, and I spread my legs unconsciously, feeling the moisture between my legs.

Did you tell her what you'd been doing?

No, I made up some lame-ass excuse about researching a term paper.

Too bad. If anything might swing her the other way, it would be the sight of her pretty roommate getting off watching other girls.

I dunno. I'm still afraid what she might think. I could smell her boyfriend's cologne all over her when she came back. I don't think she's interested in me that way.

Give it time. It's still early in the semester. She probably just needs to get a bit more comfortable around you. Your irresistible personality will eventually win her over.

So you're saying my body's not enough? ;-)

Don't be silly. Your figure is exquisite. I paused for a moment, contemplating whether to take our online conversation to the next level. *Though I still haven't seen your entire face. Don't you think we've come far enough to show the rest of our bodies to one another?*

Holly hesitated with her hands over her keyboard. For a moment, I thought she might hit the Exit button in fear of revealing her real identity.

I guess so, she said. *But I'm kind of wary about my showing my face in a public forum like this. You never know who might be recording us. I'd be horrified if somebody posted this online and my parents saw a clip of me masturbating online one day.*

I know how you feel, I typed. *I've been having the same concerns. Why don't we open a separate private chat. Do you have Skype?*

Yes, Holly said. *I use it to chat with my folks every couple of weeks.*

What's your username? Mine's gigi84.

Is that the year you were born? I thought you said you were twenty-five!

Ok, full disclosure, I sheepishly typed. *I might have stretched my age a little bit. But everyone tells me I look much younger than I really am.*

It's cool, Holly said. *Everybody has a secret identity online. I never would have guessed your age. You certainly have the body of a 25 yr old!*

Sexy enough to entice a college girl into an online affair with a middle-aged woman?

That's not middle-aged! You're barely through the first trimester. But to answer your question, yes. My Skype ID is ucgrad22.

LOL. I'm trying to slow down the clock and you're already looking ahead. Shall we log out of here and start a new Skype chat?

C u in a few minutes, sexy momma! Holly said, signing off with a playful kissing emoji.

As her image disappeared from the video window, my pussy pitter-pattered at her playful description of me. I couldn't wait to have her all to myself on a private webcam link, and I quickly exited the webpage and signed into Skype. I searched for *ucgrad22* and a profile pulled up with a thumbnail image of a pretty teenager wearing sunglasses against a seaside background. I clicked on the image and a new chat window opened, giving me three options. I could leave a text message in the chat box at the bottom of the screen, or I could send her an audio or video call request.

What the hell, I thought. *I think we're well past the preliminaries.*

I tapped on the video button and as my video stream went live, the sound of an electronic call warbled through my speakers. While I waited for Holly to pick up on the other end, I adjusted the angle of my camera so that it focused with a close-up of my face. I'd chosen to wear some skimpy lingerie this evening, and I didn't want to be too presumptuous right out of the gate. Besides, I was eager to see Holly's full face, and I figured if I set the tone, that she might follow.

After a few seconds, the bottom half of the screen filled with the familiar image of Holly's chest in her tight T-shirt. I smiled when I saw her, and she quickly tilted her screen up so that I could see her face also. My heart immediately began accelerating, not only because she appeared so close, but also because she was absolutely stunning. She had large doe-eyes, a cute upturned nose, and long auburn hair falling over her shoulders. With her bright green eyes and sprinkling of little freckles, she looked like a dead-ringer for the actress Emma Stone.

"Can you hear me?" I spoke toward my laptop's onboard microphone.

"Yes," Holly replied. "Oh my God, Jade—you're gorgeous!"

"Not bad for a thirty-five-year-old?" I smiled.

"Not bad for a twenty-five-year-old!" Holly beamed back at me.

"You're not too shabby yourself, young lady," I said. "Those eyes are to die for. Has anyone ever told you that you look a bit like—"

"Yes, I know. Emma Stone. I get it all the time. I think it's just the red hair and freckles. We gingers are always getting compared to one another. Amy Adams, Bryce Howard, Lindsay Lohan—I've heard them all."

"Sorry," I said. "I didn't mean to compare you to anybody. You're gorgeous and unique in your own right."

"No worries. It's just that I used to get teased quite a lot when I was younger."

"Not so much anymore, I bet."

"Thankfully, I seem to be outgrowing it."

"I bet you turn a lot of heads from both boys and girls on campus."

"I haven't been paying much attention. I've been focusing primarily on my studies. I don't get out much..."

"Oh my God, girl. You don't know what you're missing. With a face and body like that, you could have your pick of the litter. You could make your roommate super-jealous by bringing home a hot new boyfriend every night of the week."

"Except I'm not really into guys right now. Though I will confess, I *was* fantasizing about phalluses most of the night."

"Oh? Do tell. Real or pretend ones?"

"All your talk about strap-on dildos and double-sided cocks got me worked up all night. As soon as Jen left in the morning, I took out my vibrator and have been playing with it most of the day."

My pussy throbbed at the thought of Holly jilling herself with a dildo, as I felt a dribble of lubrication run down the crack of my ass.

"Same here. Do you have a favorite?"

Holly leaned over her bed and reached into the night table beside her bed. She pulled out a plain flesh-colored plastic dildo and held it in front of the screen for me to see.

"I just have this one. I actually pulled it out of the trash can at my house a few years ago. I think it belonged to my mother. I've been too nervous to go to an adult store to look for one of my own."

"Jeesuz, girl," I said, staring at the prehistoric sex toy. "That looks like something straight out of the eighties. Vibrators have become a lot more sophisticated over the last few years."

I reached into my side table and pulled out my favorite rabbit vibrator and held it up for Holly to see.

"This is one of my favorites. It's called The Rabbit. It twists and rolls on the end to provide an exquisite form of internal stimulation. But best of all are these little rabbit ears."

I tweaked the two silicone flaps with my fingers.

"When you turn it on, they vibrate and flap directly against your clitoris, providing the most intense type of stimulation you can imagine. The whole thing is made of super-soft silicone, so it almost feels like the real thing when it's inside you."

Holly stared at the multi-colored vibrator with wide eyes, then glanced back at her plain plastic dildo.

"I'm feeling pretty inadequate right now. Can you show me how it works? I mean—just turn it on so I can see how it moves?"

"Of course," I said, happy to indulge Holly's curiosity.

I held the vibrator vertical and turned it sideways so she could see the rabbit ears in profile view, then turned the device on. As it began making a low humming sound, a circle of beads swirled just under the transparent surface.

"See these circulating beads? They provide a sensation unlike any man can deliver."

Emma stared at the strange contraption and nodded.

"I can imagine. How else does it move?"

I pressed another button, and the tip of the dildo started rolling in small circles.

"Holy shit!" Holly exclaimed, with wide eyes. "That thing really is unlike any other cock, isn't it?"

"So you *have* experienced a real penis, then?" I said, probing for more details about her sex life.

"Well yes, just a few times in high school with a boyfriend in my senior year. But he wasn't endowed nearly as well as that thing!"

"It's a little bigger than most men's cocks, I suppose. But here's the best part." I tapped another button on the base of the vibrator and the rabbit ears started fluttering against the side of the shaft. "Can you see that," I said, pointing toward the flickering ears. "That's something else no man's cock can hope to emulate. The combined effect of these three actions will send you over the moon."

"Oh my God," Holly said. "I'm already soaking wet at the thought of having that thing inside me. I don't suppose you'd be willing to demonstrate it working for real? I mean—*inside* you?"

By this time, the insides of my thighs were coated with slippery lubrication emanating from my pussy and my clit was burning in need of some direct stimulation.

"It would be my pleasure—literally."

I unplugged my laptop and carried it with my vibrator to my bed. Then I sat up with my back resting against the headboard and placed the laptop between my legs about two feet away so Holly could see my entire body from my hips to my head.

"Mmm, I like what you're wearing tonight," Holly said, admiring my lacy camisole and matching boy-shorts panties.

"I wore it just for you," I purred, cupping my breasts and pinching my nipples through the thin fabric.

"I wish I were there to touch you like that. I want to caress every square inch of your body."

"Likewise," I said, spreading my legs further apart. "Can you take your T-shirt off so I can see your beautiful breasts while I play with myself? I've been fantasizing about seeing you naked again for the last twenty-four hours."

"Absolutely," Holly said. "In fact, let me get completely naked so I can enjoy myself properly while I'm watching you."

Holly pulled her shirt over her head as her pointy tits jiggled on her chest. Then she raised her ass and pulled her shorts over her ankles, revealing a completely bare pussy.

"Oh my God, Holly," I gasped, staring at her sexy slit and puffy labia. "Just when I thought you couldn't get any more perfect. That might be the prettiest pussy I've ever seen."

"I bet you say that to all the girls," she teased.

"I have to admit that I love every woman's vulva. But yours looks unusually—*pristine*. Almost like it's never been touched. Are you sure you've been with boys before?"

"Only a few times," Holly laughed. "Not as many times as I've used my vibrator."

"Well that skinny little thing isn't much thicker than a toothbrush. No wonder you look like you've barely been touched down there."

"My boyfriend in high school was pretty small too. I didn't know they came any bigger. Show me how that big dildo fills you up, Jade."

I had planned on giving Holly a slow striptease to get her in the mood, but when started talking dirty, I practically tore my panties and camisole off.

Holly paused for a moment as her eyes darted over her screen, appraising my body.

"Holy fuck, Jade! *You're* the one with the perfect body. I'd die to have your curves. You look like something straight out of some men's magazine centerfold."

"Or *women's*," I chuckled. "Hopefully this body works for both sides of the aisle."

Holly traced her right hand down the front of her stomach and began circling her fingers over her clit.

"It's definitely working *this* side of the aisle, I can assure you."

"Mmm, Holly, you're making me very wet."

"Wet enough for that big dildo to slide up inside you?"

"Let's see," I said, placing the end of the vibrator against my opening. I tapped the oscillating function button and the tip of the dildo began rolling over my slippery labia. As I began to insert the dildo inside my hole, Holly leaned in closer to the screen.

"Damn," she panted. "My boyfriend's cock never did anything like that. It was mostly straight in-and-out action. Usually pretty fast."

"You have no idea how good real lovemaking can be," I purred. "The trick is to take your time and let the passion slowly build. Only after you've been properly teased and stimulated, is it time for a pounding. The pleasure is so much more intense when you let it build to a boil."

"You're sure bringing me to a boil right now," Holly said, rolling her fingers over her slit. "Show me how you enjoy the rest of that special dildo. I want to watch you squirm and moan."

I raised my knees higher off the bed and tapped the second button on the vibrator. As the rotating silver beads glistened in the nightlight from my side table, the shaft slowly disappeared inside my cavern as I pushed it further inside me.

"Fuck that's hot!" Holly panted, her big doe eyes widening even further. "What does that feel like inside you?"

"It's like nothing else," I moaned. "The feeling of the beads caressing the inside of my walls while the rotating tip presses against my G-spot is simply indescribable. You've got to get one of these for yourself to truly appreciate it."

"I'll be going to my corner sex shop as soon as it opens tomorrow," Holly grunted, slipping her fingers inside her pussy. "You've certainly sold me."

"Just don't get too attached to it," I said. "It's still doesn't compare to the delicate touch of a real live, sensuous woman."

"But you said I can *combine* both sensations, with the right kind of vibrator. I might buy me one of those two-sided dildos while I'm at the store, just in case the opportunity ever arises with my roommate..."

With that image dancing around my head, I shoved the vibrator deep inside me and tapped on the rabbit ears button. As the ears began flapping against my burning clit, I humped my hips forward and back, pressing the dildo in and out of me.

"That's a sight I'd love to see," I panted, feeling the vibrations emanating throughout my body.

"I'll see if it can be arranged," Holly said, suddenly picking up her plastic vibrator and thrusting it inside her. "That is, if I can ever get past first base with her. I bet she'd enjoy watching you as much as I do. Maybe we can arrange our own little ménage à trois."

"Without her boyfriend, you mean?"

"*Definitely* without him," Holly moaned. "No boys allowed."

Holly and I watched each other holding our dildos with two hands as we fucked ourselves with increasing urgency.

"I'd like that," I panted. "But not nearly as much as being there for real. I want to feel your body pressed up against mine and make you scream in pleasure."

"You're getting pretty close to making me do that right now," Holly moaned, rolling her hips while she stared at her screen. "I'm getting close. Do you think you can cum with me?"

"Fuck yes," I grunted. "Any time. Just tell me when."

"First tell me what you want to do with me. When we get together."

"Oh Holly," I moaned, daring myself to think the unthinkable. "Everything. I want to kiss you and suck you and fuck you with every ounce of my being. We'll take our time and make it last. I'd make love to you all day long if I could."

"How do you want to fuck me, Jade?" Holly panted as her body began tensing up. The pupils in her eyes had become large and dark, signaling that she was nearing her peak. "Will you fuck me with your strap-on dildo or two-headed prick?"

"Yes," I moaned, getting even more turned on by her dirty talk. "I'll fuck you until you come all over my big dildo. I'll make you gush all over my cock while I fuck you in every imaginable way—"

"Yes, Jade," Holly groaned. "I want to feel you inside me. Make me cum all over your big dildo."

Holly was humping her hips wildly now against her plastic dildo, pumping it in and out of her pussy as her breathing became more jagged. I pressed the vibrating rabbit ears hard up against my clit and thrust my vibrator as deep inside me as I could. Within seconds, I could feel the insides of my pussy beginning to expand in preparation for a hard orgasm.

"Cum for me, baby," I groaned, feeling the first waves of passion roll over me. "Press your pussy against me and cum with me. I feel you Holly—"

"Jade!" Holly suddenly screamed, as her hips started shaking in spastic spasms. "I'm cumming!"

Her whole body began convulsing as her pointy breasts shook in tiny tremors.

"Oh baby," I growled, extending my tongue trying to reach her jiggling tits. "Mummy's coming with you. Feel me filling you up. Cum all over my big cock. Let me feel your tight pussy clamping down on me."

"Fuck yes," Holly hissed, holding her spear tightly inside her while her hips convulsed on the bed in front of her computer screen. "I'm still cumming. Oh Jade—"

Suddenly I heard the sound of a door swinging open and another girl's voice.

"What the fuck?" the girl's voice said. "I'm so sorry, Holly. I'll come back later—"

"No," Holly pleaded, peering up from the screen. "Don't leave, Jen. I've been thinking of you..."

Holly glanced down at her screen and gave me a sweet smile, then her video suddenly went blank.

Maybe she'll be getting her wish sooner than she hoped, I thought, pulling the still-throbbing vibrator out of my pussy.

3

THREE'S A CROWD

For the longest time, I stared at the empty screen, imagining what was happening in Holly's dorm room. Her roommate had surprised her in the throes of orgasm, with her naked body splayed in front of her computer and a vibrator deeply embedded in her pussy. How could anyone respond to such a sight?

There were only three possible scenarios. Either her roommate had turned tail and quickly exited the room, closing the door behind her. Or she'd continued into the dorm and gone about her usual business, pretending nothing unusual had happened. Or she'd engaged Holly directly in some way, acknowledging what she'd witnessed. It couldn't be that unusual to discover your roommate masturbating privately in the small confines of the same room. These were young women in the sexual prime of their lives. Where else could they act on their private passions but in the relative seclusion of their own room?

Holly had reached out to her friend in a vulnerable moment. Had her roommate simply brushed it off as a common practice among people their age and told Holly not to worry about it? Or had they begun a meaningful dialogue about Holly's attraction to Jen and discussed whether the feeling was mutual? Or had Jen torn off her *own* clothes and jumped into bed with Holly to begin a torrid affair?

Either way, I couldn't stop thinking about it all night. I came over and over again imagining Jen sucking on Holly's pointy nipples and probing every recess of her with her body. I wondered if Holly had been serious about running out to her local sex shop and stocking up on the latest generation of toys. The thought of she and Jen twisting their bodies together while connected by a two-sided dildo was too much. I plunged my rabbit vibrator back inside my pussy and held it tightly against my mound as I gushed all over the animated phallus.

The following night, I didn't know what to expect. If Jen had responded positively to her outreach, Holly could quickly lose interest in further contact with me. And if her roommate had shunned her advances, she might be reluctant to go back online for fear of being caught in the act again. She might even have trouble finding alone time this late at night. Her roommate couldn't be spending *all* of her free time with her boyfriend. She'd still need time to study and get caught up on her private affairs.

But there was one thing Holly said that kept me coming back. She'd alluded to the possibility of including her roommate in our online games if she got that far. *I'll see if that can be arranged,* she said. I wondered if she meant to go so far as to arrange an in-the-flesh get-together. *Maybe we can arrange our own little ménage à trois.* I'd never been with two girls at the same time, and the possibilities with three women made my head spin.

Around the same time the following evening, I logged back onto SapphicChat to see if she was still available. For over an hour, I toggled through the gallery of online visitors, but there was no sign of Holly. As sexy as some of the other candidates seemed, I had no interest in engaging with anyone else right now. There was only one person I was interested in, and my pretty college girl from UC was nowhere to be found.

I was just about to close my laptop for the night when it suddenly struck me. Maybe Holly had the same idea as me. Maybe she had no interest in wading through another collection of online strangers until she found me again. There was a good chance she was waiting for me to reconnect on our private line, via Skype. I quickly logged out of the public chatroom and launched the private app. When I logged back in, I filtered my list of contacts to display only those who were *Active Now.* Holly's familiar thumbnail appeared with a green dot beside it to indicate that she was online.

Oh my God! I thought. *She's been waiting for me!*

As my pussy fluttered in excitement, I hesitated before sending her a note.

What should I wear for this chat? What if she was with her roommate this time?

I didn't want to be too presumptuous by wearing something too skimpy and come off as some kind of floozy. What if she just wanted to chat to tell me she'd found a new outlet for her lesbian affections?

I went into my wardrobe and wrapped a silk robe over my camisole, then carried my laptop to my bed and made myself comfortable against the headboard. I paused with my hands over my keyboard, wondering how I should proceed after our last embarrassing incident. I decided to send her a text message this time, just to make sure she was free to talk.

Hi Holly, I typed. It's Jade. *Are you alone?*

Within seconds, a video call request came warbling over the line, indicating that she wanted to chat live.

Maybe I didn't scare her off so badly last time after all, I thought, clicking the Accept button.

When the call connected and our video windows went live, this time I saw Holly sitting on the bed next to another young girl wearing a UC T-shirt and skimpy panties.

My heart skipped a beat when I realized what was happening.

Could it really be? I thought. *Had she connected that quickly with her roomie and persuaded her to pull me into their affair?*

"I see you've made a new friend," I spoke into the mic, trying to conceal the excitement in my voice.

"Hi Jade," the other girl said. She appeared to be about Holly's age, and almost as pretty. With long blond hair, penetrating blue eyes, and plump rosebud lips, the pair of them looked like models straight out of an Abercrombie & Fitch commercial. "Holly's told me so much about you."

"Oh?" I said, still dumbfounded at the situation I found myself in.

"This is my roommate Jen that I was telling you about," Holly said. "I told her how you've been helping me connect with my—*feminine instincts*."

"Um, yes," I stammered, unsure how much Holly had shared with her roommate. "We've been exploring some mutual interests."

"That's not the *only* thing she's been exploring," Jen said, leaning over to give Holly a long passionate kiss on her lips.

"I'm glad to see you two have finally connected," I said. "It sounded as if Holly might never break you away from your boyfriend, Jen."

"He wasn't really my boyfriend. More of a *boy-toy* to mess around with occasionally. I've had my eye on Holly ever since we became roommates. If it wasn't for you, I might never have known she was also interested in girls."

"Not just *any* girl," Holly said, reaching out her hand to intertwine her fingers with Jen's. "Only you."

"And *Jade* apparently," Jen said, nodding toward the screen.

"We found each other by accident," I interjected, not wanting to create a barrier between the two lovers. "Holly was just trying to find an outlet for her emerging feelings, to see if they were real."

"I can see why," Jen said, leaning toward the screen. "You're just as pretty and sexy as Holly said. I think she needed a more experienced lover to help her find her path."

"Not to mention how to learn how to make love to another woman," Holly winked at me.

"Yes," Jen said, tilting an eyebrow. "She's been trying out some of her new moves on me. I should thank you for your mentoring. It might have taken us *months* to figure out all the special things we girls can do with one another."

My pussy fluttered at the thought of the two girls making out all night long.

"Oh? You've been practicing?" I teased, fishing for more details.

Jen suddenly lifted herself up and straddled Holly's hips, facing away from the camera.

"To say the least," she said. "Would you like to see? Maybe you can show us a few new moves."

I squirmed on my bed, suddenly aware of the wet spot forming in the seat of my robe.

"I'd love to watch you ravish each other. Do you mind if this old lady has a little fun while you two go at it?"

"We were kind of hoping you would," Jen said. "And you're far from an old lady. Can we see a bit more of your body? Holly said you have an amazing figure."

"Absolutely," I said, scarcely believing my luck having the opportunity to have online sex with two gorgeous young co-eds. I quickly tore off my robe and pulled down my panties, feeling the torrent of fluid between my legs soaking into my bedsheets.

"Can we see your tits, too?" Jen said. "Those are some pretty fine looking hooters."

I hesitated for a moment revealing any more of my body, out of concern this was shaping up to be a one-sided show, rather than the two-way exchange I'd enjoyed with Holly so far. It was obvious that Jen was the more aggressive partner in their relationship, and I didn't want Holly feeling embarrassed or left out.

"Am I the *only* one getting undressed?" I asked.

"No way," Holly said, pulling her T-shirt over her head. Jen quickly followed suit, and the two girls pressed their bare breasts together while they kissed passionately.

As I watched the girls rubbing their bodies together, I pulled my camisole over my head and began pinching my nipples. Jen pressed her body forward, tilting Holly down onto the bed, then they twisted their bodies so they could watch the screen from the side.

"Damn, Jade," Jen said. "Holly wasn't kidding. You have a gorgeous body. I can see how she got off so easily watching you."

"I can't hold a candle to you guys," I said, admiring the two girls' smooth, flexible bodies. "I wish everything stood as firm and perky on me as it does on you. You've got a very sexy body too, Jen."

"Talk dirty to us," she said. "Tell us what you want us to do. Holly was telling me about some of the things you like."

I guess all pretenses are off at this point, I thought. *It's time to get down and dirty.* I spread my legs and placed my fingers over my slick opening.

"I want to watch you suck on Holly's pretty nipples. Make them hard and long again, like I saw them yesterday."

Jen leaned forward and took Holly's left breast into her mouth, then turned her head to glance into the camera. I pushed my laptop away from me a few inches so they could see my pussy and hips displayed in front of the screen. As I circled my clit with the tip of my fingers, I squeezed my breast with my other hand and moaned at the sight of Holly's teat in her roommate's mouth.

"Mmm," Jen hummed, as she tickled and teased Holly's tips.

"You are one sexy momma," Jen said, popping her mouth off Holly's nipple with a smack. "No wonder I caught her coming when I walked in the door yesterday. You could put any girl over the edge with a body like that."

"Happy to oblige anytime," I panted, feeling my juices running down my thighs.

"We might have to arrange that," Jen said, smiling at the camera. "But right now, I just want to fuck my girl while you get off watching us. What would you like us to do now?"

I couldn't believe they were letting me direct the action like some kind of erotic movie director. I moved my laptop a little closer toward my body and leaned closer to the screen.

"I want to watch you *taste* her," I said. "I want to watch Holly twisting all over your face while you make her cum with your tongue."

"My pleasure," Jen said. "She *does* taste so sweet. I can't get enough of her sex in my mouth."

As Jen slithered down Holly's body toward her hips, Holly turned the laptop with her hand to allow me to take in all the action.

"You're so sexy, Jade," she purred as Jen placed her head between her legs. "Thanks for joining us tonight. I wanted to share this with you."

"*I'm* the lucky one," I said. "I'm just glad you finally connected with Jen. It's so great to see you together this way."

"You have no idea," Jen said, placing her hands beside Holly's hips and pulling her toward her. Holly gasped and arched her back when Jen's lips found her pearl.

"Yes, Jen," she panted. "Suck me right there. Lick my clit while Jade watches us.

When I saw the look on Holly's face from Jen's touch, I buried my fingers in my pussy and began rubbing my clit with the palm of my hand. By now I was soaking wet, and a huge stain had begun to spread over my sheets between my legs.

"Yes—finger your pussy," Holly moaned as she watched me jilling myself. Jen turned her face to see what I was doing then began lapping her tongue up and down Holly's slit.

"Suck me Jen," Holly moaned. "Make me cum all over your face."

"Fuck, Holly," I groaned, watching my fantasy come true. "That is so hot! You're going to make me cum soon too."

"Cum with me, Jade," Holly said. "Let me watch you squirt while I cum in Jen's mouth. I'm close—"

"Oh God," I suddenly hissed, clamping down on my fingers. As the insides of my pussy began contracting in a powerful orgasm, I pulled my fingers out of my hole and began spraying all over the computer screen. I was so lost in the throes of pleasure, I didn't care that I might be ruining my computer. Right now, I just wanted to show Holly the effect she was having on me.

"Holy fuck, Jade," Holly groaned. "I'm cumming! Spray your juices all over me!"

Holly lifted her hips off the mattress then slammed her body back down onto the bed as she grabbed the back of Jen's head. She pulled her tightly against her pussy while she jerked and thrashed on the sheets. Jen glanced out the corner of her eye toward their computer as her eyes widened watching me gush all over my camera. My image must have been blurry from the juices running over the lens, but this just seemed to get Holly even more excited.

"God, how I'd love you feel you cumming on me like that," she panted, slowly coming down from her long and intense orgasm. When her thighs finally stopped quaking, Jen lifted her head and smiled toward the camera.

"You are one hot momma, Jade," she said, wiping the back of her hand over her lips to clear some of Holly's juices off her face. "I can see why Holly wanted to see you again. This is even *more* fun with a sexy spectator."

"Sorry," I said, lifting my camisole off the bed to wipe my screen and keyboard. "I made quite a mess."

"Are you kidding me?" Jen said. "That might be the sexiest thing I've ever seen. I never even knew a woman could squirt like that."

"Only when I'm really worked up," I said. "I guess I lubricate a bit more than some women. When I come really hard, my muscles just push it out of me. I got pretty turned on watching Holly cum on your face."

"You weren't the only ones getting turned on by that," Jen said. "I'm about to burst at the seams myself."

I smiled at Jen and raised my finger to request a short break.

"Can you give me just one minute to clean up this mess before we continue? I'm afraid all this fluid might get inside my computer and short it or something. The last thing I need right now is to lose the ability to see both of you getting off together. I'll be right back."

4

JOINING FORCES

I got up and scurried to the bathroom and ran some water over a facecloth, then wrung it out and came back to the bed. I wiped the screen, camera, and keyboard with the wet cloth, then dried all the surfaces with another dry cloth. When I peered back at the screen, I saw that Holly and Jen were lying sideways on the bed, kissing one another.

"Can you guys see me clearly?" I said, hesitating to interrupt up their embrace.

They turned toward their screen and nodded.

"Perfect," Jen said. "What would you like to see us do now? Hopefully something with a little *together* action."

"Definitely," I said. "I think it's time you got some direct stimulation too, Jen." It was obvious to me that Jen was the dominant one, and I was eager to watch her fuck Holly. "Can you get on top of Holly and place your hips over hers so you're scissoring your pussies together?"

She raised herself up and straddled Holly's hips diagonally, with one knee on the outside of her hips and the other one resting just inside her thighs.

"You mean like this?" Jen said.

"Yes. Now lift Holly's right leg up so you can get more direct contact between your vulvas."

Holly lifted her leg straight up in the air then Jen placed it over her right shoulder, twisting Holly's hips sideways. Now the two girls were locked in a tight scissor position, with their pussies tightly clamped together.

"Mmm, that feels good, Jen," Holly purred.

"We haven't tried it *this* way yet," Jen nodded. "You're quite a sex coach, Jade. We'll have to do this more often."

"Any place, any time," I smiled. "But I think you two can take it from here. You're in charge now, Jen. You should be able to get plenty of direct stimulation this way."

As Jen began to swing her hips forward and back against Holly's pussy, she let out a low moan.

"Fuck, yes," she purred. "I can feel your clit rubbing against mine, Holly."

"Fuck me, Jen," Holly panted. "Fuck my cunt with your sweet pussy."

"Damn straight I will," Jen said, pulling Holly's raised leg tightly between her tits, increasing the speed of her hip movement between Holly's flared legs.

As the two girls began humping each other, I mimicked Jen's position by lifting myself up and kneeling on my bed. Then I reached over to my side table and pulled out a dome-shaped silicone cushion with a vulva impression carved in the top. I positioned the device between my legs, then I lowered myself onto it and began grinding my pussy into the artificial vulva.

"Damn, girl," Jen panted. "You've got all the toys. What *is* that thing?"

"It's just a little something I use on lonely nights to imagine I'm doing what you're doing right now to Holly. Sometimes I like to fantasize that I'm tribbing another woman instead of just using my hands or a vibrator."

"That's pretty hot," Jen moaned. "Are you fantasizing about rubbing *us* that way right now?"

"Definitely," I panted, spreading my legs wider and pressing myself harder against the cushion.

"Does that thing *vibrate* by any chance?" Holly said, winking at me.

"It does, as a matter of fact."

"Show me."

I flicked a switch on the side of the cushion, and the vulva began vibrating between my legs.

"Uhnn," I groaned, throwing my head back in pleasure.

"Yes, Jade," Holly panted as she watched me. "Fuck her like you'd fuck me. I want to watch you cum all over my pussy like you did on the screen a few minutes ago."

"I think that can be arranged," I smiled, feeling my wetness spreading over the cushion.

"God, that's hot," Jen panted, watching me fuck my artificial lover on the screen. "My pussy's on fire, Holl. I'm going to cum for you soon."

"I feel you, Jen," Holly moaned. "Caress me with your sweet lips. Spread your love all over me."

Jen wrapped her arms tightly around Holly's upturned leg and suddenly began convulsing against her hips.

"It's happening, Holl! I'm cumming! Your pussy feels so good against mine."

"I'm cumming with you, Jen!" Holly grunted. "Press your pussy against me. Feel me cumming inside you."

As I watched the two girls twisting their bodies in simultaneous orgasm, I lost all control and began spurting all over my domed lover. While the girls thrashed their bodies together, we watched each other as we screamed in one powerful, collective climax. After what seemed like an eternity at the peak of pleasure, we all collapsed onto our respective beds, panting as we peered into our screens.

"You guys seemed to enjoy that," I said. "I told you there's lots of different ways we girls can have fun, Holly."

"You weren't kidding," Holly said, trying to catch her breath.

"The possibilities become endless with such an interesting collection of toys," Jen said. "What *other* interesting devices have you got to share with us?"

I leaned over and reached into my nightstand and pulled another toy out of the drawer, being careful to hide it from their view.

"I've already shown Holly how to use my special rabbit vibrator," I said. "But my real favorite is one *two* women can enjoy at the same time."

I held up the twelve-inch-long two-sided silicone phallus and bent it playfully between my two hands.

"Scissoring is even more fun when you've got something filling you up inside."

"Holy fuck!" Jen exclaimed, with wide eyes. "That think is huge! How do you fit that inside you? I could never—"

"You don't. It's meant to be shared with your lover. Each of you takes a separate end while you fuck each other, kind of like a man. There's nothing quite like it."

"I can imagine," Jen said. "I wish we had one of those things to play with right now."

"Well, *actually*—" Holly said, reaching over her head to remove something from underneath her pillow. She held a big purple dildo up in the air and waved it sexily from side to side. "I took the liberty today when you went out for a while to get one myself. After Jade explained how these things could be used, I thought you might like to give it a try..."

"*Hell* yes!" Jen said, raising herself back onto her knees excitedly. "Show me how to use it, Holly. Maybe Jade can play along with us on her end at the same time."

"It'll be my pleasure," I said, feeling another rivulet of juices running down the inside of my thighs. "I just wish we had a *three-sided* version so we could all do it together for real."

"I didn't see one of those at the sex shop," Holly said.

"Don't worry about me. I'll improvise. I'm just happy to watch you two enjoying yourselves. Now let me see you join together using that big snake."

"Lie down on the bed," Holly instructed to Jen. "This time it's my turn to fuck you."

Jen lay down with her hips about a foot away from Holly's, while Holly inserted one end of the long dildo into her pussy. Then she pushed closer to Jen and placed the other end at her opening. As they pressed their hips together, the giant dildo slowly disappeared into Jen's cavity as she uttered a low guttural moan.

"Yes—just like that," I purred, watching the two girls begin to hump their hips together.

"What about you?" Holly said, tilting her head back toward the camera. "What are you going to do while we're having all the fun?"

"I need something moving inside me too," I said.

I reached back into my nightstand and pulled out my rabbit vibrator and leaned back against my headboard. It made a loud slurping sound as I inserted it inside me.

"Sounds like *somebody's* still wet," Holly smiled.

"It looks that way. I hope you won't be distracted if I make a little noise while you two fuck each other."

"Not at all," Jen said, pressing her pussy closer to Holly's. "We intend to make some rude sounds of our own."

"Mmm," Holly moaned. "I like the feeling of you moving inside me, Jen. Fuck me with your big cock."

"This is way better than a real cock," Jen purred, smiling at Holly. "It's double the pleasure. I can fuck my partner at the same time I'm getting filled up by her. Who needs a man when you've got so many fun ways to play with a girl?"

"Exactly," I said. "I told you there was no going back once you experienced real lesbian loving, Holly."

"I'm *never* going back," Holly moaned as Jen picked up the pace of her hip movements. "Everything I need is right here on this bed with me."

"Normally I'd agree," Jen panted, watching the fluttering rabbit ears of my vibrator rubbing up against my clit. "But I think Jade has a slight advantage with that dual-purpose vibrator. How can we get direct clitoral stimulation like you in this position?"

"No one said you can't *touch* yourselves," I said. "Half the fun of using a double-sided dildo with your partner is watching them stimulate themselves while you fuck each other. Go ahead and rub your clits with your hands."

The two girls slid their right hand over each of their mounds, then reached down their other side and clasped hands.

"That's the idea," I said. "Does that feel better?"

"Better," Jen panted, as the girls pulled themselves closer together with their interlocking hands.

As I watched them twist and roll their bodies together, I leaned forward and kneeled on the bed. I placed my rabbit vibrator underneath me then I lowered my hips, letting the pressure of the mattress insert it inside me.

"You guys look so hot together," I moaned. "Now I'm thinking about that three-sided dildo again. I'm going to have to see if I can find one of those."

"If you do, you'll have to let us know," Holly groaned, watching me hump my dildo. "I'd love to try a three-way for real someday."

"What about you, Jen?" I said. "Would you be up for that too?"

"Fuck, yes," she purred. "I'd love to squeeze those big melons of yours while we all fuck each other silly."

"I'll look into it," I said. "Right now, I want to imagine I'm there with you girls. Can you see me? I'm imagining myself fucking you both over top."

"Yes," Holly panted. "Fuck us, Jade. Press your wet pussy against our hips and gush all over our stomachs. I want to see you cum again."

"Fuck," I moaned, imagining the movement of the animated vibrator inside me as if it were two girls underneath me creating the action. "I can't hold it much longer. I'm going to cum all over both of you soon!"

The two girls clasped their hands together on both sides and pulled themselves together. As they gnashed their clits together, the dildo disappeared completely inside their pussies.

"Oh God, Holly," Jen grunted. "I'm going to cum too. Are you almost there?"

"Yes, Jen," Holly moaned, twisting her head to watch me jackrabbiting on the vibrator deeply embedded in my pussy. "Cum Jade!"

As the two girls began to pull their torsos off the mattress and look at each other with wild eyes, I felt the first wave of passion roll over me.

"It's happening!" I shouted, holding the base of my vibrator with two hands. "Cum for me, Holly!"

The two girls' mouths gaped opened in a wide yaw, then they screamed out loud as their bodies writhed against one another in mutual ecstasy.

"Fuckk," Jen growled. "I feel you, Holly! I feel you cumming against me. Cum for me baby!"

"Yes Jen!" Holly screamed as her whole body quaked in an intense orgasm, her pointy tits shaking like two trembling pyramids over her quivering tummy while the girls held each other with tensed outstretched arms.

As each of us quivered and moaned over our embedded phalluses, I couldn't stop fantasizing about what it would be like to merge together in a true ménage à trois.

If they don't have a three-sided dildo, I'll have to make one for myself, I thought, peering down at the giant puddle between my legs.

VOLUME FOUR

THE DARK ROOM

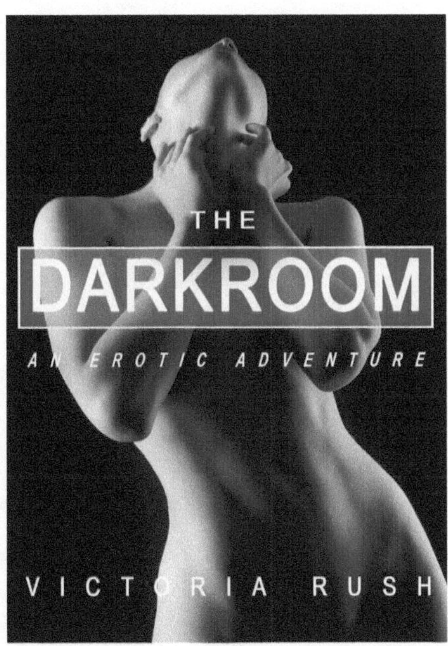

1
———

IN THE SHADOWS

After my exhilarating experience at The Dinner Party, I was ready for more sexual exploration. The idea of being watched and watching other people releasing our inhibitions in a group setting was incredibly erotic. There was something about being with strangers that took the encounter to an entirely new level.

But it was more than that—it was the *anonymity* that made it especially appealing. With my mask on, I felt empowered to try new things, to do things I would never do in my regular guise. It was like I had superpowers. With my identity hidden, I could try anything, and the results were equally surprising. The sexual feelings were stronger and the climaxes were more powerful than anything I'd experienced before.

I wanted more. But I also wanted something different. I wanted to stretch my boundaries to see how far my new powers of sexual expression could take me. What other exotic destinations might I discover in the erotic underworld?

One day late at night, I sat down in front of my computer and typed in the search words 'anonymous group sex'. Among a litany of listings for gay bathhouses, swingers parties, and wife-swapping groups, I found a cryptic heading on the bottom of the second page, reading *The Dark Room: Explore Your Sensuality*. I clicked on the link and a video opened with a naked dancer undulating under the mesmerizing effect of black and white zebra-like stripes illuminated on her body.

I watched, transfixed, as the light patterns flowed over every sensuous curve of her body. In the background, soft instrumental music added to the trance-like effect. The alternating dark and light patches provided just enough camouflage to mask her identity. But as the light parts moved over different areas of her physique, they briefly revealed her erogenous zones. The curve of her shapely breasts, a fleeting glimpse of her bare nipple, the glorious cleft in her tight round ass. She was completely naked, but I had to look carefully to recognize the naughty parts.

And what a sight it was to behold. As the illuminated stripes curved and stretched around every contour of her body, they accentuated her gorgeous figure. When she moved closer to the screen and briefly revealed her face, it had the same effect. I could see the fullness of her lips and the sensuous curve of her cheekbones. But the light never stayed in one place long enough to betray her identity, even if someone knew who was hidden behind the unusual light effects.

Now this was something completely different, I thought. *Erotic, stimulating, and anonymous.*

But where were her playmates?

As exciting as I imagined it might be to dance naked under the relative obscurity of these light effects, it would be infinitely *more* fun to participate actively with others in such a room. I scanned the webpage and noticed a heading in the menu at the top of the page titled 'Group Packages'. I clicked the link and three more video thumbnails appeared on the page: one labeled 'Men', one titled 'Women', and another marked 'Mixed'. I tapped on the first one, and another video started playing, showing multiple figures gyrating to the music.

This time, the light-projections were in different colors, shifting and bending around the moving figures like a psychedelic kaleido-scope. The bodies were masculine, with broad shoulders, muscled chests, and washboard stomachs. Occasionally, the men would brush up against one another and move their hips in a feigned anal inter-course motion, but the action was too slow and measured to be real. And the camera never strayed far below the subjects' bellybuttons, so it was impossible to tell if they were actually aroused. Even though they occasionally embraced in lip lock, it all seemed staged and dispassionate, like strippers putting on a show in a dance club.

I wasn't much interested in watching gay sex anyway, even with buff Chippendale characters such as these, so I clicked the next video thumbnail labeled 'Women'. This was definitely more my thing, and I could feel the stirring in my pussy as I reflected back on my last lesbian encounter at The Dinner Party. The video began with three slim and shapely women dancing sensuously under a new light effect. Instead of black and white alternating zebra stripes, this time the illuminated light resembled streaking raindrops.

The effect was even more captivating than the previous videos. Like an animated expressionist painting, the streaks danced across every curve and valley of the women's bodies as they swayed their hips and torsos in tantalizingly rhythmic ways. I had to concentrate even harder to catch fleeting glances of their breasts, nipples, and midsections, with the light patches even sparser than before.

At least in the women's videos, the camera panned below their waists to highlight the resplendent shape of their hips and buttocks. I strained to recognize the telltale protrusion of their mound or catch a glimpse of the mysterious slit between their legs. But as my pussy began to moisten imagining what was hidden behind the dancing raindrops splashing across their figures, the models never bent in such a way to reveal anything explicit.

Maybe this was the intention of the producers—to tease our interest just enough so we'd want to click for more information, leading to some kind of sale. This was, after all, the tried and true model for virtually every porn site—to show the viewer just enough to get them worked up until they were horny enough to pay for the real thing. Although in this case, I was still confused as to what the 'real thing' was this website was selling.

Was it just beautiful videos, orchestrated to appear as legitimate art? Were they just trying to sell me a fancy video version of a self-portrait that I could share with my husband or partner? That might be intriguing, but I was looking for more. As I continued watching the video, the three women moved closer to one another, eventually rubbing their hips and torsos together like in the all-male video. But this time, I could see their lower bodies as they caressed one another.

I watched them rub their hips and breasts together as the light streaks raced across their erect nipples. They were kissing one another far more sensuously than the men, like they were really losing themselves in the moment. It was definitely a turn-on and I imagined myself in the mix, caressing their beautiful bodies in the darkness with the streaks of light providing fleeting glimpses of their figures. As I thought about what it would feel like to have a stranger stroking my body in the dark, I slipped my fingers under my panties and began to play with my clit. But just as the action started flowing in the video, the clip suddenly ended.

Fuck! I screamed. *Just as I was getting turned on! Even a normal porno is better than this. At least they go all the way and offer some release.*

I was tempted to divert to my favorite porn site and watch some good lesbian tribbing action to get off when I noticed the last video thumbnail on the screen, labeled 'Mixed'. At least *this* one, if it was real, would be hard to hide the state of arousal that heterosexual men would experience in the presence of sexy naked women—light or no light.

I clicked on the icon, and the last video started to play. This time the light effects were in the form of multi-hued geometric circles, stretching and undulating over the curves of the naked figures like a rolling spirograph. I had to give it to the video producers—they were certainly creative in using unusual light effects that looked beautiful when projected onto shapely naked bodies.

And there was no denying that the bodies were gorgeous. Both the men and the women were firm and well-toned, with curves in all the right places. Every one of them was seriously fuckable. But much to my chagrin, the interaction between the subjects in the video once again seemed practiced and restrained. Even the men hardly seemed into it, rubbing and caressing their partners like in a cheesy black-and-white B-movie. The camera never strayed below their waistlines, but I didn't need to see their flaccid penises to recognize play acting when I saw it.

If this is what happens in these dark rooms, you can count me out, I thought.

It was all too antiseptic and 'soft-porn' for my liking. I wanted some *real* sex—actual *touching* and *penetration*—where I could feel myself and my dark room partners getting aroused and getting off. I didn't just want to be in some kind of frou-frou art production, I wanted to participate in a live orgy! I was about to click out of the website when a chat bubble popped up in the lower right corner. A text message appeared in the bubble.

'Hi!' someone named Sara wrote. 'How can I help you? Did you want to learn more about our products and services?'

Products and services? Maybe it's worth investigating this a little further after all. Let's see what other 'services' they have to offer...

2

—————

EYES WIDE SHUT

'How can I participate in these dark rooms?' I typed in the chat window.

'If you come to our studio,' Sara replied, 'you can join any room of your choosing at any time.'

Studio? This was sounding more and more like some kind of photography service to me.

'How many people will be in the rooms with me?' I typed.

'That depends what time of the day and week you come. Friday and Saturday nights are busiest, but we also schedule sessions during the day, between 2:00 and 4:00 p.m. You can book a session by clicking on the tab for Appointments at the top of the page. We normally only have two or three people in the afternoon rooms and up to ten maximum on Friday and Saturday nights.'

The word *sessions* was beginning to sound more intriguing to me. I decided to probe for more information.

'What kind of clothing should I wear in these sessions?' I asked.

'You can wear anything that makes you feel comfortable, but most of our patrons choose to wear a minimum of accoutrements.'

'Including nothing at all?'

'Yes—if that's what makes you feel most comfortable.'

I loved how Sara kept dancing around the obvious question.

'How do the people in these dark room sessions typically *interact*?' I typed.

'That depends on what you're looking for and the kind of people that join you in the room.'

I hesitated for a moment before typing my reply.

'Is *touching* permitted?'

'Absolutely. That's what makes the experience particularly enjoyable. You're encouraged to explore each other's bodies in the privacy and safety of the dark room. Subject to the consent of each partner, of course.'

Now we're talking, I thought. Exploring each other's bodies was exactly what I was looking for. But I still had lots of questions pertaining to the privacy and safety parts.

'What if I don't want somebody to touch my body? How can I ensure my personal space will be respected?'

'We have a simple rule for everybody entering any of our dark rooms. All you have to do is brush someone's body away if you don't wish to be touched. Everyone is issued a safety bracelet before entering each room. If you feel threatened or forced to do anything against your will, all you have to do is press the alert button and an audio intercom will be activated. Any violators will be immediately removed from the room. You can ask for help at any time, but we rarely receive complaints from any of our patrons.'

I paused to let Sara's comments sink in. I liked the safeguards they had set up, but I didn't like the sound of audio recordings or being leered at by a bunch of security guards.

'What kind of privacy will I have? Will any audio or video recordings be made while I'm in any of the rooms?'

'Never,' Sara said. 'What goes on in the security of the dark rooms is between you and your consenting partners.'

I liked the sound of that.

'What about the video clips on your website?' I asked. 'Those were obviously recorded. Were those actual participants?'

'Those were paid actors, using our own models. I assure you, you will never be recorded while in one of our dark rooms.'

'What about your security personnel or anyone outside the room? Can they see what's happening inside?'

'Each dark room is enclosed in one-way glass all around,' Sara replied. 'You can't see out, but outside observers can see in. This allows patrons to observe the action in the room before committing to go inside. We find this adds to the excitement level for both those watching and those being watched. But the light effects in the room are always moderated in such a way to ensure your identity will be masked. The only thing outside observers can see, including our security staff, are the silhouettes of the people inside.'

Oh my god, I thought. *That sounds so hot.*

The idea of being watched, both within the room and from outside the room, while I got down and dirty with my dark room partners sounded incredibly stimulating. I suddenly became aware of how soaked my panties had become as I continued the dialog with Sara.

'What about...*hygiene*?' I asked tentatively. 'What protections do I have against the spread of diseases?'

Sara and I finally seemed to be talking about the same thing. I decided to dispense with any further niceties and cut right to the chase.

'Every dark room participant must provide a recent blood test from an accredited medical lab,' she replied. 'You must report negative for all known sexual or communicable diseases. You'll also need to submit to a brief exam with our accredited medical doctor on staff to ensure you do not have any open sores or infections that could be spread by physical contact. This is for the safety of all participants.'

Holy shit, these guys don't fool around. A gynecological exam is never fun, but if it's performed by a real doctor and it's not too intrusive, it's better to be safe than sorry.

'Will the exam be performed by a gynecologist? Is the doctor male or female? May I ask for his or her credentials before I submit to the examination?'

'It will be with a female gynecologist for female examinations and a male urologist for male examinations. Their credentials will be on display in the examining office, which is also maintained with the utmost hygienic cleanliness. The examination is external only and very brief.'

Okay, I thought. *Now that we know exactly what we're talking about here, let's get down to brass tacks.*

'What are your fees? And is this...you know, *legitimate*? I mean, it sounds like I'm paying for sex.'

Sara paused for a moment before replying.

'This is a private club in a private residence. Whatever consenting adults choose to do with each other on private property is entirely legal. There is a modest subscription fee to join the club. You can see our fees under the tab marked Rates.'

It was all starting to come together. Just like The Dinner Party erotic club I attended a few weeks ago, they had similar terms of service. In fact, their professionalism and attention to detail made me wonder if it might be run by the same operators. I just had a few remaining questions.

'Are there separate rooms for men and women?' I asked. I was definitely ready for some more girl-on-girl action, but I wasn't ready to rule out a little hetero fun too if the mood struck me.

'We have separate rooms for men-only, women-only, and mixed gender. You may enter the single-gender room that matches your sex and also the mixed gender room, if you so wish, during your visit.'

I was definitely getting more interested by the moment and based on how fast the wet patch between my legs was spreading in my tight jeans, so was my aching pussy.

I wondered if there'd be any equipment to recline onto if things got hot and heavy enough.

'Are there places to relax in each of the rooms, or are they standing room only?' I typed.

'There is small upholstered furniture in each of the rooms, as well as Liberator sex cushions to adjust your position. Everything has neon piping around the edges to help you find it in the dark, and the coverings are laundered after each session to ensure cleanliness. Your safety and comfort is our universal goal.'

Wow, I thought. *These guys have thought of everything.*

This obviously wasn't going to be some kind of seedy swingers' party where just anybody could walk in and fuck anything that moves. This sounded like a first-class operation that was sure to titillate and satisfy all my senses.

I paused as I considered any other questions or concerns that I might have before venturing out to their club.

'How long can I remain in each room?' I said. 'And when I wish to leave, where can I go to freshen up and get dressed?'

'We have separate change rooms and showers for both men and women. Strobe lights are used in these and other public rooms of the residence to protect your identity at all times. From the moment you enter any of our dark rooms to the moment you leave the building, no one will be able to identify you. The only person who'll ask for ID is the doctor who examines you. He or she will verify your blood report belongs to you and the physician is sworn by doctor-patient privilege to maintain your privacy.'

I unconsciously exhaled a long deep breath as I began to relax. All my concerns had been addressed and all my expectations were satisfied. This was the perfect outlet I was looking for.

'Thank you for being patient with all my questions,' I typed. 'I'll check your rates and schedules and book a session in the near future.'

'It's been my pleasure,' Sara said. 'I hope our club satisfies all of your desires. Feel free to chat again if you have any more questions. See you soon!'

Satisfy my desires, indeed. I had no doubt that it would. But right now, I needed some satisfaction that no one else could give me.

I tore off my leggings and threw them on the floor as I reached into my nightstand for my favorite rabbit vibrator. Then I turned the rotating beads and rabbit ears on maximum and plunged the dildo into my aching pussy, moaning in delight as I imagined the pleasures that awaited me in the mysterious dark room.

3

FOREPLAY

As I thrust the vibrator deep inside my snatch, I watched the all-girl dark room video on continuous loop. I was absolutely hypnotized by the swirling light effects rolling over their luscious bodies. Whenever the streaks illuminated their bare nipples and mounds, it made the effect all the more electrifying. My pussy made sexy slurping sounds as my juices sopped up the slick dildo sliding in and out of my hole.

I moaned like a dog in heat thinking about what it would be like to watch and touch these women in a *real* dark room. This experience would take my Dinner Party adventure to a whole new level. Instead of just sitting and watching passively while other people did things to me, in these spaces I could participate actively with whomever I pleased. My mind raced with all the things I wanted to do with these women—and maybe even some of the men in the mixed room. I wanted to fuck and be fucked by these mysterious apparitions.

When the women in the video started touching one another and rubbing their nipples together, I lifted my hips off the bed and thrust the vibrator deeper inside me. I angled the shaft so the oscillating tip massaged my G-spot, while I pushed the fluttering rabbit ears hard against my swollen nub. I could feel my orgasm building and I opened my mouth to kiss one of the models in the video as she did the same. When the tide finally swept over me, I clamped down hard over the pulsing vibrator and spasmed a long stream of powerful contractions.

I hadn't cum this hard since Jasmin had jilled me under the dinner table at the Dinner Party retreat. As I lay on the bed rolling my hips in post-orgasmic bliss, I closed my eyes and imagined myself dancing with the geometric light effects projected on my body. For a thirty-six-year-old, I still had a pretty damn fine figure with a tight ass, perky breasts, and a yoga-toned stomach. I wouldn't be the only one in the dark room admiring the physiques of my fellow participants.

I pulled the vibrator out of my pussy and stood up to admire myself in my full-length dressing mirror. I began to sway my hips and caress my breasts like the women in the video. I looked pretty good, but something was missing. I turned off the bedroom light and closed the drapes, then opened the bathroom door just enough to emit a thin sliver of light. I moved back from the mirror until the ray of light projected a narrow beam on my body.

It wasn't nearly as fancy as the light effects shown in the dark room videos, but it was enough to make me imagine I was there. I experimented with different positions as I watched the light illuminate different parts of my body in the darkness of my bedroom. Just as in the videos, it was fascinating to see how I could briefly reveal the naughty parts by moving in and out of the light. It was almost as exciting to watch my own body as it was the models in the video, and I began to caress my curves like a stripper in a dance club.

I'll have to work on my technique, I thought, analyzing my moves.

I had to be as irresistible as the models in the video if I hoped to attract the attention of men and women with similarly toned bodies.

But that can wait for later.

Right now, the only thing I could think about was booking an appointment for a dark room session as soon as possible. My vibrator, as entertaining as it was, would be no match for the real thing. I sat down again in front of my computer and clicked on the tab marked Rates.

Let's see if I have to pay an arm and a leg to touch some of these arms and legs.

It wasn't as bad as I imagined. There was a one-time subscription fee of $300, plus another $200 for each session. *Seems reasonable,* I thought. The gyno exam alone would cost that much or more in a regular doctor's office. Two hundred bucks for two hours or more of safe, titillating sex with multiple partners seemed like a bargain.

"Sign me up!" I thought out loud, clicking the tab for Appointments.

A registration page opened where they asked me to create an account. I paused for a moment as I considered my next move. I could use an alias and a fake email account, but I knew they'd also want a credit card to pay for the subscription.

So much for nobody knowing my identity other than the doctor who'll examine me.

I looked further down the page and saw a disclaimer promising that my email and credit information wouldn't be shared with anyone else, and that I wouldn't be sent any marketing information other than the confirmation of my appointment.

What the fuck, I said to myself. *Anybody running an internet business these days knows the surest way to lose customers is to share someone's online details without consent. Besides, I reveal a lot more personal financial information when I pay bills and do my banking online—this is pretty minor in comparison.*

I filled in the required fields to complete my registration, then scanned the schedule for available sessions. All the Friday and Saturday nights on the booking calendar were grayed out for the next three weeks.

This place is popular, I thought. *I guess that's a good sign.*

I imagined that meant most sessions would be pretty full and that I'd have my pick of partners to choose to engage with. I remembered Sara saying the daytime sessions were not as busy as the night sessions, so I clicked on the first available weekday. A new window opened indicating that I was about to reserve an afternoon session for the indicated date, then it asked me to fill in the credit card information to complete the transaction. I filled in the required details then clicked the Submit button. After about ten seconds of processing time, a window popped up from my email account confirming the payment and appointment.

Well, that's it, I thought. *I'm committed now.*

I could feel the blood flowing back into my pussy as my mind already started going where I'd been fantasizing for the last hour. I stood up and positioned myself again in the sliver of light emanating from the washroom.

Damn girl, I thought, admiring my figure as my fingers strayed down toward my warm cunny. *This is going to be fun...*

4
———

PEOPLE IN GLASS HOUSES

On my appointment day, I could barely contain my excitement. I drove out to the address provided in my email confirmation and was pleasantly surprised when I arrived at the destination. As with my previous experience at the dinner party, the facility was in a large country chateau. Just like the last place, I had to provide my registration username and password to be permitted access through the security gate. I drove up the long tree-lined driveway to an even larger mansion than before.

If this was any indication of the step up in the level of services that awaited me, I was all-in. I parked my car alongside five or six other cars in the guest parking section and walked over a cobblestone path up to the front door. I tapped on the large brass door knocker and was greeted a few seconds later by an attractive young woman in a smart business suit.

I guess there'll be no naked attendants in masquerade masks this time around, I frowned. *Maybe this place is run by a different operator, after all.*

Nevertheless, the interior appointments and finishings were on a par with the previous home, and I was eager to explore its special rooms.

"You must be Jade," the woman said, taking my coat and hanging it in the closet. "My name's Ali, and I'll be your host for the evening. Can I get you something to drink? Coffee, tea, a glass of wine?"

I was pretty charged up already and thought a bit of alcohol would help relax some of the inhibitions I was beginning to feel about getting naked with a group of strangers.

"I'd love a glass of white wine if you have it, thank you."

Ali motioned to an adjoining room with large French doors.

"Feel free to relax in our waiting room," she said, handing me a piece of paper and a pen. "If you can take a few moments to review and sign this waiver, this will help ensure our expectations are aligned. I'll be back in a few minutes."

I walked into a beautiful room with tall Palladian windows and sat down on the large leather sofa. I quickly reviewed the document, which was mostly concerned with the rules of engagement in the dark rooms. Only women were permitted in the women's dark room it said, and only men were permitted in the men's dark room, but they could commingle in the mixed room. It reiterated the 'golden rule' about touching others only with consent. A simple brush of the hand or step back from an advancing partner indicated that you did not wish to be touched. Any violators would be immediately removed from the room and banned from using the facility in future. I signed the document with my alias Jade and placed it face-up on the coffee table.

I noticed some picture books lying on the table with familiar photos of naked people illuminated with similar light effects to the videos I'd watched earlier. I opened one of the books and flipped through the pages as I admired the beautiful figures of the models and the different light effects displayed in each image.

I hope the people in my dark room will be as pretty as these, I thought, feeling my panties start to dampen again.

A minute later, Ali returned with a large glass of wine, setting it down on the coffee table.

"I see you've been familiarizing yourself with our light productions," she said, noticing the open book laid out in front of me. "Did you have any questions before I take you to the viewing room?"

Viewing room? The voyeur in me liked the sound of that.

"So I'll have a chance to watch some of the dark rooms before I choose to enter one?" I asked.

"Of course," Ali said. "That's part of the fun. All of our dark rooms can be observed from the outside through one-way glass. You'll be able to watch the participants but they won't be able to see you. Most of our patrons find this to be a stimulating experience that helps put them in the mood. If you like what you see, you can then proceed to the doctor's office for a brief exam, after which you're welcome to enter your appointed rooms. Did you bring your lab test report with you?"

"Yes—of course," I said, fishing in my purse for the blood test.

Ali held up her hand to save me the trouble.

"Bring it with you and show it to the doctor when she examines you. Are you ready to head downstairs?"

"Absolutely," I said, pleased that just as Sara had promised earlier, no one had yet asked for anything that could reveal my identity.

"Allow me to escort you, then. Would you like to leave your wine glass here or bring it with you?"

"I think it's better that I leave it here. Something tells me that I'm going to need my hands free for other things."

Ali simply smiled and nodded. I followed her out of the sitting room and across a marbled foyer, where we paused at the top of a declining circular stairway.

"Our dark rooms are in the lower level, where we can control the light more effectively. There are three exits, including a direct exit to the guest parking area. You may leave at any time, or return to the main floor if you need further help."

Ali reached into one of her pockets and handed me a black wristband.

"This is your security bracelet. Please wear it at all times until you leave the building. If you feel uncomfortable at any time, all you have to do is press this button on the side of your bracelet and a security agent will come to your assistance immediately. But I think you'll find it will be quite unnecessary. Our patrons are very respectful of the stipulated rules. I believe you'll find the experience very safe and satisfying."

I nodded my head as I fastened the bracelet buckle behind my wrist.

Ali escorted me down the stairs and opened a door at the base of the steps. A white strobe light and soft instrumental music emanated through the open portal.

"It may take you a few moments to get comfortable with the flashing light, but this will protect your identity while you stay on the lower level. The light is sequenced in such a way to allow you to find your way around while also maintaining your anonymity. Each of the exits are clearly marked, as is the entrance to the doctor's office and the change rooms."

She motioned to three large glass cubes in the center of the cavern.

"Each of the dark rooms is marked according to gender. Which room would you like to see first?"

"Um..." I said, hesitating for only a moment. "I think I'd like to see the women-only room first."

Ali gently grasped my hand and escorted me to the first glass-enclosed cube. It was much larger than it appeared from the other side of the room, measuring roughly twenty feet square on each side and ten feet tall. Inside the floor-to-ceiling glass panels, I could see the familiar movement of furtive figures illuminated under the kaleidoscopic light. The rest of the room was pitch black so the only things illuminated by the projected light were the moving bodies.

I unconsciously moved closer to the glass, captivated by the swirling light effects and soft music. This wasn't some cheesy strip club with pounding music and bright lights illuminating a gaudy stage. The soft instrumental music combined with the pretty light effects projected a feeling of real class. My eyes widened as I watched the naked participants move around inside the room.

Just as in the video, they were swaying their bodies and caressing each other. But there was something different this time. Their hands and bodies were no longer touching each other with fleeting, artificial gestures. This time, they *lingered* and *probed* one another. Their action looked *purposeful*, not like the play acting in the video. Near the front of the glass, two women were locked in a tight embrace, passionately kissing and grinding their hips together in familiar motion. I could see their buttock muscles flexing as they rubbed their mounds together under the swirling light.

My eyes raced around the inside of the enclosure as I took it all in. In the far corner of the cube, I noticed some neon piping tracing the outline of a large sofa. I squinted my eyes to decipher a commingled figure twisting together as the geometric lights swept over a mass of tangled arms and legs. At first, it looked like a single person doing some kind of yoga movement, with her leg stretched over her shoulder. But as I looked more closely, I could see that the raised leg belonged to a woman lying on the sofa with her legs splayed apart. Another woman was resting on her knees, squatting between the prone woman's legs, rubbing their vulvas together, fucking her with rapid swings of her hips while she clasped the prone woman's elevated leg tightly against her breasts.

I gasped audibly and slumped over, unconsciously mimicking the movement of the woman on top.

"Shall I leave you now to enjoy the show?' Ali said, somewhere to my side.

I'd completely forgotten she was still there. I turned and saw her familiar outline flashing beside me under the white strobe light.

"Yes, I'll be fine now," I said, catching my breath and trying to sound composed.

"Wonderful," she said. "You're welcome to remain outside the rooms and watch as long as your session is booked, or enter your allotted rooms at your leisure. The entrance to the dark rooms is via the doctor's office, who'll validate your blood report and conduct a brief external exam before you move on. Remember that if you need help at any time, all you have to do is press the button on the side of your bracelet. I hope you enjoy your stay and that we'll see you again soon. Bye for now."

It was strange watching her talk as the white light flashed over her face. I could see her lips open and close in delayed jerky movements that didn't synchronize with her speech. It was a bit disconcerting and nothing like the flowing movement of the light projected inside the dark room, but it was sexy and mysterious in its own way. Just as she and Sara had promised, it was impossible to recognize her face through the intermittent flashes.

"Thank you, Ali," I said. "I'll let you know if I need anything."

I was glad to see her leave, because my pussy was pounding and my crotch was soaked from watching the action in the cube. As soon as she closed the door leading to the stairs behind her, I unclasped the top button of my jeans and thrust my hand under my panties. My fingers immediately found my opening and I inserted three fingers as far as they'd go inside me while I rubbed my palm against my aching clit. It couldn't have taken more than ten seconds for me to cum hard in my jeans as I watched the women scissoring on the couch in the dark room.

It was difficult to see the expressions on their faces under the shifting light, but I noticed the mouth of the woman on top widen as her movements became increasingly frenetic. Then she suddenly stopped and arched her back as she pulled her partner's elevated leg against her torso and spasmed her body in obvious climax. I longed to be there with them, feeling what they were feeling and listening to their moans of ecstasy as their love juices washed over one another.

After I came down from my orgasm, I suddenly became aware that I wasn't the only one standing outside the cube watching what was going on inside. I noticed another figure standing about five feet to my side, and I glanced in her direction. The flashing light showed just enough to reveal a pretty woman with long hair and high cheekbones. Although I'd never recognize her in the plain light of day, her full lips and gently sloping jawline betrayed her beauty. I glanced down at her body and noticed the bulge of her full breasts in her blouse and the curvature of her hips and ass in her tight jeans.

I blushed in the dark thinking that she might have noticed me rubbing myself in the dark like some kind of creepy flasher. But she just peered at me and smiled.

"Pretty hot, huh?" she said, in a soft, sexy voice.

"Yeah," was all I could manage to pant.

"Are you going in?" she asked, matter-of-factly.

"Definitely," I said.

"Perhaps I'll see you in a few minutes then. I'm going to watch for a little longer to get my nerve up."

"Enjoy," I said, imagining her getting just as turned on as I did watching the action in the cube. Sara was right—it was almost as much fun *watching* the action as participating in it. But I was eager to feel the touch of another woman and experience the hypnotic light effects first-hand.

But those aren't the only body parts I'll be using, I thought as I headed toward the examining room.

INTO THE LIGHT

The gyno exam wasn't as bad as I anticipated, though it was pretty embarrassing walking into the examining room with a big wet patch in the crotch of my jeans. The doctor didn't bat an eyelash and simply asked me to disrobe and lie down on the examining table. The whole thing was over in a couple of minutes.

She examined me for any sign of open sores then reviewed my lab test and checked my driver's license to verify the report. Fortunately, I'd made a recent visit to my aesthetician to clean things up down below. My smooth pussy was bald and spotless, which made the examination all the faster and easier.

When she was done, she handed me a note with a number and a key code then directed me through a door leading into the women's change room. As with the other public sections of the lower level, a soft strobe light permeated the change room. In between the flashes, I could see a few women in various stages of undress going about their business in the locker room, but I paid them no attention. Part of me wanted to search for the pretty woman who I'd chatted with briefly outside the women's dark room, but I decided it was best to respect everyone's privacy. There'd be plenty of opportunity to engage more directly once I got inside the actual dark rooms.

I located a bank of lockers with combination locks and pulled out the slip of paper the doctor had handed me. I matched the number on the slip with the corresponding locker and entered the code on the tumblers to undo the lock. Inside the locker, there was a freshly-laundered terrycloth robe and towel. I removed my clothes and placed my belongings inside the locker, then put the robe on and carried the towel to one of the shower stalls. I could still feel the vestiges of dried-up lubrication coating my inner thighs, and I wanted to be as clean and fresh as I could be going in to the dark rooms.

As I turned on the shower and stepped under its gentle spray, I reflected back to the video with the rain drop effect. I imagined myself dancing in the dark room as the light streaks flowed over my body, turning and bending my figure to reveal every sensuous curve. I opened a fresh bar of soap and rubbed the silky pod across my breasts, under my arms, and between my legs. My body felt electrified, and for a moment I was tempted to rub another one out, but I decided to save myself for the real thing. I didn't want anything tempering the pleasure that awaited me. I finished the shower, then dried myself off and returned my towel to my locker. I hesitated for a moment, deciding whether to hang my robe in my locker too, or wear it out into the open spaces of the lower level.

Screw it, I said, placing it on the hook. *This whole experience is about letting myself go and losing myself in the moment. Besides, between the strobe lights outside the dark rooms and the light show inside the rooms, no one will be able to recognize me anyhow.*

I closed the locker and scrambled the tumblers, making a mental note of my locker number and combination code. Then I walked out of change room into the open space of the lower level and looked around. It felt liberating to be stark naked in the cool air of the basement under the pulsating strobe lights.

Each of the three dark rooms were bathed with different colored and patterned light effects. On each side of the cubes, illuminated gender symbols clearly indicated who was inside. The glass cubes looked from a distance like a holographic dance show, with three different 'theaters' to choose from. I walked toward the cube displaying two familiar circle-and-cross symbols, knowing the all-girl show was what had initially attracted me to the program.

When I got closer to the cube, I noticed the light patterns inside had changed from when I viewed it earlier. This time, the patterns were in the form of orange and black spots, making the figures inside the room look like human-shaped leopards. I could make out four distinct figures inside the enclosure. Two of the women were quite slim, with tight ballerina figures. The other two were more voluptuous, with full breasts and wide, curving hips. But they all looked mouth-watering gorgeous, bathed in pretty feline leopard spots.

I was transfixed watching the women circle one another like prowling cats in the dark. It didn't take long for the figures to blend together and begin rubbing against one another. I stood spellbound as they huddled their bodies together like a group of leopards feasting over prey.

I want to be their prey, I thought, swaying my body in synchronization with the women.

I looked around the enclosure and didn't see anyone else standing in the flashing light, so I decided it was time to join the action inside the room. A sign on one side of the cube read Open. I ran my hand over the glass near the sign and felt a handle, pulling the glass door toward me. For a moment, the outside strobe light intermixed with the flowing orange spots inside the room, and I was conscious of how chaotic it suddenly appeared. I immediately closed the door and the one-way glass blocked out the outside light, returning the room to its flowing orange and black leopard motif.

By now, the four women in the room had paired off and seemed preoccupied with their partners, so I stood to the side and swayed my hips to the music as I watched the hypnotic movement of their bodies. The women circled around one another as if stalking each other. It was exciting to watch them play-act to the theme of the light show. But the acting soon turned more serious as the couples moved closer together and began rubbing their bodies together. Soon, their lips locked together and I could see them kissing passionately as the light and dark spots flowed over their faces.

I was dying to get in on the action, but I didn't want to interrupt their connection. As I watched their hands slide down each other's bodies, my hands mimicked their movement. When their hips briefly separated and their hands moved between each other's legs, so did mine. I was the odd woman out, but somehow I didn't mind. I could feel the juices flowing down my thighs as my pussy watered in sympathy with the gyrating couples.

I began circling my button and was just about to push my fingers into my slit when suddenly the light in the room was interrupted once again by someone opening the door. The shape of the body in the flashing light looked familiar, and I recognized the shoulder-length hair of the woman who'd stood beside me earlier. She closed the door, then paused for a moment as she looked around the room. Before long, she began walking in my direction then stopped about two feet in front of me. She smiled as the leopard spots flowed over her face and I suddenly felt weak at the knees once again.

Her body was even more beautiful in the buff than in her tight blouse and jeans. Her breasts were a full and firm, with a gentle ski-jump slope on the top. These were no fake balloon-shaped artificial tits—these were the real thing. I glanced further down and watched the leopard spots flowing over her hips as my mouth began to water. There was just enough light flowing over her pubic area to show that she was shaved bald like me. As she danced sensuously in front of me in the dark, her bare mound swayed slowly from side to side.

"My name's Emma," she said in a soft voice.

"Jade," was all I could reply, hypnotized by her beauty.

"Beautiful, isn't it?" she said, turning her face toward one of the couples locked in a passionate embrace.

"Stunning," I said, happy the music was playing softly enough to engage in quiet conversation.

"You look like quite a tasty feline yourself," Emma said.

"You too," I replied lamely.

Emma inched closer toward me, until we were about six inches apart. I could see her looking directly into my eyes as she smiled sexily at me.

"May I?" she asked.

I wasn't sure exactly what she had in mind, but whatever she wanted to do with me, I was game.

"Please," I panted.

She closed the remaining distance and I could feel her breasts push against mine as she locked lips with me. A jolt shot through my body as if I'd been lit on fire. I could feel the heat of her body and the perspiration on our chests as our breasts slid sensuously over one another. She slipped her tongue between my lips and I sucked on hers as we swirled our tongues together. Our hips met and we gently ground our mounds together. When she moaned in my mouth, I practically came from the passion of the moment.

There was something electrifying about being in the dark with a perfect stranger, our bodies pressed together, with these mysterious and beautiful light effects highlighting the curves and shadows of our bodies. I could feel my nipples hardening, and we separated for a moment as we tweaked them together, watching the orange spots highlighting our swollen tips.

I was hypnotized by the sights and sounds and I could feel the juices in my pussy building by the moment as they began to run down the inside of my thighs toward my knees. As if reading my thoughts, Emma's right hand began tracing a line down the side of my waist and curved over my hips toward my love box. I quivered as her hand got closer to my pussy. When she finally slipped her fingers into my cleft and traced them slowly up toward my clit, I gasped out loud.

"Yes," I exhaled onto her bare shoulder as I slumped my body against hers. I wanted her to plunge her fingers deep into me and bring me to a quick orgasm. There would be plenty of time to experiment with other things and for me to return the favor in a moment. Right now, I desperately needed to get off.

She inserted two fingers further inside me and stroked my G-spot, and our mouths joined together once again. Our tongues swirled and sucked one another while she caressed my insides. But her palm remained stubbornly fixed in place over my mound. I wanted her to move her hand over my aching clit, and I swiveled my hips in a vain attempt to create more friction. But Emma seemed to be holding back, savoring the moment, as if intentionally denying my pleasure.

"Let's move to the sofa," she said, taking her hand out of my pussy and weaving her fingers between mine as she led me to the neon-outlined rectangle at the far edge of the cube. I hardly even noticed the other women as we walked straight by them, my head was so swimming in anticipation of what Emma wanted to do with me on the sofa.

When we got to the neon lines marking the perimeter of the couch, she gently pushed me down onto its surface. When my buttocks rested on the cushion, she kneeled down beside me and kissed me hard on the lips while lowering me slowly onto the couch. Emma lay on her side beside me while she ran her left hand over my breasts and stomach, then she leaned in and sucked my erect nipples. It felt incredible and I hoped she'd soon move lower and administer the same kind of action on my aching clit.

But she seemed content with running her hands over me as she explored every curve and crevasse of my body. When her hand passed over my bare mound, I lifted one of my legs to permit freer access to my pulsating cunny. Instead, she swept her arm under my knee and pulled my other leg up until both legs were pointed straight up in the air. Then she stopped kissing me and lowered her face closer to my hips.

Finally! I thought. She's going to give me attention where I most needed it—in my aching pussy.

She positioned herself behind my exposed ass, then spread my legs apart until they formed a bent V-shape, with my thighs resting against my chest. My entire vulva was now exposed to her and I could feel my wetness trickling down my perineum toward my anus.

Now, Emma, I screamed inside. *Suck my aching twat,* I begged. *Take me into your mouth and lick my clit like you were playing with my tongue earlier. Slip your fingers inside me and fuck my twat like there's no tomor-*

row. Because right now, time is standing still and I'm not sure there's going to be another tomorrow.

Emma paused, and I lifted my head to look in her direction. She looked up at me and smiled with a mischievous grin as the leopard spots flowed over her pretty face. Then she lifted herself up and positioned her hips over top of mine as she rested her thighs on top of mine and slowly lowered her vulva until it touched mine. The feeling when our pussies touched was indescribable.

We were both aflame in passion and soaked through and through between our legs. I could feel her labia interlacing with mine in a different kind of lip lock, and I threw my head back against the sofa cushion in utter ecstasy. I began rubbing my cunt furiously against hers, listening to the sound of our juices commingling as they slurped and sloshed in glorious union. It was dirty and raunchy and sexy, and something I'd been longing to try ever since my last lesbian encounter at the Dinner Party.

Just when I thought it couldn't get any more intense, Emma shifted forward a few inches and our clits suddenly touched.

"Fuck, yes!" I cried out loud as our eyes locked in the strange orange and while shifting lightness.

Her face looked exquisite as we began to grind our pussies together and she fucked me harder. I could feel the hardness of her clit as it flicked and over mine, and I moaned in blissful abandon. I felt the ache deep in my core beginning to build, but I wasn't ready to cum yet. I wanted to savor this moment and play with Emma on the precipice of pleasure as long as I could make it last.

Emma leaned forward and began to kiss me passionately as she began fucking my gaping hole more vigorously. We both moaned into each other's mouths as we savored the union of our most private parts in the soft orange light. Suddenly, Emma lifted her face above mine and moaned an otherworldly sound. I felt a gush of liquid spraying against my open pussy, filling me with her juices. Emma was squirting her wetness against me while she came hard between my legs. Any chance of holding back my orgasm any longer quickly evaporated as I fell over the cliff, spasming a long serious of hard contractions against Emma's sex. While our bodies jerked and spasmed at the height of pleasure, we watched each other gasp and moan in the swirling lightscape.

When our climactic contractions finally subsided, Emma collapsed onto my body and kissed me softly on my lips. For the longest time, we simply lay on our sides with our legs intertwined, kissing and giggling like two little girls.

"That was incredible," Emma whispered in my ear.

"We're not done yet," I said, smiling into her eyes. "This cat still has a lot more fight left in her."

6

—————

OVER THE RAINBOW

Emma and I played for another hour or so in the women's dark room, experimenting with different positions and techniques, and we both came many more times. I was tempted to engage with some of the other women in the room, but I wanted to save myself for something else. I exchanged email addresses with Emma and we promised to stay in touch, then I exited the cube.

When I stepped back into the flashing light of the lower level, I glanced over at the men's room. There was something intriguing about watching men have sex with one another, and I was drawn to their shapes moving under a different kind of light effect. As I got closer to the enclosure, I noticed the light looked like little white tadpoles, swimming over the men's bodies while they moved about the room. Just as in all the other rooms, it was beautiful and hypnotic to watch.

Three men were facing each other near the front of the glass, grinding their hips together in a triangle formation. As they swayed their bodies, I could see they all had erections and were rubbing their cocks together in a coordinated frotting action. It was fun watching them slap their swords together like they were Three Musketeers in a playful fight.

Suddenly, the man nearest the glass knelt down and began licking the other two men's penises. It was incredibly erotic to watch him caress their hard-ons with his tongue and lips. It was hard to tell exactly how worked up the men on the receiving end of his ministrations were, but the little white tadpoles racing across their stomachs simulated the effect of sperm shooting out of their cocks.

Then the kneeling man moved up to the heads of their cocks and took both penises into his mouth. I'd heard of double penetration before, but this was an entirely different version from what I'd never seen. As the two men humped their hips slowly together, fucking the kneeling man's mouth, they began to kiss passionately. I was surprised how turned on I was getting watching the action, and I was soon ready to experience some dick of my own in the mixed room. As much as I enjoyed making love to Emma, sometimes all I wanted was a hard, throbbing cock pounding my pussy to its limits.

As I turned toward the cube housing the mixed-gender participants, my kitty beginning to tingle even more strongly. This time, the light effects stretched and curved around the figures in beautiful rainbow-colored stripes. I recognized three figures in the cube: one woman and two men. I stood entranced watching the colored stripes stretch and bend around their curves as they danced and rubbed their bodies together, much like the three men were doing in the men-only cube. But this time, the woman was sandwiched between the men as they bucked their hips against her from opposite sides.

I had to look closely to see their erections under the bands of light, but they were quite noticeable—and *large*. The man facing the woman's front side has his cock pressed up against her belly, while she stroked it sensuously with one of her hands. The man behind her had his tool between her legs and every time he swung his hips forward, I could see its head poke in and out under her mound. With her other hand, she caressed the underside of his cock and pressed it toward her opening. She turned her head and kissed the man behind her as the three engaged in an erotic tribal dance.

Not wanting to interrupt their concentration, my own hand fell to my crotch, and I began massaging my clit while I cupped and squeezed my breasts with my other hand. My mind raced ahead, thinking about all the different positions and permutations I could engage in with these three partners.

After a few minutes of erotic play, the man on the woman's backside angled his hips upward and the woman tilted her ass back to receive him. Their mouths opened in a silent moan as he slid his cock inside her. The man in front continued to hump the woman's belly, but now the woman had two hands free to clasp his cock and give him proper attention. As she and the man behind her rocked their hips together, the rainbow stripes slid over the other man's erection, making it look like a writhing anaconda.

How I wanted that cock inside me!

The movement of the man and the woman who were joined began to speed up and as I drooled from my soaking pussy, he slammed his hips against her ass, forcing her hands to move up and down on the other man's cock. She didn't need to do anything now, other than hold her hands tightly around his throbbing manhood. I was surprised how much of his organ I could see thrusting into the light, even with her grasping it hand-over-hand. It had to be at least nine inches long. As I inserted my fingers into my slit and began humping myself, I imagined directing it into my own quivering tunnel.

The three figures were now moving as one and their pace was accelerating toward an obvious climax. With one final thrust of his hips, the man in the rear slammed his cock deep inside the woman and pulled her hips toward his groin as he came inside her. I moaned out loud as my own climax rolled over me, our bodies heaving from the contractions consuming both of us. The man pulled his throbbing cock out of the woman's pussy and I could see it bobbing in the rainbow light as his seed coursed through his shaft. He leaned over and whispered something in the woman's ear, then left the room.

Now's as good a time as ever to make my entrance, I thought.

I figured I'd better get in there before the remaining couple got too hot and heavy. I wasn't sure if the man in front had come yet, but I sensed he wouldn't be disappointed to have *two* women in the enclosure giving him attention. I opened the door and stepped inside, and they turned toward me. The woman was still holding the man's dick in her hands, stroking it softly up and down. And he was still hard as a rock, in obvious need of satisfaction.

I walked up to the couple and without saying a word, I wrapped my hands around the woman's, feeling the heat emanating from the man's member. She released her hands to permit me freer access and I squeezed his pole tightly. It had to be at least six inches in circumference and even longer than I thought. I could feel him pulsating in my hands, and I leaned in to kiss him. He moaned softly as I flicked my thumb over his slick head, feeling his pre-cum leak onto my hand. The woman leaned forward and joined us in a three-way kiss while her hand cupped the man's balls.

I could feel his passion rising as the two of us gave him a glorious two-way handjob, but I wanted to save him for something else. There was no way I was going to let this beautiful cock go to waste by letting him cum in my hands. I began lowering myself, kissing his sculpted chest and washboard abs. His bush was neatly trimmed with just a bit of stubble on his pubis, and his balls were smooth as a baby's bottom. I really appreciated a man who shaved down there, especially one with such an impressive package.

When my head reached below his navel, I gobbled up the head of his tool like it was my last meal. I could only get about four inches of him inside my mouth, but I savored every bit of it with my swirling tongue. I hadn't sucked that many dicks in my life, but I knew a keeper when I saw one, and this was one spectacular johnson. While I sucked his manhood, the other woman moved behind him, squeezing his balls. Although maybe she was doing something *else* to him back there, because suddenly his hip movements escalated in urgency.

I didn't mind the idea of him cumming in my mouth, but I didn't want to siphon any of his virility before clamping another part of my body around his impressive python. I pulled my mouth off his cock and lifted myself up, licking his sweating torso with my open tongue. When I reached his face, I plunged my tongue into his mouth. The thrusting and swirling action left little doubt that I wanted to be properly fucked by him.

Screw the other girl, I thought. *She'd already gotten her piece of the action—now it was my turn.*

I turned around and began rubbing my slick ass against his dripping pole. Then I slipped his erection between my cheeks and shifted slowly up and down, giving it a tantalizing massage. He pulled back a little and grabbed his cock, trying to steer it into my anus, but I wasn't having any of that. Maybe later, if I was still in the mood, but right now I needed that throbbing monster inside my pussy. I wanted to feel him fucking me the old-fashioned way, filling me with his manhood, stimulating my G-spot, stretching me to the limit.

I reached between my legs and grabbed the sticky head of his prick and directed it toward my wet opening. He was only too happy to oblige, and after I poked it inside the front door, he slowly pushed it in all the way. I gasped at the thickness and depth of his intrusion as I clamped down on his throbbing meat like a bear trap. There was no way I was letting him escape until I was fully satisfied. He reached around and grabbed my tits with both hands, squeezing them gently while he thrust his shaft in and out of my love canal. I could feel my clitoral hood sliding back and forth over my nub as he pulled and stretched my labia with every thrust of his giant cock.

I could have easily come from this movement without any further stimulation, but as if reading my thoughts, the woman circled around and began rubbing her breasts against mine, heightening my ecstasy. As she kissed me passionately, I began moaning and grunting from the pleasure consuming me. My hands wrapped around her waist as I grasped her buttocks in each hand and pulled her toward me with each thrust of the man behind. We both panted in delight as we ground our pussies together.

Never had I felt such intense pleasure from so many different sensations at the same time. This was my first threesome, and it had already far exceeded my expectations. I would have been happy to come this way, sandwiched between two lovers, but perhaps sensing the newness of the experience for me, the woman pulled out of our lip lock and began to move her head down my body.

She cupped and played with my breasts, sucking and flicking my tender nipples with her soft, slippery tongue. I moaned, listening to the popping sound my erect nipples made when they slid in and out of her suckling mouth. I pulled her face into my chest, begging her to continue. But after a few minutes, she pulled away and moved lower. Slowly— tantalizingly—she kissed and nibbled her way down my body until she got to my soaking snatch. She paused and kissed it gently, then nibbled her way down the edges of my labia as the man slammed his cock in and out of me.

"Oh God!" I panted, practically fainting from the intensity of the pleasure building up inside me. The idea of being serviced on both ends by two different partners was driving me insane. I pushed my mound toward the woman's face and tilted my hips so my clit was level with her lips. When her tongue found my button and her lips surrounded me, I grabbed the back of her head with both hands and pulled her tightly toward me.

"Fuck, yes," I panted. "Fuck me," I shouted to no one in particular. I wanted to be fucked from both sides. *Fill me with your cock and flick me with your tongue,* I thought. *I want to soak you with my juices and feel you throbbing deep inside me.*

I slammed my mound into the woman's face and face-fucked her with all my energy as she sucked my clit into her mouth and rolled her tongue over its head. I was seconds away from having the strongest orgasm of my life.

"Yes—*yes!*" I screamed, as I bucked and whimpered from the intense pleasure racking my body. The man sensed I was about to come and I could feel his thrusting beginning to increase in intensity. I felt his hot breath on my back as he panted in unison with me. I looked down at the rainbow stripes washing over our thrashing bodies and closed my eyes, tilting my head back. This was as close to heaven as I could imagine.

When I was finally ready to come, I didn't hold anything back. I screamed like a wild animal, fucking the woman's face while the man slammed his python up inside me in a series of final rhythmic thrusts, spewing his honey inside me. I temporarily lost strength in my legs, but it didn't matter. The man's hard pole had me impaled like a cross, holding me suspended in the air as I gushed all over the woman's face.

When I finally stopped shaking and began to catch my breath, they both pulled away and turned to face me. We pressed together in a sublime three-way kiss, tasting each other's cum in our mouths. I opened my eyes and as I watched the spectrum of colors wash over our faces, and I couldn't help but smile.

I'd finally found my pot of gold at the end of the rainbow.

VOLUME FIVE

THE HAREM

1

As I walked through the open-air market in Marrakesh, I could feel my heart pounding in my chest. I'd never been to Morocco before, and the hustle and bustle of the *Souk Semmarine* was a feast for the senses. With so many tourists and locals crammed into the narrow laneways, my eyes darted from one distraction to another. While I strolled past their stalls, shopkeepers noisily hawked their wares, begging me to make an offer on everything from cheap jewelry to handbags. The pungent aroma of grilled kebabs, fresh hummus, and fried snails permeated my nose. Everywhere I looked, women in long, full-body burkas or face-concealing niqabs passed calmly by, seemingly unperturbed by the chaos of the teeming bazaar. With my long blonde hair and tight jeans, I definitely stood out like a sore thumb in this conservative muslim metropolis.

After a half hour or so, I grew tired of the peddlers confronting me, and I ducked into one of the shops to try on some head scarves, hoping to distract attention from my obvious Western appearance. When I tried a pretty pink and teal colored one on and looked at myself in the tiny mirror on the wall, the owner came up behind me, smiling at my reflection.

"Very pretty," he said. "You like?"

"Maybe," I said, mindful of the hard-sell personality of local merchants that I'd been forewarned about. "How much is it?"

"For you, pretty lady, only five hundred dirham!"

Knowing the local exchange rate was roughly ten dirham for one U.S. dollar, fifty bucks for a scarf didn't seem out of line. But I also knew that shop owners in North African bazaars were notorious for fleecing unaware tourists and that haggling was an expected and necessary condition of purchase.

"That's more than I can afford," I said, placing the garment back on the rack.

"Perhaps we can make an accommodation," he said, lifting the scarf off the shelf and placing it back on my head. "Since the colors match your eyes so perfectly."

"Um-hmm," I smiled, knowing full well he was just buttering me up for a sale.

"How about two-fifty?" I said, placing my hands on my hips defiantly.

"Ps-shaw!" the merchant scoffed. "That is well below my cost. This is an authentic Moroccan hijab. Other merchants sell this style for much more."

"Well, I guess I'll just have to go check *them* out then," I said, placing the scarf in his hands and turning to exit the stall.

"Ok, ok!" he backpedaled, catching up with me and blocking my exit. "New price, only for you. Four-fifty. But that's as low as I can go."

"That's not much of a discount," I huffed. "Other vendors have offered far better. Three hundred is the best I can do."

The man threw up his hands, wrinkling his brow with a sad puppy dog face.

"My lady, I wish I could help you, but I'm just a poor merchant with high overhead. Don't you expect me to make a profit?"

"Of course," I said. "But I know most of these items have a high markup. I think you've still got plenty of profit to work with here. Perhaps I'll come back after comparing prices with some of the other sellers."

"Wait, wait," the man said, stepping in front of me again. "I can't have you leave without purchasing something. Four hundred is my best offer. But at that price, you're practically *stealing* it from me."

I picked up the scarf again, turning it over to look for some kind of label.

"How do I know this is even made here? There's no tag."

"Oh please," the man said, crossing his arms. "Now you *insult* me. We only sell authentic textiles manufactured in this country. Look at the intricate stitching. This is hand-embroidered right here in Morocco."

"And the fabric?" I said, rolling the cloth between my fingers. "Is it genuine silk?"

The man placed the garment under an overhead ceiling light, slowly tilting it from side to side.

"Can't you see how the patina changes color when you bend the fabric? I would never sell cheap polyester at my store. This is where all the local muslim women come to purchase authentic Arab clothing."

"Okay," I said, shaking my head in surrender. "I'll offer a little more since I can tell it's a quality product. "I will pay three hundred and fifty dirham, cash. That is all I have on my person."

The merchant paused for a moment, scanning my face with a stern expression as if trying to divine my thoughts. Then he burst into a broad smile, nodding enthusiastically.

"Only for you, my pretty American," he said. "And only because I don't want to see you walking around the bazaar in a cheap knock-off sold by the other vendors."

"Good," I said, turning back toward the mirror. "Do you mind showing me the proper way to wear it? The way the local women do?"

"Of course," he said, draping the scarf over the top of my head and pulling the ends softly under my chin, tying them in a gentle knot. "The idea is to cover your hair and tie it so it covers as much of your face as possible. Our culture requires women to express their modesty by covering their bodies when they are out in public."

"Thank you," I said, pulling some bills out of my pocket and handing him the agreed-upon amount.

"Please, come again," the man said, bowing with his palms centered over his chest. "I have many more items of clothing that you would look beautiful in."

"I'll try to come back before I leave your beautiful country," I nodded. "Thank you for your time."

"Safe travels," he said, waving goodbye to me as I exited the stall.

While I continued down the main thoroughfare jostled by distracted tourists, aggressive shopkeepers, and beguiling snake charmers, I realized the thin head covering provided limited camouflage from my fair skin and Western clothing. By the time I exited the packed marketplace, I was visibly sweating and exhausted. I found a nearby cafe and ordered a strong coffee, then found a vacant table in the corner and sat down, nursing my drink.

Most of the patrons appeared to be Westerners, but on the far side of the room sat a lone man in long white robes wearing a traditional headdress, sipping a beverage. I'd always been fascinated by the clothing and customs of native Arabs, and as he appraised the boisterous tourists gathering in the cafe, he peered at them bemused. The man had dark, weathered skin and a closely cropped beard with soft brown eyes and a square jawline. Appearing to be in his late thirties or early forties, he was quite handsome, with the juxtaposition of his flowing cream-colored kaftan and his golden-brown skin making him look like a young Omar Sharif.

As he casually glanced around the cafe, he caught me staring at him, and I quickly looked away. Moments later, my gaze was drawn back to him and this time he smiled when our eyes met. When I looked away again, he stood up from his table and went to the front counter where he placed an order for something. A few minutes later, the clerk handed him two steaming cups and the man began walking in my direction.

"Excuse me," he said, approaching my table. "I noticed you were sitting alone and wondered if you'd like some company. I brought you a cup of mint tea if you'd like to sample some of our local fare."

"Um..." I hesitated, looking around the room to make sure it was safe to be seen in the company of a stranger.

Normally, I'd quickly rebuff someone who made such a bold and unsolicited advance, but there was something about his quiet demeanor and warm eyes that put me at ease.

"Thank you," I said, shifting my chair back a few inches. "That would be lovely."

"My name's Amir," he said, handing me the cup of steaming tea.

"Jade," I said, nodding politely toward him.

"That's a lovely name. It sounds Asian or Moorish, but you look much *fairer* than that."

"Yes," I laughed. "I suppose my light skin gives me away. I'm from Chicago actually, in the United States."

"I know it well," he nodded. "The Sears Tower, Navy Pier, Millennium Park..."

"You've *been* to the United States?" I said, surprised by his fluent English and knowledge of my local landmarks.

"I spent four years studying law at Columbia University and traveled throughout the country during my summers off."

"I *wondered* where your perfect English came from," I said, smiling at his handsome face. "I never would have guessed–"

"That a sheep-herder like me might be so worldly?" he joked.

"No," I stammered. "I meant–"

"It's okay," he laughed. "It's a common reaction I get from Westerners. They either expect me to be some kind of sultan or a terrorist wearing these clothes."

"I'd never judge a person simply on the basis of what they're wearing," I said, furrowing my brow in sympathy.

"That's very wise," he said, peering up at my scarf. "What about you? You seem to be a little more...*restrained* compared to your fellow countrymen."

I lifted my hand self-consciously to my scarf and chuckled.

"I felt a little exposed walking around the markets with my long blonde hair. I think I was too easy a mark for your local merchants."

The man took a sip of his tea and chuckled.

"They can be a little overbearing at times when it comes to

approaching tourists. There's something to be said for exercising a little decorum and good manners."

"I couldn't agree more," I said, lifting my cup in agreement.

"So, what brings you so far from home?"

"Just looking for a change of pace, I guess. I've never been to this part of the world and I wanted to experience the unique culture of North Africa."

"Where have you been so far?"

"Just the medina and a few of the museums. But I'd love to see more of the countryside."

"You mean the *desert*? There's really only two climate zones in the Mediterranean crescent–the fertile orchards near the sea and the barren plains of the Sahara."

"I guess I'm more drawn to the desert. Maybe it's from watching all those romantic films like Lawrence of Arabia and The Wind and the Lion. There's something about the natural beauty of the red sand and the windswept dunes that seems so peaceful and alluring. It seems to be about as far away from the hustle and bustle of the urban jungle as you could possibly get."

"Have you ever ridden a camel?"

"It's on my bucket list."

"Would you like to join my caravan for a little excursion?"

"Caravan?" I said, widening my eyes. "You're traveling in a *caravan*?"

"Yes," he nodded. "It's a modest group. A few camels, some live-stock, and my small coterie."

"Is that how you get around?" I asked, suddenly intrigued by this mysterious stranger. "Where are you from originally?"

"I was born in Jordan, but I come from a Bedouin family. We're nomads, moving from country to country, buying and selling live-stock and living off the land."

"So you really are a–"

"Goat herder?" he laughed. "In a manner of speaking. But as the leader of my tribe, I'm officially considered a *sheikh*."

"But what about Columbia...?"

"My wealthy parents sent me there hoping for bigger things for me. But I prefer this simple life. There's something to be said for the freedom and stress-free life of a traveling vagabond. I get to meet interesting people in all the countries along the North African peninsula."

"Just like Sean Connery in the movie The Wind and the Lion," I smiled.

"I suppose, insofar as being the king of my domain and living a nomadic lifestyle. So what do you say? Do you feel as brave as Candice Bergen?"

"As I recall, she didn't exactly go *willingly* into the Sahara wilderness with her would-be captor. And I don't have any romantic intentions..."

"No worries," the man said. "You can stay as long or as short as you prefer, or even just for a day trip through the edge of the desert on one of my camels. I assure you that I have plenty of *other* distractions at my disposal."

I pinched my eyebrows, appraising the mysterious man in luxurious robes. I had no doubt that he had little trouble attracting beautiful women wherever he traveled.

"How would this work exactly?" I said, crossing my arms. "I've never run off with a strange man into the desert before."

"I understand your hesitation," he said. "My camp is just outside the city limits. You can join my troupe for an authentic Bedouin dinner while you stay with my other wives in a separate tent. If you feel so-inclined, you're free to join us on the next leg of our journey toward Algiers. I'll be happy to pay for your safe passage back to Morocco if that's where you've made return travel arrangements."

I paused for a moment, scanning his face for any sign of ill intent. I'd heard about the legal practice of polygamy in certain Arab countries, and far from turning me off, the idea of being surrounded by other women who could satisfy his sexual needs gave me a certain degree of comfort.

"That won't be necessary," I said. "It shouldn't be too difficult to change my airfare if necessary. But how can I be sure you don't intend to steal me away like Sean Connery and add me to your stable of harem girls?"

"That's not the way we operate," he laughed. "As you probably learned from watching that movie. Honor is the most important character trait among we Bedouin. But of course, I would encourage you to leave a message with your friends and family before you leave."

The man took a menu scrap from the table and scribbled something on the paper.

"This is my full name. I'm well known in most towns along the coast. The last thing I need is the American cavalry hunting me down like in the movie. I assure you, this is an honorable offer between friends. You have my word on that."

"Can you give me a day to think it over?" I asked, still not convinced this was a good idea. But the lure of joining a real caravan through the Sahara Desert was awfully tempting.

"Absolutely," Amir said. "If you decide to join me, let's meet in this cafe at the same time tomorrow. If you're not here, I'll understand and there will be no hard feelings. But if you do decide to come, we can take a taxi to the outskirts of the city where my aide will meet us and escort us by camel to my camp at the edge of the desert."

"How will I keep from falling off?" I smiled.

"It's not as scary as it looks to ride a camel," he said. "There are comfortable and secure saddles, and they walk quite slowly. But if you're still worried, you can always ride tandem with me."

"I'm sure I'll be fine," I smiled, turning my wrist to check the time. "Thank you for your kind offer, Amir. I look forward to meeting you again tomorrow at five p.m. And thank you for the tea."

As I rose to leave, he stood along with me, extending his hand.

"I hope to see you again, lovely Jade," he said, clasping my hand softly. "And keep an eye out for those carnival barkers. Best to keep your hijab on while you're walking about town."

"Will do," I said, heading toward the exit door.

After I left the cafe, I closed my eyes, inhaling the warm arid air of the Moroccan town square. Something told me that my North African adventure was about to take an interesting new turn.

2

———————

For the next twenty-four hours, I vacillated back and forth on whether to entertain the handsome sheikh's offer. On the one hand, I'd always dreamed about trekking through the Sahara Desert on a camel. But I knew that traveling into the wilderness with a total stranger was not without its risks. He could easily abduct or molest me, with no guarantee that the local police would make any effort to find me or hold him to account. I knew that muslim law was highly skewed in favor of the man's rights and that women were often ostracized or worse for any kind of perceived sexual indiscretion.

The following morning after enjoying a light breakfast, I approached the front desk of my riad to enquire about the mysterious man. If he was as important and well-traveled as he claimed to be, I figured the staff of one of the best hotels in Marrakesh would have heard of him. But if he was an unknown or persona non grata, I'd simply ignore his invitation and remain in the relative safety of the downtown tourist areas.

"Excuse me," I said, slipping Amir's handwritten note across the counter towards the attending clerk. "Can you tell me if you've heard of this man?"

The clerk squinted at the writing then looked up at me and smiled.

"Of course," he said. "Mr. Haddad is one of our frequent guests. Would you like me to see if he's staying at the hotel?"

"Um, no, thank you," I said. "It's just that he invited me to take a tour with his caravan and I wondered if this was, you know–*safe* or irregular."

"I can't vouch for how often he entertains Westerners in his cavalcade, but he is often seen in the company of attractive young women such as yourself, and I've never heard of any complaints or misconduct. The Sheikh is widely respected as a man of honor and prestige in these parts. I'm quite sure that you would not only be safe, but indeed well-protected while under his guardianship."

"Thank you," I said, placing the note back in my pocket.

As the hour approached for our planned reconnection, I packed a light duffel bag of overnight clothes and sent an email to my best friend Hannah from back home.

Han,

Enjoying my trip to Morocco so far. Will send more pics soon. I've accepted an invitation to go on a private caravan tour of the local desert with a prominent bedouin leader. His name is Amir Haddad. Apparently his family is quite prominent in Jordan.

If you don't hear back from me in a few days, contact the local embassy to see if they can track my whereabouts. I know this sounds crazy, but I've always dreamed of traveling the Sahara on camelback, and you only live once!

Talk soon,

Jade

I knotted my silk scarf under my chin, then placed a wide-brimmed straw hat on my head and headed back towards the cafe where I'd met the sheikh the previous day. With my heart beating a million miles an hour, I strolled past the bustling souks wondering what I'd gotten myself into.

When I entered the cafe and saw Amir sitting in the corner with his legs crossed sipping a cup of tea, he smiled and stood as I approached his table.

"I'm glad you decided to join me again, Jade," he said, holding out his hand as he supported me while I lowered myself onto the adjoining chair. "I was afraid that I might have scared you away with my rather direct proposition."

"I went back and forth considering it, to be honest," I said. "But I asked around, and you were truthful about your reputation. Apparently, I'm not the *first* tourist you've entertained in this manner. But I left your credentials with the U.S. Embassy just in case."

"I would expect no less from such a wise and pretty lady," he smiled. "May I order you a cup of tea?"

I looked at my watch and glanced outside at the lengthening afternoon shadows.

"I'm already pretty charged up about this adventure," I said, concerned about traveling at night deep into the outback. "Shouldn't we head out to your camp while there's still good light?"

"As you wish," he said, standing up and extending his hand as he surveyed my wardrobe. "I see you've come well prepared for the elements. Though I'm not sure about that hat. You look more like *Audrey Hepburn* in Breakfast at Tiffany's than Candice Bergen in The Wind and the Lion."

I smiled at his genteel manners while he opened the cafe exit door for me then hailed a passing taxi. After we got in the cab and he gave the driver directions in arabic, he glanced down at my overnight bag.

"It looks like you're intending to stay for a while," he smiled. "I must not have scared you *too* much with my abrupt proposition."

"I've heard it's a pretty big desert," I said, pulling my handbag closer toward me. Unbeknownst to my host, I'd included a can of pepper spray under my belongings in case he got the wrong idea. "A girl can never be too prepared on these kinds of expeditions."

"Indeed it is," he smiled. "Did you know that the entirety of the Sahara Desert is even bigger than the continental United States? But never fear—my caravan has enough provisions to keep us comfortable for as long as you choose to stay."

As the taxi sped towards the outskirts of the city, I watched the passing scenery as it became progressively less populated and more barren. Within twenty minutes, the dusty streets soon gave way to grassy hillsides. When we crested the final ridge and I saw the open expanse of the desert stretching out in every direction, I gasped. The late afternoon sun cast long shadows over the undulating red sand dunes, making it look like a different *planet*.

"Is this your first time seeing the desert?" Amir asked, noticing my wide eyes surveying the eerie landscape.

"First time up close and for *real*," I nodded in a daze. "It's even more magnificent than I imagined."

"It has a way of transporting you," he nodded. "There's something about the open vistas and the way the sun reflects over the shifting sands that's quite captivating. Perhaps now you can begin to appreciate how I'm are attracted by its allure."

"It *is* mesmerizing, I grant you," I said. "But how do you navigate your way across this moonscape? There are no roads or landmarks to know which way you're headed?"

"We navigate by the shadows of the sun during the day and the stars in the evening. Plus, the desert isn't all sand. There are bluffs and oases and mountain ridges that point our way. We bedouin have traveled the deserts of North Africa for thousands of years. We know it as well as the back of our hands, as you Americans say."

"I'll have to take your word for it," I said, suddenly feeling the dryness in my mouth. "But something tells me I should have packed more bottles of water in my overnight case. How far away is your camp?"

"It's only twenty or thirty minutes by camel ride," Amir said as the taxi skidded to a stop at the end of the road. Nestled in a shaded dale of the hillside, I noticed a dark-skinned Arab man in a long tunic tending to three camels. "My aide brought an extra ride for you. Don't worry about the water. We've long-since learned how to manage our scarce resources in the parched desert."

Amir paid the taxi driver then escorted me to the dale where he introduced me to his servant.

"This is Ali," Amir said, motioning toward the other man. "He'll look after all of your needs during your stay with us."

The man bowed slightly at the waist, acknowledging me as Amir's guest. I found it a bit strange that Amir didn't introduce me by name, but I assumed it had something to do with the customs of his tribe and his status as leader of the clan.

I glanced at the three oddly shaped animals nibbling on grass besides us. With their long knobby legs, U-shaped neck, and large hump in the middle of their back, they looked like a cross between a llama and an oversized donkey. Towering at least two feet over the top of my head, I was already starting to get vertigo imagining myself trying to balance on top of their precarious mounds.

"These are a lot *taller* than I imagined," I said, noticing an absence of stirrups hanging from their woven cloth saddles. "How will I ever get on top of it?"

"You don't climb up on a camel like you would a horse," Amir said. "They kneel down for you to get on top of them."

He mentioned something to his aide in arabic and Ali pulled on the long hair on the side of one of the camels, then the animal knelt down on the ground with its front knees and lowered its back end until its belly was lying flat on the ground.

"Wow," I said. "That's certainly convenient. Have you trained them this way only for your guests, or is this the way *everybody* mounts a camel?"

"They're very domesticated," Amir said. "It's easy enough to climb atop a standing camel if you know how, but this certainly makes it a lot easier."

"I'll say," I nodded, seeing the top of the cloth saddle now resting at hip height.

"But you still need to be careful to hold on to the pommel at the front of the camel's saddle to make sure you don't get bucked off when it stands. It jerks forward and back as it rises, and if you're not used to it, you can easily be thrown."

Amir said something to Ali and he held out his hand, motioning for me to climb atop the saddle of the resting camel, and I swung my leg up over his hump and sat down on the surprisingly comfortable seat. Although the frame appeared to be made entirely of wood, I noticed a padding of straw and palm leaves under the thick woven blankets draped over its flanks.

"Okay," Amir said. "Now grasp the knob on the front of the saddle tightly and clamp your legs against the side of the camel as he rises."

I did as Amir instructed, then Ali tapped the side of the animal and it lurched forward lifting its back end, then it stepped forward with both front legs until it was fully erect. My body swung wildly as it see-sawed up to a standing position, and I could feel my heart beating as I stared down at the ground ten feet below me.

"Are you good?" Amir called up to me, seeing the fright in my eyes.

"Yes, as long as I don't fall off," I grunted. "But how do I *steer* this thing?"

"Don't worry about that," he laughed. "Ali will lead your camel with a tether behind his animal. But watch out as he begins to walk. They have a bit of a jerky gait. Try to relax your body and let it sway with the animal's movements. Are you ready to head out to our camp?"

I nodded my head then Amir and Ali mounted their camels, heading out in a straight line toward the open desert with Amir in the lead. It didn't take long for me to get used to my camel's rhythmic up-and-down gait, and as I began to relax, I looked out over the vast expanse of russet-colored dunes at the exquisite beauty of the desert. Looking like a giant Rothko painting, all I could see was an endless sea of golden waves juxtaposed against the brilliant blue sky.

The air was hot and dry, and I blinked as sprinkles of sand dusted up into my eyes from the strong wind sweeping across the dunes. More than once I had to grab my hat from falling off my head from the gusts shooting overtop the crescent-shaped hillocks. As I watched the long shadows of our three camels traipse across the soft turf, I smiled at the serene beauty and solitude of the glittering landscape. I wasn't sure what awaited me at Amir's camp, but for the time being, the gentle loping of my camel and the whisper of the warm Saharan breeze lulled me into a blissful, trancelike state.

3

Thirty minutes later, I noticed a clump of trees on the horizon, and I squinted through the shimmering haze wondering if it was a mirage. But as we got closer, I saw a small collection of tents nestled among the palms and a flock of livestock grazing on the grass surrounding the perimeter of the encampment. Hardly believing my eyes, I called ahead to Amir, wondering how anything could grow in this barren wasteland.

"Is this your camp?" I shouted over the howling wind.

"Yes," he said, pulling his camel up beside mine so I could hear him better.

"I thought my eyes were playing tricks on me at first," I said, shaking my head in astonishment. "How does any vegetation survive out here without any water?"

"The desert is riddled with a labyrinth of underground aquifers," he said. "In certain places, natural springs bring the water to the surface, feeding the surrounding vegetation. At other oases, manmade wells tap the aquifers, supplying much needed water to traveling caravans such as my own."

"I thought oases were just a figment of Western movies. I had no idea they actually existed in the middle of the desert."

"There are actually quite a few scattered across the Sahara," he nodded. "But because of the vast size of the desert, it can take many days on camel to travel between them. They've been the lifeblood of we bedouin for centuries."

As we got closer to the camp, I noticed a large herd of camels and scores of sheep and goats grazing quietly in the grass.

"And there's enough water to feed all those *animals* too?"

"Yes," Amir said. "The aquifers are practically endless. There's a veritable ocean of water underneath this arid surface. Did you know that the Sahara was once an enormous sea before the Earth's shifting plates separated the large continents of Eurasia and Africa?"

"I had no idea," I said, growing increasingly impressed with Amir's knowledge of world history and geology. "But why do you have so many camels and livestock? You must have quite a large entourage."

"Actually, it's mostly just me and Ali and my stable of wives. The animals are primarily used to transport our gear and provide food for our band."

"Wow, you really *are* a self-contained entity out here in the middle of the wilderness, aren't you?"

"Everything we need is supplied by the animals and the desert," he nodded.

"And your *wives*," I smiled, peering ahead toward Ali plodding along in front of us, wondering how he satisfied some of *his* more primal needs.

"Yes," Amir smiled. "And my wives."

When we reached the edge of the trees, I noticed a group of women kneeling in the sand preparing food. They all wore loose-fitting tunics and cotton headdresses that wrapped tightly around their heads and faces, providing protection from the overhead sun and the dusty wind. As our retinue approached the center of the camp, the women looked up and stared at me like I was from another planet. They all seemed young and strikingly beautiful.

Maybe Amir doesn't need to entertain Western women after all, I thought.

The two men dismounted their camels, then Amir tapped my

animal and he knelt onto the ground, where Amir offered his hand to help me dismount. Then he led me into one of the two large tents in the campground where an attractive dark-haired woman roughly my age was folding clothes in the corner of the enclosure.

"This is my wife, Laila," he said, introducing me to the woman. "Laila, Jade will be joining us for dinner this evening, so please make sure she has everything she needs."

She turned around and smiled at me with her piercing eyes. I was surprised how beautiful she looked bereft of any makeup or other embellishments. Her wraparound headdress framed her pretty face, highlighting her high cheekbones and golden-brown skin.

"Pleased to meet you," Laila said, bowing slightly at the waist.

It was hard to discern her figure under her layered cloak, but my pussy fluttered when I saw her face flush slightly in modesty.

"You speak *English*?" I said, surprised by her absence of any discernible accent.

"Yes," she said. "My family is from Cairo and we learned English in elementary school. I'm a bit rusty, so it will be nice to have a native speaker to help me brush up on my skills."

"We'll be having dinner when the sun goes down," Amir interrupted. "Then I'll be providing some special entertainment in my tent later on. You may wish to put on some warmer clothes, as it can get quite chilly outside after dark. I'll see you in another hour or so."

After Amir exited the tent, I peered at Laila with a quizzical look. "*Entertainment?*"

"Never fear," she chuckled. "He often entertains visitors with a traditional arab dance. Though it's usually for the benefit of other men. This is the first time he's brought a Western *woman* into his camp."

"I guess I should be honored then," I shrugged, wondering exactly what kind of dance he had in mind.

Laila peered at my cut-off capri pants and light linen blouse and smiled.

"Would you like to change into something more comfortable? As

Amir said, it gets quite cold at night and you'll want a bit more protection against the blowing wind."

"Sure," I said, happy to adopt the local customs during my brief visit with the group.

"If you'd like to remove your clothing, I can store them in a safe location while you stay with us."

"*Everything*?" I said, wondering what arab men and women wore underneath their long garments.

"It's more comfortable that way," she said. "Unless you need to wear something because it's that time of the month...?"

"No, thankfully," I chuckled, curious how they also managed *that* aspect of their personal hygiene.

As I began to remove my clothing, Laila peered at me, noticing the strange tan lines around my bra and upper arms. I paused for a moment before pulling off my panties, and her eyes widened when she saw my shaved pubis. I felt like a bit of a freak, realizing that she and the rest of the women rarely went outside with any exposed skin and almost certainly abstained from any kind of intimate grooming.

Laila fetched a neatly folded garment from the corner of the tent then opened it up to reveal an ankle-length tunic with long sleeves and an opening at the top. I held up my arms and she draped it over my body, stepping in close to me as she peered into my eyes. She smelled of jasmine and lemongrass, and my heart fluttered as her full lips neared my mouth when the garment fell over my shoulders. Then she wrapped a long cotton scarf over my head and under my chin, fastening it with a bobby pin at the ends to hold it in place.

I guess they're not completely bereft of Western conveniences, I smiled.

When she finished, she stepped back and nodded approvingly, smiling at the unusual appearance of a Western woman dressed in traditional arabian garb.

"Do you have a mirror or something to view myself in?" I asked, intrigued to see what I looked like.

"I'm afraid we don't," she said. "It is not part of our culture for women to primp over their external appearance. But I assure you that you look quite beautiful."

"Thank you," I said, reaching into my bag to retrieve my phone. I tapped the screen a few times then handed the device to Laila. "I know this must sound terribly touristy of me, but would you mind taking a picture of me? My friends back home will never believe that I got myself into this arrangement, and I'd love to have a keepsake of my visit to your camp."

"Okay," Laila said, squinting her eyes at the phone. "But this is a little different from the phones I remember using in my youth. How does it work?"

"Just step back and angle the phone until you see my entire body on the screen, then tap the red button at the bottom to capture the image."

Laila did as I requested and I heard the familiar shutter sound when the phone took the picture. She handed it back to me and I tapped the thumbnail image in the lower corner of the screen to view the full-size image. I laughed when I saw myself encased in the flowing robes, with only my pale face peering through the wrap-around fabric.

"That's certainly a different look for me," I said, feeling the soft fabric brushing against my hardening nipples and bare mound. "But I have to admit, it's a lot more comfortable than my usual attire. Is it comfortable to wear in the heat of the day?"

Laila pulled the fabric up over my shoulders and I felt a puff of air press up from the floor toward my exposed pussy.

"The cotton fabric breathes nicely, and the loose fit permits the wind to flow over our bare bodies underneath," Laila smiled.

"Yes, I can see that," I said. "I'm *already* beginning to appreciate the extra freedom of movement in this dress. Although I don't imagine you call it that in your native language."

"We women refer to it as a *thawb*, but when men wear similar robes, they call it a kaftan."

I nodded, beginning to understand the various ways arab culture subjugated women under the control of men. I crossed my arms, beginning to feel the chill as the sun began to set over the horizon.

"Do you think this will this be warm enough in the evening?"

Laila pulled a wool blanket off the pile of clothes in the corner and placed it over my shoulders.

"This shawl will help keep you warm," she smiled. "And it can also be used as a bed covering later on at night."

"Speaking of," I said. "I see you don't have any traditional beds in the tent..."

"We bedouin can't afford such luxuries," Laila laughed. "Everything has to be light enough to pack onto the backs of our camels when we move from one location to the next. We sleep on woven blankets on the soft sand. I think you'll find it's quite comfortable, actually."

"Does everyone sleep in this one tent?" I said, peering at the limited amount of floor space in the twenty-by-twenty-foot enclosure.

"All of the *women*, yes," Laila nodded. "The men have separate tents, of course. Everything is tightly controlled in our caravan. Nothing goes to waste."

"So I'm beginning to learn," I smiled, imagining myself lying on the soft desert sand next to the covey of beautiful women at night.

"Are you hungry?" she asked.

The mention of food made my stomach grumble. I suddenly realized that I hadn't eaten since early in the morning.

"Oh yes, very."

"Come, let's show you how we prepare our traditional bedouin meals."

Laila led me outside, where a large open fire cackled in a sand pit with a wooden frame erected overtop of its perimeter. The women sat in a large circle around the flame, hunched over in their long robes, kneading their hands into large porcelain bowls.

"It smells heavenly," I said, breathing in the fresh scent of milk and spices. "May I ask what the women are preparing?"

"It's a rice dish infused with fresh goat milk, lentils, and chopped onions, seasoned with saffron and turmeric."

"So you're all *vegetarians*?"

"Oh no," Laila said. "We also eat goat meat and lamb. But that's usually reserved for special occasions, like when we have a guest such as yourself."

"I see," I said, noticing Amir flipping open the canvas door of his tent and walking in our direction.

"I see that Laila has gotten you into some more comfortable clothes," he nodded approvingly. "Are you ready to enjoy our traditional bedouin dinner?"

"Absolutely," I said. "I don't know if it's this desert heat or the long camel ride, but I'm famished!"

"Well, we won't delay any longer then," he said, brandishing a curved knife from under his kaftan. He walked up to one of the younger sheep grazing quietly at the edge of the pasture and he grabbed the animal by the back of its head, calmly slicing its throat. The lamb staggered for a moment in shock, then fell to the ground twitching its legs for a few seconds, then lay still as the blood from its neck coated the desert sand. Seconds later, Ali approached the dead animal, and using a longer knife proceeded to slice open its belly, pulling out its entrails.

"Oh my God," I dry-heaved, turning away from the scene of the gory slaughter.

"You've never seen a live animal killed before?" Amir said, seeing my discomfort.

"Never up close and in person like this," I coughed, trying to keep myself from retching.

"But you eat meat?"

"Yes, it's just that–"

"You Westerners are insulated by your supermarkets and hidden slaughterhouses from the act of killing and preparing the animal."

"Yes," I said, realizing how hypocritical it was of me to be offended by the practice of killing live animals for consumption.

"A halal slaughter is considered the most humane way of killing an animal in our culture," he said. "The animal hardly feels a thing before it loses consciousness and quickly bleeds out."

"I'll take your word for it," I said, watching Ali skin the animal and thread a stake through its mouth as he placed it over the fire pit.

"I hope this won't diminish your appetite for the meal. Everything should be ready in another half hour or so."

"I'm sure I'll be fine," I said, smelling the scent of the fresh meat cooking over the pit. "I just need a moment to collect myself."

"Come join me then by the fire while the women make the final preparations."

Amir motioned to a blanket spread out on the sand about ten feet away from the fire, and he held my hand while I sat down on the mat.

"So, what do you think of our little caravan so far?" he said, sitting down cross-legged beside me.

"It's certainly *authentic*," I said, peering at the group of young women preparing the dishes in the circle around the fire. "But I'm wondering about the ratio of men to women in your troupe. Are all of these women your wives?"

"Not in the *legal* sense," he said. "I prefer to think of them as my courtesans."

"They're all so young and pretty. How did they come to join your caravan?"

"I bought them," Amir said nonchalantly.

"You *what*?"

"I know this is a custom frowned upon in the West. But it is quite common in conservative muslim cultures, especially among we bedouin. Families consider it an honor for their daughters to be indentured to a prominent sheikh such as myself."

"And when they get *older*? Do you simply dispose of them when they no longer suit your fancy?"

"They're sold off to other prominent men as maids, nannies, and cooks. The women are always treated well, generally enjoying lives far more comfortable and secure than in their own impoverished families."

"And in the meantime, they travel in your caravan for your own amusement?"

"Well, as you can see, they perform many *other* useful functions. Nobody goes for want in my troupe. Everyone's needs are fully satisfied."

"What about *Ali's* needs?" I said, noticing his servant dutifully turning the roast lamb on the fire spit. "Does he also enjoy the company of these attractive ladies?"

"He would never dare *touch* one of my women for fear of instant execution," Amir said, suddenly clenching his jaw. "But he's well compensated for his service to the caravan. He satisfies his more primal needs in the many small towns along our route."

"I see," I said, watching him remove the charred carcass from the spit then carving it up into smaller chunks and passing them around the circle. Each of the women took a piece and sliced it up into bite-sized portions, mixing them in with their bowls of rice.

"Come," Amir said, taking two bowls and placing them in front of us. "Let's not be concerned about such indelicate matters over dinner. Let's enjoy our feast under the stars of this magnificent canopy."

He picked up his bowl and dipped his hand into the dish, pinching skewers of meat and rice between his fingers and bringing it to his mouth. Looking around the circle, I saw the rest of the entourage doing the same, and I picked up my bowl not wanting to be rude, following their lead. The food was surprisingly moist and tender, with the milk-infused rice keeping all the ingredients bound together, making it easier to take bite-sized chunks in my fingers. I hummed appreciatively at the piquant taste of the freshly prepared ingredients, soon forgetting about the unsettling scene that I'd witnessed with the young lamb moments before.

As we all ate quietly around the circle, my eyes scanned the faces of the pretty young women peering at me curiously across the dancing flames of the bonfire. It didn't take long for my mind to wander to what *other* forms of entertainment they used to keep themselves amused when Amir was otherwise occupied. Surely, he couldn't keep *all* of them satisfied at one time, I thought. As my pussy twitched from the cool desert breeze wafting up under my fluttering robe, I began to look forward to sleeping on the soft desert sand later in the evening.

4

———————

After dinner, Amir invited Laila and me to his tent to enjoy the planned entertainment. He motioned for two of the girls to prepare for the event, and they left the circle while the rest of the women cleaned up the dishes. When I entered his enclosure, I was surprised at how large it was for one person. More than twice the size of the women's shelter, it was bedecked with persian rugs, beautiful tapestries, and a large wood-frame bed with luxury linens.

Wow, I thought, shaking my head in dismay. *Arab men really do enjoy all the advantages in this culture.*

Amir invited the two of us to sit on the plush carpet in the center of the tent, then he fetched a heart-shaped guitar from the corner and sat down between us with the instrument cradled between his legs. A few moments later, I heard two women's voices outside the front door of his tent and Amir replied to them in arabic. When they pulled back the flap and entered the room, my eyes flew open in shock. Instead of their usual long robes and wraparound headdresses, they wore a skimpy ornamental bikini costume.

Their long black hair was held in place by a beaded headband with long tassels hanging down over their eyes, festooned with little silver bells. Dangling from their tasseled bikini bottom hung a knee-length black cloth that provided a modicum of modesty to cover their crotch area. But the rest of the costume left little to the imagination, showing the deep cleavage between their tightly compressed breasts and their exposed bellies and thighs glistening in the soft candlelight of Amir's tent.

Shifting from the ultra-conservative full-body covering of their traditional frocks to this bawdy costume was a shock to my system, and I soaked up the women's taut, sexy figures like I hadn't seen a near-naked body in weeks. Which I damn near *hadn't*. Suddenly realizing that I hadn't felt the touch of another woman's body since I left home, my pussy throbbed while I ogled the sexy girls standing only a few feet in front of me.

"Are you ready to watch a real arabian belly dance?" Amir said, noticing my pupils dilated in excitement.

"Definitely," I smiled, eager to see the two women gyrate their bodies next to me.

He nodded toward the two girls and they stepped back a few feet, then he picked up the guitar and began strumming a rhythmic folk tune. As the melody filled the cabin, the two women began to undulate their hips in unison, matching the beat of the song. My eyes flickered over their bodies, absorbing the sensuous spectacle while their stomach muscles flexed and their navels swayed from side to side like two winking eyes. As they stepped forward and back in perfect harmony, they snapped the castanets on the tips of their fingers together, providing a rhythmic accompaniment to Amir's lilting melody.

Just when I thought this guy couldn't get any more suave and sophisticated, I thought. *He even plays the guitar perfectly.*

In another place and time, I might have fallen for his seductive demeanor, but for the time being I was utterly hypnotized by the sensual moves of the two beautiful women dancing before me. As I watched their eyes gazing at us behind their swinging ringlets, I tried to place how old they were. Their bodies hardly had an ounce of fat, and their skin was as soft and supple as a teenager's. Knowing many arab countries had few restrictions against marrying much younger women, I wondered if they were even of legal age. As if that actually mattered out here in the middle of the desert.

Amir softened the strumming of his guitar and the girls eventually slowed their movement to a stop, then he turned toward me and smiled.

"What do you think of our traditional arab music and dance?" he said to me.

"It's beautiful," I said, shifting my position on the warm carpet, suddenly realizing how wet I'd become watching the two girls. "And very sensuous."

"Yes, it is," he said. "Do you have a particular request?"

I shook my head, unsure what he meant at first, then I cleared my throat when I realized he was talking about the music and not what I wanted to do with the girls.

"You mean like a Western *song*?"

"Yes," he nodded. "I always like to satisfy my guests' preferences."

I thought for a moment about a song that resonated with me that was also slow enough to fit with the girls' style of performance.

"Do you know the Bob Marley song Waiting in Vain, but played in the style of Annie Lennox?"

"Of course," he said. "It's one of my favorites."

He began strumming his guitar again, and the familiar melody of the song filled the tent while the two girls swayed their hips in harmony with the rhythm, clapping their castanets softly to provide gentle background accompaniment. A few moments later, Laila began humming the tune and Amir turned toward her, encouraging her to join him.

From the very first time I laid my eyes on you, girl, she sang with an angelic voice. *My heart said follow through. But I know, now, that I'm way down on your line...*

I turned to face her, amazed that she knew the lyrics to the song and enthralled by her gorgeous tone.

But the waiting feeling's fine, she cooed, meeting my gaze. *So don't treat me like a puppet on a string. 'Cause I know how to do my thing...*

Suddenly my thoughts echoed back to earlier in the day when she slipped my robe over my naked body, and the way she peered at me as she leaned in toward me.

Had she felt the same sexual attraction I'd had for her when we first met?

As she sang the words, she looked into my eyes and smiled while I tapped my feet rhythmically against the soft carpet.

I don't want to wait in vain for your love, she sang, gazing at me directly as my mouth parted in a spellbinding stupor. Suddenly, I couldn't wait to get out of Amir's tent and back into the women's enclosure where I could lie next to her on the warm desert sand under my soft wool cape.

As the song wound down and the girls' movement slowed to a stop, Amir placed his guitar to one side and reached around behind him, placing two odd-looking drums on the mat in front of him. Made of different-sized hollowed-out ceramic bowls with dried animal skins stretched over top, they looked like homemade bongo drums. As if on cue, Laila reached beside her and picked up a wooden reed instrument fashioned in the manner of a flared flute.

"That was beautiful," I said, peering at the two of them. "I don't think I've enjoyed that song as much as I did just now. This whole experience has been a feast for the senses."

Amir smiled as he pulled the drums in closer toward his knees.

"I'd like to finish with song I wrote myself for this kind of occasion," he said. "Unfortunately, I can't sing as well as Laila and her mouth will be otherwise occupied during this tune, so you'll just have to enjoy the *other* elements of the performance," he said, nodding toward the two belly dancers.

As he began beating on the drums with two hands, Laila picked up the flute-shaped instrument and began humming another arabic tune, tapping her fingers rhythmically over the holes on top of the shaft. The girls began swinging their hips slowly at first, but as Amir began increasing the pace of his tapping, they gyrated their hips faster and faster, turning their bodies around as I watched their buttock muscles flexing and shaking under the silk tassels hanging down from their tight bikini bottoms. As Laila matched Amir's escalating backbeat in pace and volume, the girls grew increasingly animated with the shaking of their bodies, looking like they were building up to some kind of climax.

While they shook their bodies with increasing passion and fervor in the form of a simulated sex act, I found myself shifting my weight again on the warm carpet underneath me, growing progressively wetter from their suggestive body movements and facial expressions. Amir became increasingly energetic pounding his drums with his two hands, and I noticed that he was staring at the girls with a lustful look in his eyes. The sexual tension in the room was now at a fever pitch, and as he banged out the last part of the performance, I saw a light sweat dripping over his brow. When he finished the song with two loud bangs on the drums, for a few moments everything in the tent became still as I listened to the sound of everyone's heavy breathing.

"Did you enjoy our little performance this evening?" he said, turning to face me after a long pause.

"Yes, very much," I panted, suddenly realizing how much the performance had raised my *own* heartbeat.

"If you'll excuse me now," he said, looking at the two scantily clad girls in front of him and motioning for them to stay behind. "I think it's time for me to turn in now. Laila will look after your sleeping arrangements. I'll see you again in the morning."

"Thank you," I said, as Laila and I stood to leave. "I'm sure I'll sleep very soundly this evening."

When I followed Laila out the front flap of Amir's tent, I noticed a dark shadow moving away from the perimeter and I recognized Ali's shape in the flickering moonlight. I shook my head realizing that he'd been spying on the erotic performance through a hole in the tent and picked up my pace to catch up with Laila.

"It's as simple as *that*, is it?" I said, referring to Amir's unbridled control over the girls. "He only has to nod, and the women submit to whatever his request?"

"Unfortunately, yes," she said, peering at me with sad eyes. "He's bought and paid for us, and we have to do whatever he says."

"Even if that means sleeping with him whenever he demands?"

"*Especially* that," she said.

"You seem somewhat less eager than the other girls," I said.

"He's had his way plenty enough times with me," she shrugged. "Thankfully, he now prefers the younger girls. Did you at least enjoy the performance?"

"Yes," I said. "It was very–*stimulating*. But honestly, I enjoyed your singing more than anything else. You have a gorgeous voice. Even when you played the wind instrument, I couldn't take my eyes off of you."

"Thank you," she said, noticing me pull my wool shawl over my shoulders to protect against the biting desert wind. "You have a very intoxicating manner about you as well. Come, let's get out of this cold desert air and bundled underneath something warmer."

When we entered the women's tent, all the other girls were already lying fast asleep on their blankets on the sand, with only one small open spot left in the corner of the enclosure. Laila laid a large blanket down over the space, then nonchalantly pulled her dress up over her shoulders, folding the robe and headdress on the ground next to the blanket. I couldn't help staring at her voluptuous body, highlighted by the lone flickering candle next to the makeshift bed. Her breasts were full and firm, resting high on her chest with dark medallions encircling her thick, pointed nipples. Her bare hips curved sensuously around the dark patch of pubic hair on her mound, tapering to long but muscular legs. In the dark shadows of the enclosed pavilion, she looked to me like some kind of sexy Amazon.

Then she picked up a large woolen blanket and threw it over her shoulders, lying down on the carpet peering up at me.

"Are you just going to stand there, or are you going to get under the covers and help keep me warm?"

"In the *buff*?" I said, unsure what the proper protocol was for women sleeping together in the tight confines of the communal tent.

"It's more comfortable that way," she said. "The less washing of our clothes that we have to do, the better. We prefer to air them out overnight. Besides, the sheepskin feels so much better against your bare skin. Come join me if you feel brave enough."

I pulled off my shawl and lifted my thawb over my shoulders, placing them gently on the sand on the other side of the blanket, then lifted the fluffy duvet and nestled in next to her.

"Oh, I'm feeling brave enough," I said, turning to face her.

"Good," she said. "Because those dancing girls weren't the *only* thing distracting my attention this evening."

5

———————

Laila turned her body toward me, then shifted her weight closer, wrapping her legs around my hips. I could feel her soft bush caressing my bare mound as she pressed her breasts firmly against my chest. I placed my hand against the side of her head and leaned in to kiss her, and our tongues melded together in a different kind of erotic dance.

"Laila," I whispered. "I'm so happy we have a chance to sleep together. I've wanted you from the moment I laid eyes on you."

"Why do you think I joined the two of you in Amir's tent?" she said, smiling into my eyes. "I wanted you all to myself."

"Weren't you worried that I might have stayed with *him* instead?"

"Possibly," she cooed. "He certainly knows how to put on the charm when he wants something."

"I already made it clear to him that I didn't come here for *romantic* reasons," I said. "Besides, men don't really do it for me any longer."

"Oh?" she said. "You prefer the company of women?"

"Only *certain* ones," I purred, grinding my pussy against hers.

"Do you mind if I examine you more closely?" she said. "I've never seen a Western woman up close and naked before. You're very–*different*."

"Absolutely," I said. "I've been fantasizing about you strumming your fingers over something other than that *flute* for the last half hour."

"Mmm," she groaned, moving further under the blanket.

As she nibbled her way down my body, I felt her hard nipples etching a line over my trembling stomach. When her mouth reached my breasts, she circled my teats with her warm tongue then sucked them hard into her mouth as she squeezed my mounds with both hands. Unlike the tender manner of most new lovers, I reveled in her rough and dominant style of lovemaking. If this was the way arab women made love to one another, I was ready to be taken.

I placed my hands on the back of her head and pulled her harder against my chest, burying her face between my cleavage. Then I lifted my right knee and pressed it between her splayed legs until it stopped against her wet vulva. She sighed as I began to rock my hips forward and back, stretching the skin of my thigh over her burning pussy.

"Lick me down below," I panted, rolling my hips frantically against her belly. "I need to feel your hot lips on my pussy before I explode."

"Soon enough," she said, blowing softly on my belly as she inched her way down toward my aching snatch.

But when her face reached my shaved mound she paused, feeling my bare skin while she rolled the sides of her cheeks against my soft flesh, kissing me softly at the apex of my slit where my labia merged together at the top of my clit.

"Oh *God* yes," I panted, feeling her warm lips touching my sensitive organ for the first time. "Lick my slit and taste my juices. See how wet you've made me."

She pressed her head a few inches lower, then ran her flat tongue over the length of my folds, lapping up my dripping juices.

"Yes, I can see that," she purred. "You taste much better than goat's milk over rice."

"Yes," I gasped. "Suck on me like a tender lamb. I want to feel your tongue probing every part of me."

Laila curled her tongue as she mashed her face between my legs, pressing it deep into my hole. I grabbed her head, pulling her harder against my cunt, rubbing her face up and down my dripping crease. There was something about the raw act of fucking her naked on the desert sand that I found incredibly arousing. Seeing her wrapped up in her full body covering and suddenly feeling her naked body writhing next to mine took me to new heights of pleasure.

"Mmm," I groaned. "I need you to suck my button now. I want to feel your tongue on my clit. Suck me, Laila."

"Hmm," she purred, moving her head higher up on my slit.

When she surrounded my jewel with her lips I almost came right away, but she seemed to sense my heightened state of arousal and for a long moment she held her head still between my legs while she felt my clit pulsing in her mouth. But when she began rolling her tongue over my nub in slow sensuous arcs, bathing me with her warm saliva, I couldn't help moaning out loud.

"God, yes," I panted. "That feels so good. I needed this so badly."

"Mmm-hmm," Laila nodded, feeling my juices running down her chin and neck.

I could feel my passion beginning to rise and I could have come quite easily from the action of her tongue alone on my raging clit, but what she did next took me to an entirely new level of ecstasy. She slipped two fingers of her right hand into my hole and buried them knuckle deep while stretching her little finger further down my perineum and circling it over my tender anus.

Fuck me, I thought. *This girl really knows how to make love to a woman.* I wondered just how much extra-curricular activity went on at night in the privacy of the women's tent while the other men were sleeping. I had no idea, but I was certainly interested in finding out.

When she began curling the two fingers inside me toward my G-spot, I arched my back and began grunting like a wild animal. I couldn't hold back the floodgate of pleasure any longer as my orgasm suddenly overtook me like a freight train.

"Yes, Laila!" I wailed. "I'm going to come, baby. I'm going to come all over your pretty face."

Part of me wanted to warn Laila about my tendency to squirt when I was this wet and worked up, but there wasn't any time. I suddenly felt the muscles of my pussy begin to clench uncontrollably, gushing my pent-up juices all over her slippery face and the soft blanket below us.

"Uhnn," she groaned, seeming to enjoy my orgasm almost as much as I was while she felt the walls of my pussy contracting powerfully on her fingers still deeply embedded inside me.

It must have taken over a full minute for me to stop coming in her arms with the most powerful orgasm I'd had in months. When I finally began to calm down, I collapsed onto the moist blanket and turned to kiss her softly on her lips.

"Thank you," I said, running my fingers through her hair. "I really needed that."

"You seemed to be already pretty worked up. Did you get that excited watching the two girls performing their special dance?"

"I have to admit that I did," I nodded. "I don't know if it was because I was so surprised to see their almost naked figures or because of the way they were moving their bodies, but it didn't just put *Amir* in the mood for some extra nighttime fun."

"So you're attracted to women also?"

"Definitely," I said. "I find women are more adept at satisfying my sexual needs, just as you were a few moments ago. In fact, your special expertise suggests this wasn't the first time you've made love to a woman either."

"Of course not," she smiled. "What do you think we girls do with ourselves in this tent when we're left to our own devices?"

"*All* of you?" I asked, feeling my juices dripping out of my slit once again at the thought of the pretty girls having a group orgy in their little pleasure dome.

"Um-hm," Laila nodded. "There are twenty women but only one penis in our traveling caravan. How *else* do you think we satisfy our needs?"

"What about poor Ali?" I said. "Isn't he ever allowed to get in on the action?"

"Amir would never share the women he's bought and paid for with another man. It would be considered a violation punishable by death if he so much as *looked* at one of us the wrong way. Besides, with his hooked nose and foul-smelling breath, none of us would ever be interested in him that way."

"Well I'm certainly interested in *you* that way," I smiled, threading my thigh again between her legs toward her steaming pussy. "It's my turn to give you the kind of pleasure you just administered to me."

As I began to move my body lower under the blanket, Laila suddenly stopped me, flipping me over onto my back.

"Why don't we *both* share the pleasure this time?" she said, rolling her body on top of me and lifting my left leg while she pressed her wet vulva against my pussy.

"If you insist," I said, smiling up at her.

"I want to watch you this time while I make love to you," she said. "I've never made love to a white girl before."

I smiled at her reference to me as a white girl, even though we were both technically caucasian. But there was no denying that she was considerably darker than me, and I felt a similar sexual attraction to her exotic appearance.

"I'm sure it's not so different from the *other* girls you've fucked," I said, feeling her thick bush pressing against my bald pubis. "Other than being *bare* down there."

"Like a little girl," she grunted, beginning to grind her twat against mine.

"Does that turn you on?" I said, reaching up to pinch her thick nipples as her large breasts swayed overtop my chest.

"Maybe," she said. "I've never felt a woman's bare *kus* before."

"Not even when you experimented when you were younger?"

"Never like *this*," she panted, rocking her hips more rapidly against mine as the sound of our wet pussies slapping together filled the cabin.

"Fuck my girly pussy, Laila," I teased her, recognizing that she was getting turned on by the naughty imagery. "I want to gush all over your furry snatch when we come this time."

"Yes," she huffed, throwing her head back in pleasure as we squeezed each other's breasts tightly with both hands. "You're so wet and slippery down there. I like the feeling of your bare sex against me."

"Would you like to try it yourself sometime?" I said, lifting my hand to her face as she sucked my thumb into her mouth. "Perhaps I can groom you myself while I'm here."

"I'm not sure Amir would appreciate me defiling my body in a way that's not in accordance with muslim custom."

"But you already said he rarely shows interest in you that way. This can just be between the two of us. It will grow back within a few weeks after I leave."

"I'm not sure I'm going to *want* you to leave after this," she said, pulling my leg up higher as she wrapped her arms around it, pulling it tightly between her sweating breasts. "Come with me, Jade. I want to feel your juices mingling with mine when you climax this time."

"*Fuck* yes," I panted, just waiting for her signal. "Grind your pussy against mine. I'm going to cum all over your hairy bush. Here it comes, baby."

"Uhnnn!" Laila suddenly grunted, throwing her head back in rapture, and for the second time that evening, I felt my body pushing over the precipice as another powerful orgasm washed over me and I began squirting jets of liquid all over Laila's twitching pussy.

As we watched each other's bodies convulsing atop one another in the dim light of the tent, I suddenly heard the soft squealing sounds of the other women around us while they pleasured themselves listening to the two of us. Something told me my little caravan excursion was about to stretch out into a longer adventure than I'd planned.

6

———

The following morning, Laila and I rose at the break of dawn and got dressed, heading outside for breakfast. Amir was already sitting around the fire pit with a scattering of women preparing the meal. He smiled when he recognized me wearing my thawb and invited the two of us to sit beside him.

"Did you sleep well last night?" he asked me.

"Yes, thank you," I said. "I found it surprisingly comfortable sleeping on the desert sand."

"It's fine as long as you have a thick blanket underneath you. The grains have a way of finding their way into every nook and cranny of your body if you're not careful out here. I prefer to sleep a few inches off the surface myself."

I peered around the circle and recognized the two girls from last night's belly dance performance back in their long robes and head-dresses, baking flatbread atop a curved metal hotplate.

"That smells wonderful, whatever it is you're making," I said, choosing to ignore his none-too-subtle intimation about our sleeping arrangements.

"Fresh flatbread and yogurt," he said, motioning to the tall trees surrounding the encampment. "With a side portion of dates, harvested directly from these palm trees."

I shook my head in awe at the simplicity of their nomadic lifestyle.

"I'm amazed how self-sufficient you can be simply from what you carry with you across the desert."

"Yes," he nodded. "Our goats provide milk, cheese, and yogurt, and the sheep provide all the meat we need. Everything else is supplied by the markets we visit along the fringe of the desert on our caravan route."

"If you don't mind my asking," I said, watching the women flipping the sizzling flatbread over the metal hotplate. "How do you pay for the extra materials? I mean, how do you earn hard *currency* while traveling across the desert?"

"Primarily from our livestock," Amir said. "Our animals are quite prolific, and there's a strong demand for these animals wherever we go. The camels in particular are very valuable commodities since they live for so long and can travel long distances without any water."

I glanced at the herd of camels grazing on the sparse grass and drinking from a wooden trough next to the well.

"And they're able to carry your entire entourage with all of its regalia across the open desert?"

"Yes, they're very strong and hardy animals. We'd never be able to survive out here in the middle of the desert without them."

The girls placed some of the fresh flatbread on individual plates along with bowls of yoghurt and chopped dates, then passed them around the circle to the now fully assembled group.

"Please—eat up," Amir said. "You'll need your strength if you plan to stay with us a little longer. The desert provides, but it also takes away. Your body burns a lot more calories in this sweltering heat."

I watched him dip his flatbread into the bowl of yogurt and pick up the dates with his fingers, and I followed his lead. Everything tasted incredibly fresh and delicious and when I finished my plate, I licked my fingers clean like the rest of the group.

"Oh my God," I sighed. "I could get used to this way of life. Everything is so simple and easy out here. Even the food tastes better than what I'm used to at many five-star restaurants. Talk about farm to table!"

"Are you enjoying it enough to *join* us on the next leg of trip to Algiers?" Amir smiled.

I paused for a moment, remembering what I'd told Hannah before I left my hotel in Marrakesh.

"How far away is it? I told my friends they should expect to hear back from me in a few days."

"It six or seven days by camel ride. But we'll be sleeping out in the open most nights under the stars. We only set up camp when we stop near towns or at the few oases along our route."

"I think I can manage that," I nodded, smiling at Laila remembering how much I enjoyed sleeping next to her on the warm sand last night. "But only if you let me help clean and pack up like everyone else. If I'm going to join your troupe for a few days, I want to feel like a productive member of the tribe."

"If that's what you wish," Amir nodded. "Laila and Ali can look after whatever you need. Will you have any trouble making return travel arrangements from Algiers?"

"It shouldn't be a problem," I said. "As long as it has an international airport."

"Indeed it does," he said, standing to leave. "I'm going to collect my things while Ali begins dismantling the tents. We'll be setting out within the next hour."

I was surprised how quickly the group broke down the camp, neatly arranging all the tent poles, coverings, and contents atop the backs of the camels. When we were ready to leave, we filled our saddlebags with enough water to last us for a few days, then we headed east two-abreast atop the remaining camels. It was quite a sight watching the long train of animals traipsing through the pretty sand ripples lining the undulating desert with nothing to keep us occupied but the shifting shadows of the sun and the howling desert wind.

At nighttime, we circled the camels and livestock around us to provide a modicum of cover from the blowing breeze, then laid down on our individual blankets and woolen duvets to keep ourselves warm. I missed sleeping with Laila and more than once thought about sneaking under the covers to join her, but I dared not risk disturbing Amir and Ali who were sleeping nearby.

After three days, we came upon another small oasis and set up the tents once again to provide a respite against the searing overhead sun. I was thrilled to have another chance to make love to Laila in the relative privacy of our own tent, and after the girls fell asleep, she let me shave her mound with the travel razor I'd packed in my bag, using goat's milk and yogurt as an improvised shaving cream. Afterwards, I licked her clean as she knelt over my face writhing in pleasure while I sucked her bare vulva and clit into my mouth.

But the following morning, something happened that forever changed the course of my dreamlike desert adventure. As I flipped open the flap of our tent to fetch some water from the well, I noticed Fatima, one of the girls who'd performed the belly dance a few nights earlier, lifting a pail out of the well while Ali snuck up behind her, trying to lift her robe while he pulled his erect penis out from under his kaftan. When she ducked aside to evade his unwanted advance, he suddenly lost his balance and tumbled head over heels into the well, screaming all the way down until I heard a loud splash when he fell unconscious at the bottom of the pit. Fatima looked around her with frightened eyes and we she saw me watching, she rushed toward me crying, throwing her arms around me wailing in arabic.

Not wanting her to be discovered, I ushered her quickly into our tent and explained to Laila what had happened. A few seconds later, Amir emerged from his tent alarmed by the commotion, calling out Ali's name. Suspicious when he didn't immediately hear his reply, Amir went back into his tent and came out carrying a flashlight, pointing it down into the well. When he saw Ali's body floating face-down in the pool of water, he turned toward our tent and stormed toward it, angrily flipping open the door covering.

He glared at Laila with steely eyes and a red face, speaking loudly to her in arabic. She said something back to him and shrugged her shoulders, feigning ignorance at what had just transpired. He then approached each of the girls separately, asking them if they knew what had happened. But we got to Fatima, he noticed that she was shaking and he placed his hand under her chin, raising her face to meet his angry gaze. She shook her head, afraid to admit any involvement in the incident, but when he saw her dried tear tracks, he grabbed her hair, dragging her outside.

I looked at Laila bewildered and asked what was going on.

"It's not good," she said, following Amir outside. "Just stay close to me and don't say anything."

"Why don't we just tell him the *truth*?" I said. "That it was an innocent mistake, and that she was just trying to protect herself from Ali's unwanted advance?"

"It doesn't work that way," Laila said, shaking her head. "The scales of justice are tipped greatly in favor of the men in our culture. If she were discovered to have been involved in his death, even incidentally, it wouldn't end well for her."

"So what happens if nobody's willing to talk?"

Laila gritted her teeth as she watched Amir remove his long curved knife from under his belt and place it over the fire. I watched the steel grow red-hot in the flame, then he pulled Fatima's head back and placed the hot blade next to her face. He said something angrily to her and she shook her head frighteningly. Then he forced her mouth open as she slowly extended her tongue. He placed the flat side of the knife on it and she screamed as the blade made a horrible sizzling sound against her flesh.

"What the *fuck*..." I said, stepping toward her trying to intercede.

"Don't," Laila said, grabbing my arm.

"But what he's doing to her in *inhuman*," I protested. "She's just an innocent bystander–"

"This is the way justice is administered in the bedouin culture. When there's a dispute involving a serious crime and no one comes forward to admit guilt, the men administer what is called a *bisha'a*, which is a type of trial by ordeal. The accused person is forced to lick a hot piece of metal and if the tongue shows any sign of a burn or a scar, this is considered a sign of guilt."

"Of *course* her tongue will burn!" I exclaimed. "He just placed a red-hot *knife* against her flesh!"

Amir removed the knife from Fatima's mouth, then doused her tongue with a ladle of fresh water. Then he peered closely at it and threw her down on the sand, cursing at her in their native tongue.

"So what happens now?" I said to Laila.

"If a woman is convicted of this type of crime, she's usually sentenced to death, often by public stoning. But Amir won't do it himself. He'll have to take her to a local tribal court where judgement will be formally handed down and administered by the muslim council."

"You've got to be kidding me," I said, hardly believing what I'd just seen and heard.

Amir turned around noticing that Laila and I had witnessed the entire scene, and walked toward us with flaring nostrils.

"I'm sorry you had to see that," he said to me. "But what Fatima did was a serious crime that cannot be ignored. She will have to face the consequences of her actions. Laila, I want you to coordinate with the other women so we can pack up the camp immediately. We'll be heading out to Algiers as soon as possible to have Fatima's fate decided."

"Wait!" I said, stepping toward Amir in desperation. "I saw the whole thing. She didn't do anything wrong. Ali assaulted her and she was simply trying to defend herself. It was just an accident when he tripped and fell into the well."

Amir paused for a moment as his eyes flashed over my beseeching face, then he shook his head dismissively.

"She must have done something to provoke him," he said. "He couldn't have fallen so easily into the well. We will see what the tribal council decides in Algiers."

"And if she's found guilty?" I said.

"She'll be put to death immediately," Amir said, turning to head back to his tent.

I tried to follow after him, but Laila grabbed my robe, holding me back.

"He can't get away with that!" I said, turning toward her. "It's barbaric!"

"Unfortunately, this is the way of our culture. If a muslim woman is even *suspected* of fraternizing inappropriately with a man other than her husband, Sharia law dictates that she be summarily executed."

"By public *stoning*? What about the guilt of the *man*? What if it's simply one person's word over another?"

"In our culture, the man is always presumed innocent since they have free rein over the women and females are instructed to refrain from fraternizing with anyone other than their husbands."

"I'd hardly refer to what they were doing at the well as *fraternizing*. There's only one place for everybody to collect water out here. It's inevitable that there'll be some form of close contact among such a small group in close quarters. Surely something can be done–"

"I'm afraid we have no control over the situation," Laila said, looking at me sadly. "It's out of our hands now."

Later that evening, we stopped in the middle of the desert to rest for the night and grab a bite to eat, and everybody sat around the campfire looking sadly at each other. Nobody dared say a thing, knowing full well what Amir's intentions were. I peered at Fatima, shivering next to the fire as Laila wrapped her arms around her, trying to provide a modicum of comfort. When we dispersed after the meal to make our individual beds in the sand, I took Laila aside and peered into her eyes.

"We can't just let this poor girl be unjustly punished for a crime she didn't commit," I pleaded.

"What would you have us do?" she said. "*He's* the one with all the power and the control. We can't just overpower him and run away."

I crossed my arms and shook my head at the absurdity of the situation.

Laila paused for a long moment, then looked up at me through narrowed eyelids.

"There might be *another* way we can extricate ourselves from this unfortunate situation," she said. "What if we steal away in the middle of the night and take all the camels with us? He won't be able to follow us, and he'll run out of water long before he gets to Algiers."

"But he'd *die* out here in the middle of the desert without any food or water!" I said.

"It's either him or Fatima," she said. "Who do you think is more deserving to live? The innocent girl who did nothing other than try to protect herself from a violent rape, or the man who summarily judges her based on his ludicrous code of honor?"

"But he seemed to be so–"

"Sophisticated, and a man of the world?" Laila said. "There are two sides to every man, and this one is no different. He may have been educated in your country, but I assure you that his morals and underlying character have been indelibly shaped by his family affiliations and the culture of his tribe. Are you prepared to do what has to be done?"

I paused for a moment, trying to think of any other conceivable options, then I grudgingly nodded. I couldn't believe that my exciting desert adventure had suddenly turned into a deadly serious conspiracy where two people's lives lay in the balance.

7

Laila and I waited until we heard Amir snoring under his blanket, then she roused each of the girls, telling them about our escape plan. Everybody got up and tiptoed through the sand toward the camels, then we tethered them together and mounted them carefully, slowly leading them away from the rest of the livestock herd.

"What about the goats and the sheep?" I whispered into Laila's ear, who I'd paired up with on the lead camel.

"We haven't got time to gather them together and we can't risk disturbing Amir–"

Suddenly I heard a man's voice yelling in the darkness, and I turned to see Amir rising from his sleep and begin chasing after us. Laila kicked the sides of her camel and the whole train burst into a gallop, creating a dusty trail behind us. Amir screamed and shook his fists as he tried to catch up with us, but he was no match for the fleet group of camels, and within seconds he disappeared behind us in the thick cloud of dust.

"*Jesus*," I said to Laila after we'd put a few hundred meters between us. "Are you sure this is going to work? Now we're *all* unwitting accomplices in this sordid affair."

"We're at least three days' camel ride to the nearest village on the outskirts of the desert," she said. "It would take three times as long to cover that distance on foot. There's no way he can survive in this stifling heat for that long without water."

"And the *rest* of the animals?"

"They're a bit more hardy. We can come back for them a little later when the coast is clear."

I peered behind me to see the other girls following behind Laila's camel in single file.

"What will you and the others do now that you're no longer part of Amir's caravan?"

"I plan to send them back home to their families when we get to Algiers. This many camels will fetch more than enough money to arrange safe transit to their home ports."

"What about *you*? Won't people be looking for Amir at some point if he doesn't show up? Surely his family–"

"I plan to be long gone before anyone raises any suspicions. I've got some extended family in the Andalusia region of Spain where I can lay low for a while. I'm more worried about you. Did you tell anyone that you were going to join Amir's caravan? The local authorities won't take kindly to finding out you might have been involved somehow in his disappearance."

I paused for a moment trying to remember the details of the message I'd sent Hannah before I set off to see Amir at the cafe.

"Just my best friend back home," I said. "I gave her Amir's name and told her to alert the U.S. Embassy in Morocco if she didn't hear from me in a week or so."

"You'd best clear out of this region at your earliest opportunity then," she said. "It will be difficult for the local police to hold you to account once you're out of the country."

"But I didn't do anything–" I began to protest.

"We're *all* implicated now. If they find Amir's dead body, they could trace any one of us to the deed. Technically, we'd all be considered accessories to the crime."

"Christ," I sighed, feeling my heart suddenly racing at the implications of what we'd done. "What the hell have I gotten myself into?"

"Don't worry," Laila said, patting my thigh reassuringly. "The desert soon buries anything that doesn't move. He'll never be found, and we'll all be long gone before anyone raises any suspicions."

"What about *Ali*?" I said. "Won't another caravan eventually find his dead body at the bottom of the well?"

"Perhaps, but with any luck it should be pretty decomposed by then. Whoever finds him will have difficulty connecting him to Amir's disappearance."

Suddenly I had a queasy feeling in the pit of my stomach, and I wrapped my arms around Laila's midsection, resting my head against her back as I peered at the never-ending hills of red sand dunes.

"How will you find your way through this wasteland all the way to Algiers?" I asked.

"The shadows of our camels will guide the way. It shows which way the sun is pointed, and all we have to do is head east and north until we reach the Mediterranean coast. From there, it should be easy to track our way to the city."

"You're a pretty smart cookie," I smiled, clutching her closely. "These girls were pretty lucky to have such a strong leader to get them out of this predicament."

"I hope they'll be happier now that they're freed from Amir's grip," she nodded. "But I'll be sad to see some of them go. I've grown quite attached to these girls after all this time we've spent together in the desert."

Twelve hours later, the sun began to fade over the horizon and Laila stopped the group to set up camp, laying out our bedrolls amongst the circle of resting camels. Most of our food was still packed in the saddlebags and we enjoyed a peaceful dinner of rice, cooked legumes, and sweet dates. Everybody seemed much more relaxed around the campfire, chatting and giggling amongst them-selves in their native arabic.

When we finished eating, we retired to our beds but soon discovered in our haste to leave the previous camp that we hadn't brought enough bedrolls and blankets for everybody to sleep on separately. Taking charge of the situation as always, Laila nestled the blankets together then we lay down as a group, not bothering to take off our robes to protect ourselves against the encroaching desert chill. It didn't take long for everyone to snuggle together for extra warmth, and before long I felt the telltale sensation of someone's fingers sliding up the bottom of my smock.

I turned around and saw Fatima smiling at me in the soft moonlight, and she leaned in to kiss me. Whether she was trying to express her gratitude for my helping to save her or she was just curious about feeling my fair skin, I couldn't be sure. But either way, I was happy to accommodate her newfound intimate interest in me. As we began to kiss more passionately, intertwining our tongues and pressing our bodies together, she pulled my robe up over my hips, caressing the outside of my thighs and my round buttocks.

But when her hand curved around to my bald pubis, she gasped and uttered something in arabic. I heard Laila reply to her in the darkness on my other side, and Fatima giggled as Laila rolled over to sandwich me between the two of them. Suddenly I had two pairs of hands caressing my body from both sides, and I moaned as they slipped their fingers between my thighs, caressing my vulva from two ends. I pulled Fatima's smock higher, feeling her fluffy bush caressing my bare mound, and I groaned in her mouth as her fingers found my pleasure spot and she began rubbing my clit in soft circular motions. But when I felt Laila's fingers press inside my slit and begin finger-fucking me from behind, I began rocking my hips, moaning more loudly.

When the rest of the girls began to realize what the three of us were up to, it didn't take long for the entire group to devolve into a moaning, slithering mass of naked bodies writhing under the thick jumble of cotton robes and woolen blankets. I pulled Fatima's dress all the way over her shoulders and squeezed her bare tits while she played with my clit and moaned into my mouth. It didn't take long for the combined action of her manipulation of my clit and Laila's caressing of my vulva to bring me to the brink of pleasure. As the two women pressed their bodies tightly against mine, I felt my orgasm overtake me and I jerked my body spastically, gushing all over the two girl's hands.

Fatima said something again to Laila, and she responded in arabic, then Fatima moved her body down closer to my midsection, apparently fascinated by my unusual bare mound and my propensity to squirt when I came. When she spread my legs apart, the other girls stopped what they were doing to peer at my dripping bald pussy glistening in the moonlight. Before I knew it, I had a clutch of pretty young girls kissing and probing every part of my body as Laila propped her head up on her elbow, smiling at me.

"Holy shit," I said to her. "You weren't kidding about how these girls like to stay entertained when the men aren't around. I think I've died and gone to *heaven!*"

"Welcome to the club, baby," Laila said, leaning in to kiss me as I felt a deluge of tongues and fingers converging on me while they sucked and nibbled on every square inch of my body. The multitude of erotic sensations soon brought me to the edge again, and I screamed in ecstasy as my whole body convulsed in another intense orgasm. Fatima suddenly pulled away from licking me while the whole group watched my pussy twitching and squirting my juices all over her face and my bare legs.

"Oh my God," I purred to Laila, after I came down from my high. "I could seriously get used to this. Are you *sure* you want to disband this group of horny young vixens?"

"Not for a couple more *days* at least," she smiled, rolling her body on top of me, grinding her dripping mound into my pliant face.

As I began to eat her pussy, the girls swarmed over top of me like a bunch of buzzing bees, rubbing their wet pussies and hairy bushes over whatever open flesh they could find on my pinned body. One of them positioned herself between my legs, pulling her pussy tight against mine and began scissoring me in a prone 'X' position while some of the other girls sucked my nipples and toes. Before we all fell asleep in a steaming pile of sweaty flesh, I must have come at least a dozen more times sucking, caressing, and fucking every one of the girls in one position or another.

As I lay on the soft desert sand surrounded by the bevy of beautiful women, I looked up toward the sky at the cloud of stars shimmering above me like a blanket of sparkling sequins. Suddenly the troubles at the previous camp seemed a hundred miles away, and I smiled at one of Amir's last comments to me. *The desert gives and takes away indeed*, I thought, as I drifted off to sleep.

8

For the next couple of days, we rode slowly through the desert, stopping periodically to relieve ourselves and snack on dried dates and flatbread. At night we reassembled the blankets in one large group and resumed our wild orgy under the stars until we all fell asleep, completely spent and satiated. I almost regretted seeing the dusty buildings on the edge of Algiers as we approached the city from the west, and I squeezed Laila's tummy softly to express how much I dreaded the thought of leaving her.

She parked me and the rest of the girls out of sight behind a tall dune so as not to arouse suspicion, then she led the camels three at a time into the local trading market, where she sold them at a relative bargain. It was approaching dusk by the time she returned to fetch all of us, then she took us down to the docks to arrange clandestine travel for each of the girls to return to their original towns. She gave each of them enough money to pay for the remainder of their passage, then the two of us walked along the waterfront while we talked about our next steps.

"That looked easier than I *thought* it would be," I said after all of the girls had boarded their individual ships to head home.

"These merchant seamen will transport anything for the right amount of money," she nodded.

"What about the harbormaster? How did you manage to bypass all the usual paperwork and document controls?"

"The protocols for onboarding and offboarding passengers on cargo ships are far looser on the North African coast than in Europe or America," she said, sliding her fingers and her thumb together to indicate the payment of a bribe. "Nobody seems to have a problem looking the other way as long as you grease their palms a little bit."

"How can you be sure the ships' captains will *complete* the transaction now that they've already been paid?"

"Because I promised to have them paid an *equivalent* amount once the girls safely complete their journey on the other end."

"All of this is made possible from the selling of a few *camels*?"

"Um-hm," Laila nodded. "Amir paid to take us *away* from our homes, now he's indirectly arranged to pay for them to get back."

"I'm not sure this was exactly the way he envisioned it," I frowned, trying not to think about how much he was suffering in the middle of the desert without any food or water.

"I suppose not," she chuckled. "Though I don't think *any* of this went down the way he imagined."

"So what now?" I said, peering over the Mediterranean as the sun began to set on the horizon.

"We pretend like none of this ever happened," she said. "You go back home to America, and I slip across the sea to start a new life in Spain. It shouldn't take long for us to put all of this unpleasantness behind us."

"It hasn't *all* been unpleasant," I said, grabbing her hand and pulling her into an alley to give her a long, passionate kiss. "I'll have far more *happy* memories to hold onto than this one unfortunate affair."

"Mmm," she nodded, pressing her body up tightly against me.

"Well isn't *this* a happy little reunion," a familiar man's voice suddenly cackled from the shadows.

Laila and I swung around to see Amir blocking the exit to the alley, brandishing his glinty curved knife.

"I knew the two of you were up to no good the moment I saw you ogling each other during the belly dance performance in my tent. And now it's time for the lot of you to be held to account for your transgressions. Right after you tell me what you've done with the other girls."

I stared at Amir with my mouth agape in a mix of shock and confusion.

"How–"

"Did I manage to get all this way on foot?" he said. "Your first mistake was leaving me with all the livestock. Their milk and meat can sustain a man for a long time in the desert. Plus, I was lucky enough to catch another passing caravan after a couple of days. If you two hadn't dawdled taking your time crossing the desert, you might have made a clean getaway by now." He paused, running his eyes up and down our bodies. "Of course, I didn't have any *other* distractions encouraging me to pause for a little entertainment in the evenings."

"So I suppose you've alerted the elders by now and arranged for us to be taken before the council to be properly punished?" Laila said, stepping in front of me and placing her arm around me protectively.

"In due course," he said. "First I needed to *find* you before you slipped away. I'm afraid your fate, along with the rest of my little harem, has already been sealed, Laila." Then he turned toward me, clucking his tongue. "As for my pretty Western friend, I'm sure we can find a dark prison somewhere in the bowels of this medieval city to let her rot away the rest of her miserable life."

Amir lurched forward, placing the knife under Laila's neck.

"Now *tell* me where the rest of the girls are!" he sneered.

Suddenly, Laila reared back, kicking Amir as hard as she could between his legs and he hunched over, dropping the knife onto the ground. She quickly picked it up and before he could regain his composure, she sliced it across the front of his neck in one quick and silent motion. He clutched his throat, looking at us with wild eyes, then he fell to his knees, collapsing onto the cobblestone pavement. As a thick pool of blood seeped out of his jugular vein onto the darkened stones, the life slowly drained out of his eyes, and he suddenly became still.

"Holy *fuck*, Laila," I gasped. "You *killed* him!"

"It was either him or us," she said nonchalantly. "He got what was coming to him."

"What the hell do we do now?" I said, looking around frantically to see if anyone else had witnessed the scene. "We can't just *leave* him here. He can be traced back to us."

Laila paused for a moment as she peered around the wharf to get her bearings, then she nodded toward a nearby dock.

"We'll have to drag him to the edge of the jetty and dump him into the water. There's no one around and it's dark enough for us to dispose of the body. Grab a leg and help me pull him toward the pier."

I shook my head, hardly believing how fast our plan had unraveled and wondering what would happen if anyone saw us. But I knew Laila was right. Between the front desk attendant at my hotel in Morocco and my email trail to Hannah, there was more than enough circumstantial evidence to connect me to Amir's disappearance. The best chance for both of us to get away before the police caught wind of any malfeasance was to dispose of the body and exit as quickly as possible.

We each grabbed one of Amir's legs and after checking to make sure the coast was clear, we carefully dragged his body the thirty feet or so across the narrow roadway lining the wharf and dropped his lifeless body into the murky water at the edge of the pier. We watched his body slowly sink into the deep water, then we ducked into another alley to decide what to do next.

"So what do we do now?" I said, shivering from a combination of shock and the encroaching chill.

"You've still got your travel bag and papers," she said, nodding toward my clutch case. "You need to get changed back into your Western clothes as soon as possible and catch the earliest flight out of the country. With any luck, you'll be long gone before anyone finds any evidence of foul play. I'll pay for safe passage to the continent and try to slip into Spain undetected. Right now, we both have to get the hell out of here."

"Okay," I said, wrapping my arms around my body to keep myself from shaking. "But will I ever see you again? I hate leaving you this way..."

"It's best we make a clean break," she said, pulling me close against her breast. "We don't want anyone connecting us together after this. You'll be fine. I'll think of you whenever I'm sleeping alone under my woolen blanket."

I paused for a moment, darting my eyes across her pretty face. I hated the idea of leaving so abruptly, but I knew we didn't have any other choice. I opened my travel bag and scribbled my address on a piece of paper.

"This is my address back home in America," I said, handing her the paper. "Just do me one favor. Write me once you get situated in Spain and send me your address. It'll be safe to see you again once this all settles down. I'd love to be able to stay in touch."

"Okay," Laila said, folding the paper and tucking it away into her robe. "But you need to go now. I want you to catch the earliest flight out in the morning. I'll contact you once I get settled."

She leaned in towards me, clasping the sides of my head with both hands.

"This has been the most amazing adventure of my life," she said. "I'll never forget these few days we've shared together, my beautiful sweet, American girl. Safe travels, my love. We'll talk again soon."

Then she turned and walked briskly down the wharf into the inky darkness without looking back. I watched her robes billowing in the cool evening breeze until she disappeared in the mist, then I changed out of my thawb in the darkness of the alley and put my Western clothes back on, hailing a cab to the airport. I was lucky enough to catch the seven a.m. flight to Paris with a connecting flight to Chicago later that day. As my jet lifted off the runway and turned north over the Mediterranean Sea, I peered down at the wide expanse of sparking blue waves, smiling at how it reminded me of the golden sand ripples in the desert.

After I got home, a few months passed without hearing from Laila, and I began to fear that she might not have made it out of the North Africa. But when I received an airmail letter postmarked Seville, Spain, I tore it open and read the contents breathlessly.

Jade,

I hope this letter finds you well and fully recovered from our little desert adventure. I've thought of you often since we departed so suddenly in Algiers and miss having your smooth, supple body snuggling up next to me. You may be happy to know that I've grown quite accustomed to your Western-style grooming habits and I always think of you whenever I touch myself on dark, lonely nights. If ever you find the time to come visit me, I've enclosed my new address below.

Love always, Laila

Oh my God, I exhaled, happy to hear that she'd made it out safely. And the fact that she still had fond memories of our time together and even thought of me whenever she touched herself intimately made my heart dance and my panties moisten. As I sat in my chair rereading her letter over and over again and smelling the delicate scent of jasmine and lemongrass infused in the paper, my fingers trailed a path down between my thighs as I separated my legs slowly.

Maybe this won't be the end of my arabian adventure after all, I smiled to myself.

Three somes

THE LESBIAN COLLECTION

VICTORIA RUSH

2 + 1 = a hundred ways to have fun...

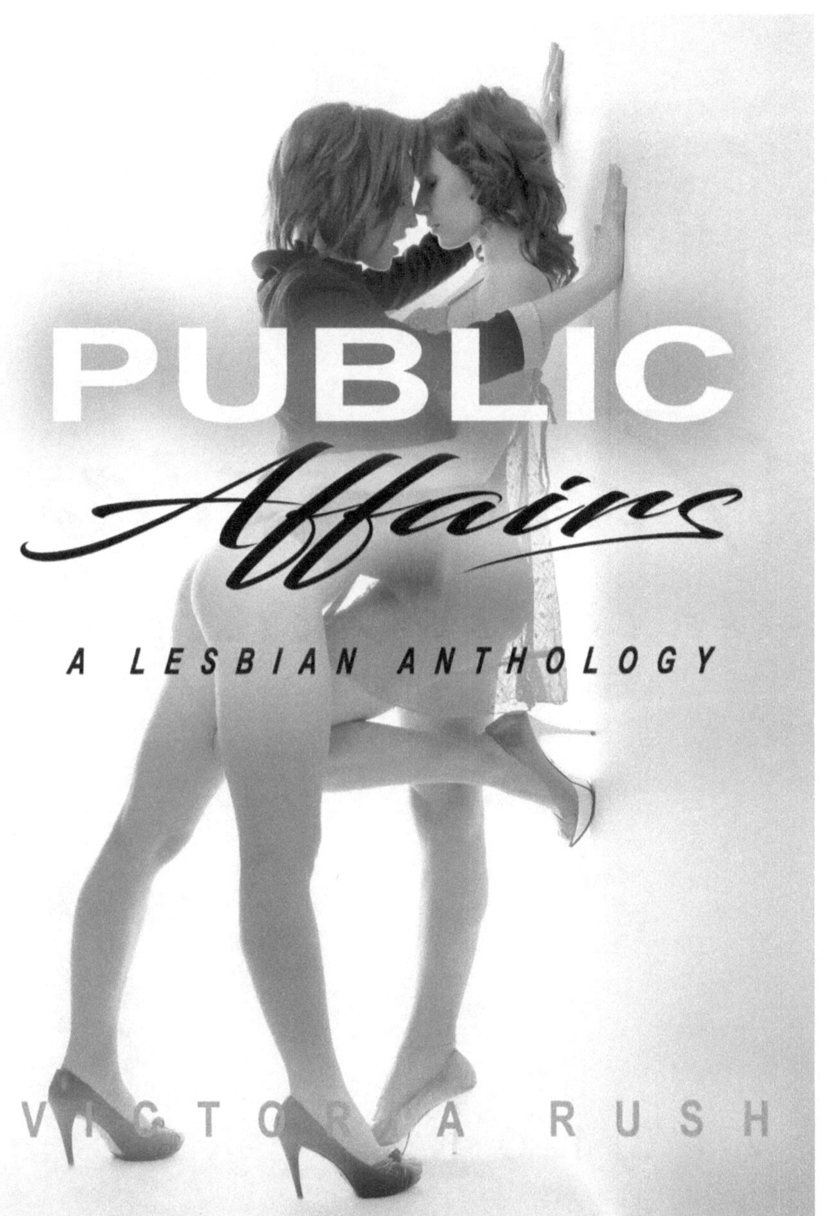

PUBLIC
Affairs
A LESBIAN ANTHOLOGY
VICTORIA RUSH
Sometimes the biggest turn-on is knowing you might get caught...

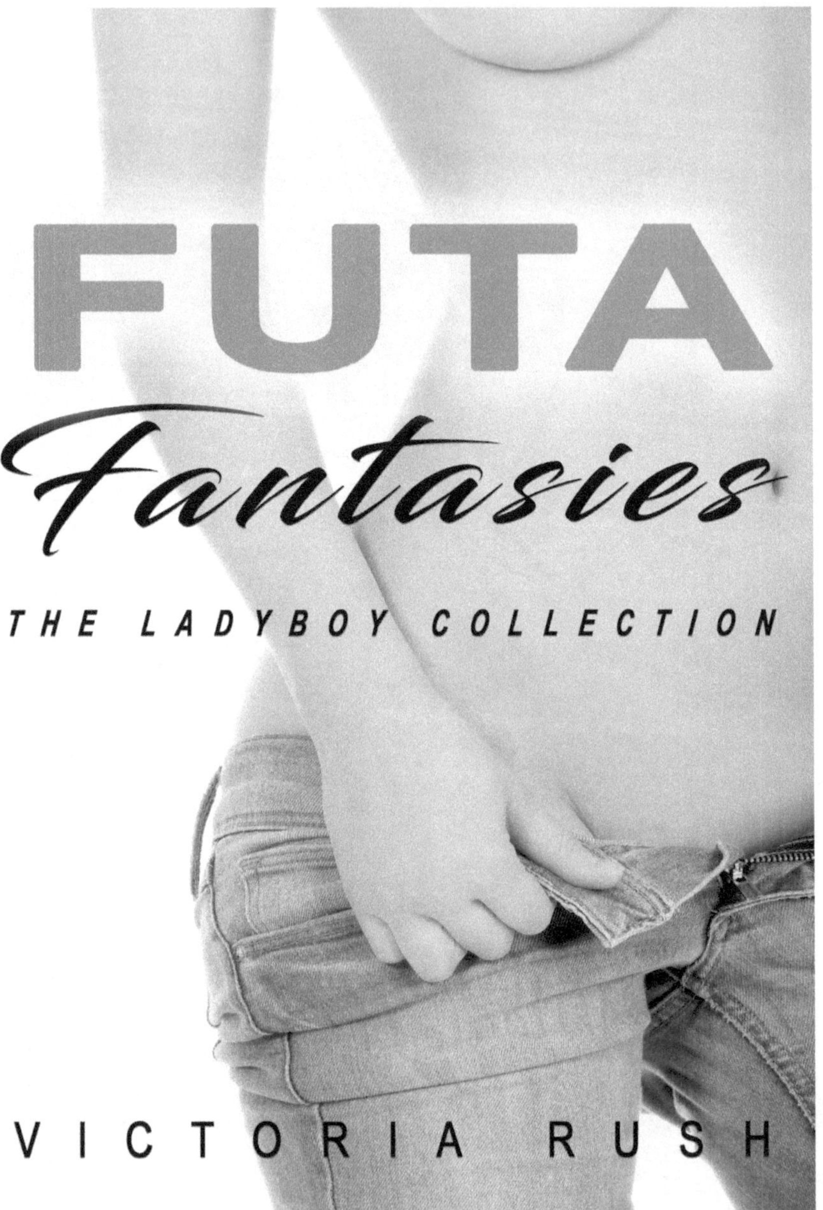

FUTA

Fantasies

THE LADYBOY COLLECTION

VICTORIA RUSH

Some girls have got a little more to work with than others...

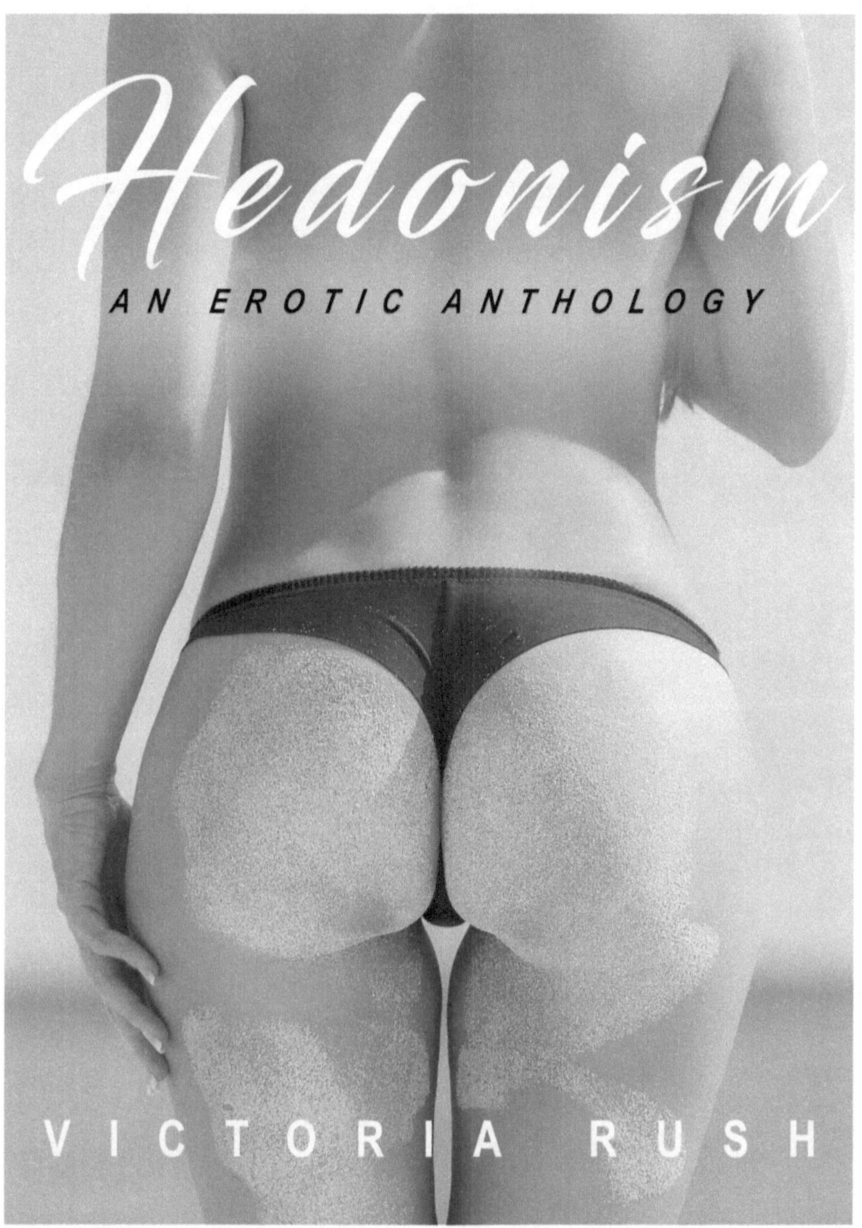

Sometimes all you need to spark up your love life is a little change of scenery...

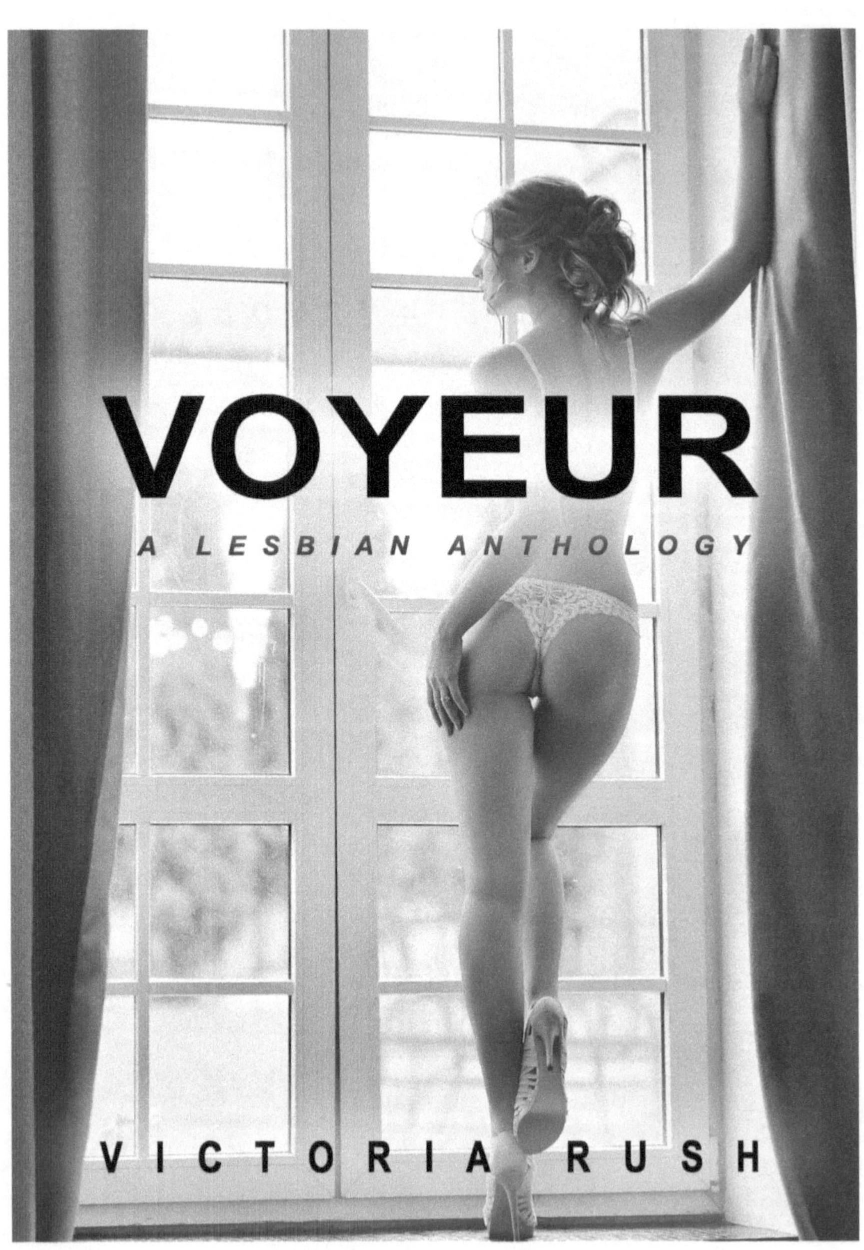
VOYEUR
A LESBIAN ANTHOLOGY
VICTORIA RUSH
Sometimes it's more fun to watch...